"Laxness is a poet who writes to the edge of the pages, a visionary who allows us a plot: he takes a Tolstoyan overview, he weaves in an Evelyn Waugh-like humour: it is not possible to be unimpressed"   FAY WELDON, *Daily Telegraph*

"It is a novel (a world) that transmits something of the wonder of life, its strangeness, its goodness, occasions for stubbornness, and the stoicism of people – people everywhere"   MURRAY BAIL

"*The Fish Can Sing* meanders beautifully . . . Laxness's view of a child's bounded universe has humour and a light touch"
ISOBEL MONTGOMERY, *Guardian*

"Icelanders aren't bleak so much as blessed with a refined sense of humour and an ability to see the hand of God in even the smallest things . . . an uplifting novel"   MICHAEL MELLAR, *Observer*

"Put whatever you are reading now to one side and buy this book. You won't regret doing so . . . To read Laxness is to discover a writer who is genuinely *sui generis*. He embodies the Joycean idea that nothing is more universal than the local perfectly described. Iceland itself is a presence in his books: the cold, the country's strange, blasted landscape and the rural basis of its society . . . Above all else the writing of Laxness is beautiful"
EAMMON SWEENEY, *Sunday Tribune*, Dublin

"A strange and beautiful tale"   ZULFIKAR ABBANY, *The Times*

"One of this great writer's most unusual and attractive books"
Kirkus Reviews

HALLDÓR LAXNESS (1908–98) was born near Reykjavík, Iceland. His first novel was published when he was 17. The undisputed master of contemporary Icelandic fiction and one of the outstanding novelists of the twentieth century, he wrote more than 60 books and his work has been translated into more than 30 languages. He was awarded the Nobel Prize for Literature in 1955.

MAGNUS MAGNUSSON KBE is an Icelander who was brought up in Scotland. Although justly celebrated for his achievements as a television presenter and for his journalism, he is also the translator of several volumes of classical Icelandic sagas and modern novels.

Also by Halldór Laxness and published by The Harvill Press

INDEPENDENT PEOPLE

Also by Halldór Laxness in English translation

WORLD LIGHT

THE HAPPY WARRIORS

THE ATOM STATION

PARADISE RECLAIMED

CHRISTIANITY AT GLACIER

Halldór Laxness

THE FISH CAN SING

Translated from the Icelandic by
Magnus Magnusson

THE HARVILL PRESS
LONDON

First published with the title *Brekkukotsannáll* by Helgafell, Iceland, 1957
First published in Great Britain by Methuen & Co. Ltd, 1966

This paperback edition first published in 2001 by The Harvill Press

4 6 8 9 7 5

Map by Emily Hare

The Harvill Press
Random House, 20 Vauxhall Bridge Road, London SW1V 2SA

Random House Australia (Pty) Limited, 20 Alfred Street, Milsons Point
Sydney, New South Wales 2061, Australia

Random House New Zealand Limited, 18 Poland Road, Glenfield
Auckland 10, New Zealand

Random House South Africa (Pty) Limited, Endulini, 5A Jubilee Road
Parktown 2193, South Africa

The Random House Group Limited Reg. No. 954009
www.randomhouse.co.uk/harvill

A CIP catalogue record for this book is available from the British Library

ISBN 1 86046 934 5

Designed and typeset in Baskerville by Libanus Press Ltd, Marlborough, Wilts

Papers used by Random House UK Limited are natural, recyclable products made from wood
grown in sustainable forests. The manufacturing processes conform to the
environmental regulations of the country of origin

Printed and bound in Great Britain by
Bookmarque Ltd, Croydon, Surrey

Contents

NOTE ON PRONUNCIATION

The only extra consonant in Icelandic used in this translation is ∂ (ð), the so called "crossed d" or "eth", which is pronounced like the voiced *the* in *breathe*.

The pronunciation of the vowels is conditioned by the same accents:

> á as in *owl*
> é as in *ye*, in *yet*
> í as in *seen*
> ó as in *note*
> ö as in French *fleur*
> ú as in *moon*
> y as in *seen*
> æ as in *life*
> au as in French *oeil*
> ei, ey as in *tray*

ARCTIC

Latrabjarg

BREIDAFJORD BAY

Hvammsfjord Bay

Helgafell

Snaefells Peninsula

Stapi   Borgarnes

FAXA BAY

Borgarfjord Bay

Akraness

Seltjarnarness

Skerjafjord Bay

Njardvik   Alftaness   Hafnafjord   Hellis Heath

Skagafjord Bay

Skagi Peninsula

Hvit River

Husafell

Langjokull Glacier

Mount Esja   Strokkur

Pingvellir

Vatnasmyri

Sogid River   Huita River

Pjorsa River

Reykjavik

Cathedral

Hringjaraby

Brekkukot

3 4 5 6
Long Street

7

South Street

++ 2
+ +

Tjorn Lake

8 & 9

1 Churchyard
2 Gabriel's Tomb
3 Hotel d'Islande
4 Gudmunsen's Store
5 Isafold Office
6 Fridriksen's Bakery
7 Althing House
8 To Hvammskot Farm
9 To Soga Stream

C I R C L E . . . .

⊙ Holar

Langaness

Hofsjokull
Glacier

Vatnajokull Glacier

Laki
Crater

Mount
Hekla

Skaftafell
Distritis

Myrdalsjokull
Glacier

Landbrot

ATLANTIC OCEAN

0   40miles

1

A STRANGE CREATURE

A wise man once said that next to losing its mother, there is nothing more healthy for a child than to lose its father. And though I would never subscribe to such a statement wholeheartedly, I would be the last person to reject it out of hand. For my own part, I would express such a doctrine without any suggestion of bitterness against the world, or rather without the hurt which the mere sound of the words implies.

But whatever one might think of the merits of this observation, it so happened in my own case that I had to make do without any parents at all. I will not say that it was actually my good fortune – that would be putting it too strongly; but I certainly cannot call it a misfortune, at least not so far as I myself was concerned, and that was because I acquired a grandfather and a grandmother instead. It might be closer to the truth to say that the misfortune was all my father's and my mother's: not because I would have been a model son to them, far from it, but because parents have even more need of children than children have of parents. But that is another matter.

Anyway, to cut a long story short, I must tell you that to the south of the churchyard in our future capital city of Reykjavík, just where the slope begins to level out at the southern end of the Lake, on the exact spot where Guðmundur Gúðmúnsen (the son of old Jón Guðmundsson, the owner of Gúðmúnsen's Store) eventually built himself a fine mansion-house – on this patch of ground there once stood a little turf-and-stone cottage with two wooden gables facing east towards the Lake; and this little place was called Brekkukot.

This was where my grandfather lived, the late Björn of Brekkukot who sometimes went fishing for lumpfish in springtime; and with him lived the woman who has been closer to me than most other women, even though I knew nothing about her: my grandmother. This little turf cottage was a free and ever-open guest-house for anyone and everyone who had need of shelter. At the time when I was coming into this world, the cottage was crowded with people who would nowadays be called refugees – people who flee their country, people who abandon their native homes and hearths in tears because conditions at home are so desperate that their children cannot survive infancy.

Then one day, so I have been told, it happened that a young woman arrived at the place from somewhere in the west; or north; or perhaps even east. This woman was on her way to America, abandoned and destitute, fleeing from those who ruled over Iceland. I have heard that her passage had been paid for by the Mormons, and indeed I know for a fact that among them are to be found some of the finest people in America. But anyway, without further ado, this woman I mentioned gave birth to a baby while she was staying at Brekkukot waiting for her ship. And when she had been delivered of the child she looked at her newborn son and said, "This boy is to be called Álfur."

"I would be inclined to name him Grímur," said my grandmother.

"Then we shall call him Álfgrímur," said my mother.

And so the only thing this woman ever gave me, apart from a body and soul, was this name: Álfgrímur. Like all fatherless children in Iceland I was called Hansson – literally, "His-son". And thereupon she left me, naked as I was and with only that curious name, in the arms of Björn, late fisherman of Brekkukot, and went on her way; and she is now out of this story.

And I now begin this book with the old clock that used to stand in the living-room at Brekkukot, ticking away. Inside this clock there was a silver bell, whose clear pure note as it struck the hours could be heard not only all over Brekkukot but up in the church-yard as well. In the churchyard there was another bell, a copper bell, whose deep resonant tones carried all the way back into our cottage. And so, when the wind was right, you could hear two bells chiming in harmony in our little turf cottage, the one of silver and the other of copper.

Our clock had a decorated face, and in the middle of the

ornamentation one could read the legend that this clock had been made by Mr James Cowan of Edinburgh, 1750. It had no doubt been built to stand in some other house than Brekkukot, for its plinth had had to be removed so that it could fit under our ceiling. This clock ticked to a slow and stately measure, and I soon got the notion that no other clock was worth taking seriously. People's pocket-watches seemed to me to be dumb infants compared with this clock of ours. The seconds in other people's watches were like scurrying insects having a race, but the seconds in the timepiece at Brekkukot were like cows, and always went as slowly as it is possible to move without actually standing still.

It goes without saying that if there were anything happening in the room you never heard the clock at all, no more than if it did not exist; but when all was quiet and the visitors had gone and the table had been cleared and the door shut, then it would start up again, as steady as ever; and if you listened hard enough you could sometimes make out a singing note in its workings, or something very like an echo.

How did it ever come about, I wonder, that I got the notion that in this clock there lived a strange creature, which was Eternity? Somehow it just occurred to me one day that the word it said when it ticked, a four-syllable word with the emphasis on alternate syllables, was et-ERN-it-Y, et-ERN-it-Y. Did I know the word, then?

It was odd that I should discover eternity in this way, long before I knew what eternity was, and even before I had learned the proposition that all men are mortal – yes, while I was actually living in eternity myself. It was as if a fish were suddenly to discover the water it swam in. I mentioned this to my grandfather one day when we happened to be alone in the living-room.

"Do you understand the clock, grandfather?" I asked.

"Here in Brekkukot we know this clock only very slightly," he replied. "We only know that it tells the days and the hours right down to seconds. But your grandmother's great-uncle, who owned this clock for sixty-five years, told me that the previous owner had said that it once told the phases of the moon – before some watchmaker got at it. Old folk farther back in your grandmother's family used to maintain that this clock could foretell marriages and deaths; but I don't take that too seriously, my boy."

Then I said, "Why does the clock always say: et-ERN-it-Y, et-ERN-it-Y, et-ERN-it-Y?"

"You must be hearing things, my child," said my grandfather.

"Is there no eternity, then?" I asked.

"Not otherwise than you have heard in your grandmother's prayers at night and in the *Book of Sermons* from me on Sundays, my boy," he replied.

"Grandfather," I said. "Is eternity a living creature?"

"Try not to talk nonsense, my boy," said grandfather.

"Listen, grandfather, are any clocks other than ours worth taking seriously?"

"No," said my grandfather. "Our clock is right. And that is because I have long since stopped letting watchmakers have a look at it. Indeed, I have never yet come across a watchmaker who understood this clock. If I cannot mend it myself, I get some handyman to look at it; I have always found handymen best."

2

FINE WEATHER

When I was not in the living-room listening to the strange creature in the clock, I was often outside playing in the vegetable garden. The tufts of grass between the paving-slabs reached to my waist, but the dockens and tansies were as tall as I was, and the angelica even taller. The dandelions in this garden were bigger than anywhere else. We kept a few hens, whose eggs always tasted of fish. These hens would start their clucking when they were pecking for food around the house early in the morning; it was a comfortable sound and I never took long to fall asleep again. And sometimes, around noon, they would break into their cluck-ing again as they strutted about in their hen-run, and once again I would fall into a doze, entranced by this brooding birdsound and the scent of the tansies. Nor must I forget to thank the bluebottle for its share in this midsummer trance; it was so blue that the sunshine made it glint green, and the joyful note of earthly life vibrated ceaselessly in its well-tuned string.

But whether I was playing in the vegetable garden, or out on the paving, or down by the path, my grandfather was always somewhere at hand, silent and omniscient. There was always some door standing wide open or ajar, the door of the cottage or the fish-shed or the net-hut or the byre, and he would be inside there, pottering away. Sometimes he would be disentangling a net on the drystone dyke; or else he would just be tinkering with something. His hands were never idle, but he never seemed to be actually working. He never gave any sign of knowing that his grandchild was nearby, and I never paid much attention to him either, and yet somehow I was always involuntarily aware of him in the background. I would hear him blowing his nose with long pauses between each blow, and then taking another pinch of snuff. His constant silent presence was in every cranny and corner of Brekkukot – it was like lying snugly at anchor, one's soul could find in him whatever security it sought. To this very day I still have the feeling from time to time that a door is standing ajar somewhere to one side of or behind me, or even right in front of me, and that my grandfather is inside there, pottering away. So I think it only right, if I am to talk about my world, that I should first of all give some account of my grandfather.

The late Björn of Brekkukot was born and bred in this part of the world; his father had been a farmer here in Brekkukot in the days when it had been a farm with its own meadows on the south side of the Lake, where, later, peat-pits were dug to supply this future capital city with fuel. In those days there were Danish governors ruling over Iceland. But by the time my story starts, an Icelandic governor had been appointed; he was called the King's Minister because he was under the thumb of the Danish king in just the same way as was the Althing we had for a so-called Parliament. When my grandfather was born there were barely two thousand people living in the capital; in my own childhood there were nearly five thousand. In grandfather's childhood the only people who counted were a few government officials (who were called variously "the gentry", or simply "the authorities"), and a few foreign merchants, mainly Jews from Schleswig and Holstein who spoke Low German and called themselves Danes; for in those days Jews were not allowed to do business in Denmark itself, only in the Danish duchies and colonies. The rest of the town's inhabitants were cottagers who went out to the fishing and sometimes owned a small share in a cow, or had a few sheep. They had little rowing-boats, on which they could sometimes hoist a sail.

In my grandfather's boyhood everyone was self-sufficient as far as fish was concerned, except for the gentry and the merchants, who lived on meat, for the most part anyway. But as the community grew and began to develop into something like a town, with some basic divisions of labour, and there began to be artisans and harbour-workers who had no opportunity of going to sea for themselves, and as a little money began to circulate, one or two people started to make a livelihood by catching fish for their neighbours' larders.

One of those who made his living in this way was my grandfather. He was not a ship-owner in the sense of being in big business; nor did he own shares in a boat with others. He was never one of those who dried fish on a scale large enough to trade with merchants and accumulate gold and silver in a chest and then suddenly start buying up land or plots of ground or taking shares in a decked ship, as was then becoming the fashion. Nothing like that. When the weather was fine it was his custom to row out to sea early in the morning from the landing place at Grófin or Bótin, with one or two helpers in his boat, and put his nets out somewhere just beyond the islands – or at the very most, perhaps, they might paddle the boat out as far as Svið. When he returned, grandmother and I would be waiting at the landing place with a bottle of coffee wrapped in a sock and a slice of ryebread in a red handkerchief. Then grandfather would go off with his catch in a wheelbarrow and sell it in the town for ready money, either in the street or from door to door. During the winter season, or late on in the summer, he would catch mainly cod and haddock, and sometimes also plaice and small halibut; no other fish counted. If any of the fish were not sold at once, my grandfather would clean them at home and hang them up on spars in the fish-shed, for drying into stockfish.

During the last few months of winter he would stop going out to the fishing, as it was called, and turn his attention to lumpfish, which he would look for among the seaweed either in Skerjafjörður or out at Grandi. I am not sure if it is generally known that there is a distinct contrast between the male and female lumpfish; the male is one of the most beautifully coloured fish to be found, and tasty to match, but the female is less highly thought of and is usually salted down. In the south, out on the Nesses, spring is said to have arrived when the lumpfish season starts and the bark-coloured sails of the Frenchmen are glinting out in Faxaflói.

Towards the end of March my grandfather would be down in the town with his wheelbarrow every morning, just as people were getting up, to sell fresh lumpfish. Those who row such a short distance out to sea are not usually reckoned as fishermen at all in Iceland – I doubt whether my grandfather ever saw the open sea in his whole life. Nor would it be correct to say that he ran a fishing business, even though he dabbled about in the seaweed with a helper or two, or put out a net a stone's throw away from the shore. In other countries, someone who rowed out in a small boat early in the morning and had fish at your door by breakfast-time would certainly be called a fisherman; indeed, my grandfather himself looked a little like those fishermen in foreign paintings, except that he never wore boots, let alone clogs, but always the traditional home-made moccasins of treated hide known as "Icelandic shoes", or "thin-shoes". When he was out rowing in rain or heavy seas, he would put on trousers and smock made of hide treated with train-oil. But when he was going round the town he always wore those green Icelandic thin-shoes, and blue woollen stockings with a white border on top, made by my grandmother; if it was wet he would tuck his trouser-ends into his stockings, but however much mud or mire there was in the streets, there was never a spot to be seen on grandfather's stockings or shoes.

He grew his whiskers in a collar round his chin, like those Dutch or Danish fishermen you see in pictures, and his hair hung in long white locks cut square at the bottom. When he was not wearing his sou'wester, he had on a broad-brimmed black hat of the kind that is called a clerical hat in Germany but an artist's hat in Denmark, with a shallow crumpled crown and red silk lining. This hat was never new, as far as I can remember, but it never became old either, and the creases in it always remained the same. It blew off once, and after that he got my grandmother to sew on two tapes, which he would then tie under his chin when the weather was windy.

In our fish-shed, half of which was used for storing fishing-gear, the lumpfish would be hung until late spring, along with dried catfish, halibut, and haddock. Sometimes my grandfather would boil fish-liver over an open fire to the south of the fish-shed; and the rancid smell of the lumpfish, mixed with the odour of liver-oil and sediment, would blend with the scent of growing grass and tansies and angelica, and the peat-smoke from grandmother's chimney. About the time that the bluebottle was laying her eggs the stockfish had to be fully cured, for this was the time for the fish-shed to be emptied. Every single stone in the walls of our cottage glistened with fish-scales, as did the spars of the fish-shed and the peats in the stack to the north of the shed. You could also see the glint of scales in the mire that formed between the shed and the cottage when it was wet; and every single thing within our plot of land was smeared with liver and oil, right out to the turnstile that revolved horizontally on its axle in the garden gate behind our cottage. In the southern-most corner of our plot, farthest from the cottage, was grandfather's store-shed; it, too, was divided into two compartments, with a deal floor in one of them where all sorts of supplies were stored, for it was our custom to buy all our household necessities at half-yearly intervals; the meat we salted down ourselves in a barrel to last the whole year. At the other end of the shed lived Gráni and Skjalda; so the smell of oil and the tang of smoke at our place was mixed with the scent not only of grass, but of a horse and cow as well.

And still this day of high summer continued to pass . . .

And now, as I sat there in the vegetable garden playing by

myself on this summer day, with the bluebottle buzzing and the
hens clucking and grandfather's net-hut half open and the sun
shining from a sky with as much brightness as a sun can have in
this mortal world, I saw a man come walking past the wall of
the churchyard, staggering beneath a monstrous load on his
back, a cram-full bushel sack. He jostled his way with the sack
through our turnstile-gate, which was only about two feet wide,
so there was no mistaking that he was on his way to visit us. I
really cannot remember whether I knew him then, but I always
knew him when I saw him thereafter. He was one of those
odd-job-men who lent a hand occasionally; he went out in the
boat with grandfather sometimes, or helped him clean the fish.
He had a little place in the Skugga district, I think, and a
brood of starving children, but that does not concern us here.
I think he was called Jói of Steinbær. I am only telling what
happened to him at Brekkukot because I have never been able to
get it out of my mind, and because my own story would somehow
not be complete if I did not record it here. But before I tell this
story, I want above all to warn people against thinking that they
are about to hear something epic or spectacular.

The man laid his sack down on the paving at the cottage and
seated himself upon it, wiping the sweat from his brow with his
sleeve. He addressed himself to me, a mere boy at this time, and
said, "Is your grandfather, Björn the skipper, at home?"

When my grandfather came out of the net-hut and round to
the paving where the sun sparkled on the fish-scales, the visitor
rose from the sack and fell to his knees beside his burden, took
off his cap and began to wring it, lowered his head and said, "I
stole these peats from you last night, Björn, from your peat-stack
over there next to the wall of the shed."

"Is that so?" said my grandfather. "That was a wicked thing to
do. And it's only about a week since I gave you a sack of peats."

"Yes, and I've scarcely slept a wink all night because of my
conscience," said the thief. "I didn't even have any appetite for
my coffee this morning. I know I'll never have another day's
happiness until you have forgiven me."

"Quite so," said Björn of Brekkukot. "But at least you can try to stand up straight while we are talking. And put your cap on."

"I feel as if I will never be able to stand up straight again all my life," said the thief, "let alone put my cap on."

My grandfather solemnly took a pinch of snuff:

"Yes, it's hardly to be expected that you would be feeling light-hearted after a deed like that," he said. "Can I offer you a pinch of snuff?"

"Thank you for offering," said the thief, "but I feel I scarcely deserve it."

"Have it your own way," said my grandfather. "But in a case like this I need to do a little thinking. Won't you come inside and have a cup of coffee while we discuss this?"

They left the stolen goods in the middle of the paving and went inside. And the sun shone on the sack of peats.

They went into the living-room.

"Have a seat and show us some cheer," said my grandfather. The thief put his crumpled cap beneath the chair and sat down.

"Yes, it's wonderfully fine weather we're having now," said my grandfather. "I do believe there has been fishing-weather every single day since April."

"Yes," said the thief, "it's wonderfully fine weather."

"I have seldom set eyes on such spring haddock as this year's," said my grandfather. "Rosy-fleshed, and fragrant."

"Yes, such blessed haddock," said the thief.

"Or the growth in the meadows!" said my grandfather.

"Yes, you can certainly say that," said the thief. "What growth!"

My grandmother served them. They went on discussing the season on sea and land while they swilled their coffee. When they had finished the coffee the thief stood up and said thank you and shook hands. He picked his cap up off the floor and made ready to take his leave. My grandfather accompanied him back out to the paving, and the thief went on wringing his cap between his hands.

"Are you perhaps going to say anything to me before I go, Björn?" said the thief.

"No," said my grandfather. "You have done something which God cannot forgive."

SPECIAL FISH 13

The thief heaved a sigh and said in a low voice, "Ah, well, Björn, you have my warmest thanks for the coffee; goodbye, and may God be with you now and for ever."

"Goodbye," said my grandfather.

But when the visitor was on his way out through the turnstile-gate with his cap, my grandfather called out to him and said, "Oh, why don't you just take that sack with you and whatever's in it, poor chap. One sack of peats doesn't matter a damn to me."

The thief turned back at the gate and came and shook my grandfather's hand in gratitude again, but could not say a word. He turned his head away while he put on his cap. Then he shouldered the sack of peats once more and edged himself with it through the turnstile the way he had arrived in that fine weather.

3

SPECIAL FISH

I have now described how my grandfather was a man of orthodox beliefs without its ever occurring to him to ask God to model Himself upon men, in accordance with that strange passage in the Lord's Prayer which says: "Forgive us our trespasses, as we forgive them that trespass against us." My grandfather said plainly to the fellow from Steinbær: "God cannot forgive you, but to me, Björn of Brekkukot, it doesn't matter a damn." So I cannot help suspecting that my grandfather had a special scale of standards for most of the things that happen in the life of a fisherman.

To corroborate this, I shall now mention briefly the question of fish as we saw the matter at Brekkukot – or rather, the moral law relating to fish. It could be said that my grandfather's ideas about the fishing industry had only a limited relevance in the rapidly evolving society that during my boyhood was developing beyond the turnstile back-gate of Brekkukot; on the other hand, we had not yet reached the stage of becoming palpably aware of that society which was beginning to ferment all around us. At any rate I can assert that I was brought up with an assessment of money very different from normal banking values.

I think that our own standard had its origins in my grand-father's conviction that the money which people consider theirs by right was unlawfully accumulated, or counterfeit, if it exceeded the average income of a working man; and therefore that all great wealth was inconsistent with common sense. I can remember him saying often that he would never accept more money than he had earned.

But what does a man earn, people will ask? How much does a man deserve to get? How much should a fisherman accept? The devil alone can tell. Nowadays anyone who rejects the bank's valuation would have to solve complicated moral puzzles on his own several times a day. But these problems never seemed to baffle my grandfather nor cause him any anxiety; difficulties which in most people's eyes would have led to endless complica-tions were disposed of by my grandfather almost without thinking, with the easy assurance of a sleepwalker who strolls along a ledge halfway down a hundred-foot precipice – yes, I am tempted to say with the same disregard for the laws of nature as a ghost passing through locked doors.

I was not very old when I got an inkling that some of the fish-ermen felt aggrieved at my grandfather because he sometimes sold fresh fish for the pot cheaper than others did; they called it underhand to compete at cut prices against good men. But how much is one lumpfish worth? And what is the value of a pound of haddock? Or plaice? One could answer just as well by asking, What does the sun cost, and the moon, and the stars? I assume that my grandfather answered it for himself, subcon-sciously: that the right price for a lumpfish, for instance, was the price that prevented a fisherman from piling up more money than he needed for the necessities of life.

In accordance with the economic law of supply and demand, people were inclined to raise the price of fish when catches were meagre or the weather unfavourable – all except Björn of

Brekkukot. If anyone came to him and said, "I shall buy everything you have on your wheelbarrow today at twice or even three
times the usual price," he would just look blankly at the person
who was making such an offer, and continue to weigh one pound
after another in his scales, or to hand people one lump-fish after
another from his wheelbarrow according to what each person
needed for his pot – and at the same price as usual.

But then came the days when catches were plentiful and the
weather was fine and there was an abundance of all kinds of good-
quality fish; and those days came more and more often as time
passed, especially after the decked ships had begun to shovel fish
out of Faxaflói by the boatload – not to mention the trawlers. Yet
when supplies were plentiful and most fishermen felt compelled
to lower their prices in the streets, it never occurred to my grandfather to lower his; he sold his catch at the same price as he
always did, and then the fish on his barrow became by far the
most expensive. In this way my grandfather Björn of Brekkukot
rejected all the fundamental rules of economics. This man kept in
his heart a secret money-valuation of his own. Was this standard
right or wrong? Was the bank's standard perhaps more right?
Or the standard at Gúðmúnsen's Store? It may well be that my
grandfather was wrong, yet not wrong enough to discourage most
of the regular customers at his wheelbarrow from trading with
him also on those days when his fish was more expensive than
anywhere else. Everywhere in town, even as far as Árnapóst and
all the way up to Mosfell district, what's more, one could hear
people maintain that Björn of Brekkukot's fish tasted better
than other fish; people believed that Björn of Brekkukot in some
mysterious way hauled better and finer fish from the sea than
other men could. And for that reason everyone wanted to buy
from Björn of Brekkukot, even on the days when his fish was
more expensive than anywhere else.

4

WHAT IS THE VALUE OF THE BIBLE?

I have now said something about fish, but I have not said anything yet about the Bible. I cannot leave this subject without referring briefly to the price of the Bible in our house.

My grandfather Björn of Brekkukot was no bookman. I never knew him to read anything other than the family *Book of Sermons* by Bishop Jón Vídalín – unless one counts that he sometimes ran his eye over the advertisements in the *Ísafold*. He read aloud from Vídalín every Sunday just after noon. He usually read correctly (although he sometimes made mistakes) but never really well, and he always laid special emphasis on two things: to get the proper pulpit drone into his reading, and not to skip any of the figures which gave book, chapter and verse references to scriptural citations – sometimes several times in each sentence. But he never expanded these abbreviations when he read them; instead he would say, for instance, Mark, Rom, Cor, and Hab. Nor did he ever use ordinals among the numbers that accompanied these references, and he paid no attention to commas or other punctuation marks between the numbers. Instead of reading, for instance, "First Corinthians, thirteenth chapter, fifth verse" (written as I. Cor, 13: 5), he would read out "One Cor a hundred and thirty-five". But he never deviated from the special manner of reading that people in Iceland once used for God's Words, a monotonous and solemn chant in a high-pitched tone that dropped a fourth at the end of a sentence. This style of reading bore no trace of worldliness, although it had certain affinities with the mumblings of some of the mentally deranged. The artist is no longer born in Iceland who knows this particular chant.

I am quite unable to say what thoughts were aroused in my grandfather Björn of Brekkukot by these references in the *Book of Sermons* to ancient eccentrics from the far end of the

Mediterranean, enhanced by the rigidly systematic theology of German peasants, such as one finds in the Venerable Jón Vídalín. Many people would consider such a spiritual exercise as his readings to be no more than an empty formality. I can swear on oath that I never heard him make any reference to anything contained in these Sermons, nor was I ever aware of any other pious activities on his part besides those Sunday readings. Furthermore, I have not managed to find anyone who can remember having heard Björn of Brekkukot ever refer to any theological, moral, or philosophical doctrine in the Sermons. I have no idea whether my grandfather took notice of everything in it, or nothing. If he believed it all, he was just like those theologians who store their theology somewhere in a locked compartment of the brain, or rather, perhaps, like those travellers who carry a bottle of iodine in their luggage and take care to keep it tightly corked in case it leaks and ruins their belongings. To be honest, I think my grandfather Björn of Brekkukot would not have been significantly different if he had lived here in Iceland in pagan times, or if his home had been somewhere in the world where people never read Vídalín's *Book of Sermons* but believed instead in the bull Apis, or the god Ra, or the bird Colibri.

From all this it must be obvious that we were not bookish people. Any reading that was done in our house was done chiefly by visitors who brought their own books with them. Sometimes there were stories which they read aloud for the whole household, or else they took to reciting ballads. Overnight visitors often left their books behind with us, sometimes as payment for their lodgings, and that is how our library, small and haphazard as it was, probably came into being. I shall refer to that later.

But though various books happened to land in our house, no one noticed that we had no Bible until old Thórður the Baptist began staying with us; and this brings me at last to the matter that was uppermost in my mind.

It is too well-known to need mentioning that according to an ancient Icelandic price-scale, the cost of a Bible is equivalent to that of a cow – and that means an early-calving cow, or else six well-fleeced lambing ewes. This price is written on the title-page of the Bible edition that was printed in a remote mountain valley in northern Iceland in 1584, and as is known, Icelanders have never believed in any other Bible than this one; it was printed with tasteful vignettes and decorative woodcuts and weighs five pounds, and is very like a raisin-box in shape. This volume has always been available in the better churches in Iceland.

As happened so often in summer, a visitor once came to the door of Brekkukot and said that he had just arrived on the steamer. Two or three summers later, he stayed with us for several weeks at a time. I can still remember how he came walking past the churchyard wall in a clerical coat (as Prince Albert coats were called in Iceland), wearing a hard hat of the kind called a half-keg, to distinguish it from a whole-keg, or tile hat. He wore a rubber collar buttoned at the back of the neck. This was old Thórður, or as he called himself, Thórður the Baptist. But what made me sure that this was another peat-thief on the way was the strange circumstance that this frock-coated man, who seemed at a distance to be one of the gentry in every respect, was carrying on his back a gunny sack stuffed with what looked to me like peats; but to cut a long story short, it was not peats he was carrying on his back, but Bibles – and that was all the luggage he had. I shall say nothing about how it happened that a frock-coated gentleman arriving from abroad on the steamship itself should make straight for our turf cottage at the outermost edge of civilization, where dandelions grew on the roof, rather than move into the Hotel d'Islande where he would have acquitted himself well among all the officials and foreigners.

Thórður the Baptist was a large man of imposing presence, with the kind of face whose chin seemed to have been pushed up forcibly from below, and an exceptionally well-formed Roman nose which curved down towards the cleft in the chin. His mouth was so tightly closed when he was not holding forth that his lips disappeared somewhere inside his mouth and were nowhere to be seen; but on his upper lip, the weakest and most insignificant part of the whole person, there sprouted a short and extremely well-trimmed moustache. He always screwed up his eyes so that they seemed to be sieving the light.

What old Thórður's title of Baptist was meant to signify we never really knew, nor did we care; indeed, we never saw him baptize a single living soul. It was said that he had landed up in some religious sects in Scotland and Canada and had given them his allegiance, and now received his bread from them; but there can hardly have been much left of that bread, since he chose to lay his head in one of the few free hostelries that have existed in the world in this century or the last. It was probably his business to proclaim in his native town the word of that Lord who believes in Baptists. It would never occur to me to doubt that old Thórður spoke from divine inspiration, if any man ever did; such was his exaltation in preaching that he never cared whether there was anyone within earshot or not when he preached, except that, if anything, I think he preferred to have no one; and indeed it seldom happened that he had any audience at all, unless some boys happened to be hiding in a nearby barrel to find out what so excellent a cleric was proclaiming with such zeal to no one. Unfortunately I had neither the intelligence nor the maturity, and perhaps not even sufficient curiosity either, to try to penetrate the kernel of Thórður the Baptist's message, any more than I wanted to fathom my grandfather's sermon-readings.

It is a matter of simple fact that Icelanders have always been notoriously indolent, and it may well be that Thórður both knew his countrymen all too well and was a good Icelander himself; for if it ever came about that one or two idlers happened to drift in his direction when he was standing alone in a deserted square, preaching, he invariably turned away and showed the honourable assembly his back. This he considered the most effective way of converting Icelanders. I remember walking past him down at the harbour one evening in a northerly gale of rain and fog, while he was preaching with great force and conviction at some wheelbarrows which were lying upside down a short distance away; he stamped on the ground with both feet to lend emphasis to his words and thumped the Bible with might and main to reinforce his arguments, and the froth flew from his lips in all directions. He was preaching against the unseemly and disgraceful practice of baptizing children:

"It is nowhere found written in this Holy Book," he cried, thumping the book. "Not by so much as a word or a letter or a dash or a dot is it found written in the Holy Book that innocent children should be baptized. Whosoever maintains that it stands anywhere written in Holy Scripture that innocent children have to be baptized does so on his own responsibility – and must take the consequences."

When old Thórður the Baptist had done his baptistical duty out here in Iceland, it was his mission to go next to Norway and preach there for a time; and it is considered conclusive proof of the great difference between Norwegians and Icelanders that no sooner had Thórður the evangelist set foot on land in Bergen than hosts of people were crowding round him to hear his message, so that the police and even the army had to be called out frequently to protect the old and infirm from being trampled underfoot, or to prevent partisan groups who were for or against this messenger of the Lord from rioting and inflicting mortal injuries upon one another.

Apart from the meagre income which old Thórður may have had from the Scots and the Canadians for turning the Icelanders and Norwegians from the practice of child-baptism, I think that the Baptist had no other belongings than those Bibles he carried in a gunny sack on his back from country to country; at least, no one knew him to have any other valuables in his possession.

The day now dawned when the Baptist was to leave Iceland and travel to Norway to preach fire and brimstone to all those who practised child-baptism in that country.

Each time he had previously stayed at Brekkukot for a month or six weeks on his summer travels he had invariably tried to repay the hospitality with a Bible, but my grandfather Björn had always excused himself from accepting such a gift on the ground that it was not the custom at Brekkukot to take precious belongings from people just for letting them sleep. On the other hand, my grandfather on previous occasions had not refused some trifling Christian pamphlets as token gifts from Thórður the Baptist. But Thórður was now tired of giving small presents, and refused even to contemplate leaving any gift smaller than a Bible on his departure.

"If you do not accept a Bible from me this autumn, Björn," he said, "I shall take it that you no longer consider yourself my friend; and besides, I could then never let it be known that I had stayed at your house again."

"I don't know how genuine your Bibles may be, my lad," said Björn of Brekkukot. "But in my time it was not known for Bibles to be printed in tiny letters on sheets of toilet-paper."

"My Christian conscience is my pledge that this Bible I have brought with me is good and genuine, lawfully printed and faithfully translated from the original languages by the Bible Society in London."

"In *what*?" said my grandfather.

"London," said the Baptist.

"What's that?" asked my grandfather.

"It is the capital of the British Empire," said the Baptist.

"Well, that may be so," said my grandfather. "I know nothing about that. The proper Bible here in Iceland was translated and printed by the late Right Reverend Guðbrandur at Hólar in the north. I have seen that Bible with my own eyes in the Cathedral here. It says in it that it costs a cow. That is our Bible."

Thórður the Baptist said, "I refuse to retract one word from my claim that my London Bible is a genuine Bible, even though it costs no more than seventy-five *aurar*."

"Do you think that the Right Reverend Guðbrandur was trying to rob us Icelanders when he put the price of the Bible at one cow?" said my grandfather. "No, my lad, the Bible which the Right Reverend Guðbrandur published was at the right price. And if the Bible was worth an early-calving cow in the past, then it is so still. A Bible that costs half a hen! Pshaw!"

"And my salvation, which stands as a pledge for my Bible – is that worth no more than dirt, perhaps?" said Thórður the Baptist.

"I'm not concerning myself with that," said my grandfather. "You'll have to wangle yourself out of that one yourself, my good man. And we shall be just as good friends whether you go up or down."

Thórður the Baptist was intending to leave on the steamship the following morning. But during the evening, when grandfather went to wind the clock for the week, what did he happen to find but one of Thórður's cheap Bibles hidden inside the clock?

Without a word my grandfather took the book out of the clock. This was at the time when our Skjalda was about to calve for the first or second time. Next morning, when the Baptist had kissed everybody goodbye and had gone outside with the rest of his Bibles in his sack for the Norwegians, and had reached the turnstile-gate – who should be standing on the path outside the gate but my grandfather Björn of Brekkukot, waiting for him with a cow in tow?

"Well! I'm glad I found you in time to kiss you goodbye," said the Baptist.

"God give you good day, my boy," said my grandfather. "And since you have left behind a genuine Bible, by your own account, I am now going to give you a genuine cow; for one gift deserves another."

"Yes, you have always been full of fun, my dear Björn," said the Baptist, and was through the gate and trying to kiss my grand-father as he went past; but he could not reach him.

"We do not kiss until we are even," said my grandfather.

The cash equivalent of the Holy Scriptures gazed lazily at the moors to the south and swished her tail in the morning calm.

"My ship is leaving," said the Baptist.

"Here is Skjalda's halter," said my grandfather.

Then they kissed, and while they were doing so, my grandfather slipped the rope into the Baptist's hand, and came back in through the turnstile. But when the Baptist had led the cow a stone's-throw away or so he dropped the halter and took to his heels in the direction of the town.

Then my grandfather pulled the London Bible out of his trouser pocket and said to me, "You are fast on your feet, my boy; run after Thórður the Baptist and give him back his book."

The Baptist was old and short-winded, and it did not take me long to catch up with him. I gave him his book, and he thrust it into his sack without a word, and carried on towards the ship.

5

TWO WOMEN AND A PICTURE

I have written about everything at Brekkukot, both indoors and out, which can be given a name; but I have scarcely said a word yet about my grandmother, who was certainly not some useless ornament about the place. On the other hand, if she were likened to the heart of the house, one could say exactly the same about her as one does about healthy hearts in general, that whoever is lucky enough to have such a heart is quite unaware of having a heart at all.

But since people have been invited into the living-room at Brekkukot time and time again in this story already, I think the time has come to mention the housewife and hostess, however briefly. I say "however briefly" because I never really knew the woman; for instance, I was almost grown up before it ever occurred to me, quite accidentally one day, that she might perhaps have a life story like other people. What I have to tell about her here is really how little I knew about her.

All the same, it was probably she who brought me up, so far as I have been brought up at all; at least, I believe that she had a greater part than several other people in making me the way I am. But it was not until after I was fully grown that I noticed her sufficiently to feel that I really saw her. Suddenly one day I simply felt that she was probably closer to me than anyone else in the world, even though I knew less about her than anyone else and despite the fact that she had been in her grave for some time by then. It is anything but easy trying to speak of a person one knows so little about but who is nevertheless so close to one.

She was an extremely thin and fragile-looking woman; nevertheless when I first came to know her she had already reached an age which is beyond the reach of most people, however fabled they are for strength and stamina; and she lived for at least another quarter of a century after that. I cannot remember her otherwise than bowed and toothless, with a bit of a cough and red-rimmed eyes from having to stand before the open fire in the kitchen-smoke of Brekkukot, and before that in other cottages whose names I did not know. There might sometimes have been a little soot in the wrinkles of her face, and her head would dither slightly when she looked at you with those mild eyes of hers. Her hands were long and bony.

My grandmother had a cousin who was probably fifteen years younger, although she aged more quickly and lasted less well, and this was Kristín of Hríngjarabær up on the hill at the north end of the churchyard; she had been housekeeper to the old bell-ringer, now dead. Once, as so often before, my grandmother and I went to pay a visit to Kristín's house. Our path lay through the churchyard. It was at the time of year when the flies were in their element. The two old women talked together in that curiously distant tone which is like the sound of the bell-buoy off Engey, or of a fiddle up north in Langanes; a fine sound for lulling you to sleep. When we had finished drinking coffee and I felt I could not fall asleep any more that day, and was waiting for my grandmother to say her goodbyes so that I would get the shiny new ten-*aurar* piece which Kristín always gave me as a parting gift for being such a good boy, I leaned against the sill of the window that looked over the churchyard and across Skerjafjörður all the way south to Keilir, and began to amuse myself by killing flies. A little later we said goodbye and I got my beautiful ten-*aurar* piece from Kristín.

But when we had reached the middle of the churchyard on our way back home, my grandmother said to me, "There is one thing you must never do, little one, for it is wicked."

"What's that, grandmother?" I asked.

"Never kill flies in other people's houses," said my grandmother.

"Is Aunt Kristín so fond of her flies?" I asked.

"No," said my grandmother. "But it is she who lives at Hríngjarabær."

How relieved I was that my grandmother had not admonished

me in front of Aunt Kristín, who only gave me ten *aurar* because I was such a good boy.

Since I have now almost inadvertently brought these two women together into the story, I must not delay any longer in telling a little about what I thought most remarkable in their relationship: in both their living-rooms there hung a picture which was quite unlike all the other pictures on their walls. The other pictures were there by chance; at our house, for instance, there was a picture of two angels flying upright with a garland of flowers between them, and one of a girl advertising Sunlight soap, another one of the late psalm-composer Hallgrímur Pétursson (one of the most dismal-looking men I have ever seen in a picture), and finally a few pictures of Icelandic-American families who had been given shelter at Brekkukot while they were waiting for a ship to take them to America; these people had achieved "good times" in America, as the saying went, which consisted of clearing away boulders and uprooting tree-stumps or digging ditches, and then posing in collar and tie in a photographer's studio. The same sort of haphazardness applied to the pictures in Kristín's house at Hríngjarabær. But the picture which I am now going to describe was special; it was a photograph in profile of a young man looking upwards. He seemed to be seeing in a reverie some far-off wondrous sight; and in particular, the clothes he was wearing lent the picture an air which was quite alien to our life here; a stiff white collar, a gleaming shirt-front, and a tail-coat with glistening silk lapels, and over and above that, a rose in the buttonhole.

Even more remarkable, however, was the discovery I soon made that this was the son of Kristín of Hríngjarabær, and consequently related to us at Brekkukot – Georg Hansson, who "nowadays", as the old woman said, was called Garðar Hólm.

One fine day or other when I was contemplating this picture of Garðar Hólm, I could not resist asking my grandmother, "Does Garðar Hólm have a home anywhere? Or is he perhaps just an angel?"

"Little Georg?" she said. "No, I suppose he no longer has a home anywhere, poor creature."

"Why didn't he stay put at home with his mother, our Aunt Kristín at Hríngjarabær?" I asked.

"He took to travelling," she said.

"How did he do that?" I asked.

"It is ill-fortune that causes people to travel," said my grandmother.

"What ill-fortune?" I asked.

"We won't talk any more about that, little one," she said. "He was a nice little boy, Kristín's little Georg, when he was playing here in the churchyard. Very like you. But he took to travelling."

I was silent for a long time, pondering in my mind this ill-fortune which was graver than any ill-fortune known to people in Brekkukot; and finally I asked, "Why do people go on these travels, grandmother?"

She replied, "Some people just give up and leave their farms; or their homes are taken from them; some people lose their reason; a few can see nothing but America; or else the poor wretches have done something wrong and are sent away over mountains and deserts, rivers and sands, to be put into prison."

"Have you never done any travelling, grandmother?" I asked after a long pause.

Peering down at her knitting to see if she had dropped a stitch she said, "Oh yes, I have travelled. I travelled once all the way from Ölfús in the east to the south here. We went across Hellisheiði."

"Wasn't it terribly bad, grandmother?" I asked.

"We won't talk about that, little one," she said. "What's past is past."

A long time went by before I summoned up enough courage to mention the luckless Garðar Hólm again. But on one occasion when I was alone with Aunt Kristín at Hríngjarabær I said to her, "Why is Garðar Hólm always travelling?"

"He's singing, of course," she replied, rather brusquely; and from then on I always noticed that every time her son's name was mentioned, she seemed almost to become angry. Although I was more than a little surprised at such a reply, I did not dare for a long time to go into it further, and went on gazing respectfully at the picture.

"Don't you know that singing is the noblest thing on earth?" said the woman, as crossly as before.

"Can he sing high?" I asked.

"What do you think, child?" she said. "No one in Iceland can go so high. But he can also get deep down. That's his old harmonium in the corner there. And here's your ten *aurar*. And now try not to ask questions about things you don't understand and which don't concern you."

I longed for the time when I would be thought clever enough to have secrets disclosed to me; but until that time came I went on pondering this difficult problem.

6

PROPER TITLES AT BREKKUKOT

It is strange, considering how intimately I knew Brekkukot, so intimately indeed that I felt I had lived there even before I was born, and despite the fact that this woman, my grandmother, had taught me how to speak and think and ended by teaching me to read – it came as a complete surprise to me when someone told me many years later that she had never had a bed to sleep in, in her own home. I then had to acknowledge that the only times I had ever seen her asleep were in her kitchen when she was sitting on the lower stone of the hearth, which jutted out a little, and leaning back against the upper stone; her head would sink forward and her hands with their knitting would drop into her lap and the restless needles would be stilled for a while; and there was only a faint glimmer in the fireplace. I am told that no one ever saw her go to bed in the evening; but if there was an empty pallet available somewhere she may perhaps have stretched out on it for an hour or two in the middle of the night, or else contented herself with leaning back against those hearthstones. What is certain is that if she slept, she never went to sleep before everyone else had retired; and no matter how early anyone rose in Brekkukot, she was always up and about already and had made the coffee or even cooked the porridge. And I can remember, too, with absolute certainty that the fire in her hearth never went out during all the time that I was my grandfather's and my grandmother's son there at Brekkukot.

I have already described how this woman impressed upon me never to kill flies in other people's houses. Now I just want to mention one or two other doctrines that she taught me.

When Skjalda was put out each morning late in the summer and I had to drive her to the pastures, this cow had the bad habit of putting her head over the bit of fencing round the swede-patch and starting to eat the leaves off the swedes. The fencing was actually rather old and dilapidated by then, rotting and moss-grown, and in several places did not reach as high as the tansies and angelica and the docken clumps, so it was not perhaps the animal's fault that she paid no attention to such a fence; but if she managed to get at the swedes she became so enthusiastic that she paid no heed to me even when I whipped her with all my might and main with a docken-switch. I had just learned a few swearwords by then from various good people, and when the cow refused to budge despite all the beating, I used to shout, "You damned old cow, Skjalda!" and a few other sentiments of that kind.

That summer a man from Borgarfjörður on his spring trip to the capital had left his dog with us at Brekkukot by mistake. The wretched cur stayed with us all summer, waiting for his master to come and fetch him on his autumn trip. He looked just like any other old sheep-dog. He was very bored at Brekkukot, because he was always thinking about his master and wondering how on earth the man had managed to forget him. He often lay with his head on his paws at our turnstile-gate or on the paving at the door of the cottage, with his eyes open and that rather pathetic expression of doggy melancholy on his face; and it did not help matters that the dratted cat was always prowling somewhere around him – a brindled stray who had also settled in with us.

The dog was a guest himself and could not bring himself to chase cats on an alien farm. My grandmother would sometimes toss him some fish-skin and bones if she happened to pass near him, and always with the same words: "Here you are, creature!" or else, "Help yourself, you brute!"

The dog was the only animal I ever heard her address disrespectfully apart from the cat, and she never mentioned the cat without a slight grimace of distaste, as if this creature were some abominable family fetch which had dogged her and her kin from time immemorial. The cat was called Brand, and never had other than four titles of address: "that devil", "that disgrace", "that pest", or "that bane". Never on any occasion did my grandmother pat the dog or stroke the cat; yet she had a constant supply of fish-skin and bones in the pocket of her skirts. I should add that she was nevertheless the only person in the house to whom these two stray creatures attached themselves unconditionally and unreservedly. Wherever she went around our plot of land, even if it was only to the clothes-rope, they were both round her at once and almost on top of her, the dog with boisterous affection while the cat rubbed herself against my grandmother's leg with her tail held straight up in the air and ending in a handsome hook at the tip. Whenever my grandmother had to slip over to see Kristín at Hríngjarabær the animals were always at her heels until she reached the churchyard gate, which she never allowed them to pass through, of course.

And now to return to the point where I left off, with the cow standing with her head inside the fence eating the new-grown swedes – this was a good opportunity, I thought, now that we had a dog around the place; and I set the dog on the cow.

As the day wore on it became very warm. The dog lay on the paving with his head on his paws and his eyes open and was undoubtedly thinking about his master and wondering why he never came. I was sure that the poor creature could not sleep for sheer boredom. So I sat down beside him on the paving and started to pat him on the head, as people had done to me when I was small. Then I began to sing to the dog the following little poem which I had composed myself, to a tune that I made up as I went along and which was so moving that I burst into tears as I sang it:

> "Dearest blessed doggy mine,
> Whom other dogs adore,
> Fly with the doggy angels fine
> To the doggy heaven's door."

When it was nearly six o'clock my grandmother came out to have a look at the swedes in this fine weather; she walked past me as I played in the grass, and seemed not to notice me. But while she was looking at the swedes, with her back to me, I was sure I heard her say, as if she were talking to herself, "I hope I didn't hear correctly this morning, that someone in this house was using ugly words about the cow."

"It wasn't me!" I shouted.

"At least I hope that no one has ever heard Björn of Brekkukot doing that," she said.

"The cow was at the swedes!" I said.

"I know few things more wicked than speaking ill of a cow," my grandmother said, "except perhaps setting a dog on her. The cow gives us our milk. The cow is mother to us all. 'Little cow, little cow, have you any milk now.' 'The blessed beast' is what one says about the cow."

I said nothing. She went on peering under the leaves to see if there were any swedes ready for the soup-pot yet. And as she stooped over them, I heard her say as if to the swedes, "I wonder who was blessing a dog out here in front of the house today?"

"I can't remember doing that!" I cried.

"I thought I heard someone blessing a dog," she said. "My ears were probably deceiving me. About dogs one says 'the brute', 'creature', or 'wretch'. At least no one has ever heard Björn of Brekkukot saying nice things to a dog."

7

BARBED WIRE AT HVAMMSKOT

Our horse, Gráni, was pastured on a distant moor out at Sogin, and occasionally he had to be fetched when he was needed for work. It is no exaggeration to say that at that time, Sogin was one of the farthest points of the atlas. There is a modern town at Sogin now, and no one who enters this paradise could suspect that a few decades ago there were horse-grazings there. When Gráni had to be fetched, it was a journey that took the best part of a day. At Sogin there was a little moorland brook called the Soga Stream; it was comparatively easy to jump over it. And yet this stream for some reason or other formed a most sinister impression on my grandmother's mind. She never really wanted me to go to fetch the horse by myself, but always in company with some other boy who was also going to fetch a horse and who could pull me out of the stream if I were to fall in.

"Be careful of the Soga Stream", was always the last thing she said when we were setting off. And when we arrived back with the horse or horses in the evening, the first thing she always asked was: "Was there much water in the Soga Stream today?" If there were ever a downpour when Gráni was out on the moor and there was a chance that he would have to be fetched in a hurry, the old woman could be heard muttering, "My, my, what a lot of water there must be in the Soga Stream today."

And now one day, as had happened so often before, I was sent off to fetch our horse out at Sogin, accompanied by a few other boys who were on the same errand.

This was about the time, not long after the Boer War, when the Barbed-wire Age was beginning in Iceland. This special commodity, which is banned by law in most countries except for military purposes and was indeed said to have been invented during the Boer War, has pacified the Icelanders more than any other foreign product one could name; and whereas in other countries there are severe penalties for putting this wretched stuff up in the open in peacetime, in Iceland barbed wire became the most desirable luxury commodity in the land for a while, next only to alcohol and cement. There are few things over which the nation has united over so wholeheartedly as stringing this glorious material round every part of the land, over hill and dale, heath and moor, right up to the mountaintops and out to the farthest sea-cliffs. At first, many people behaved as the Boers had done towards the English, and simply climbed over the barbed wire wherever they came to it, but then the Althing passed a law declaring barbed wire to be inviolate in Iceland. These laws were made more far-reaching by special local regulations in some districts and towns, including our town of Reykjavík; here, a by-law about barbed wire was issued to the effect that anyone caught climbing over these sacred boundary-fences would have to pay a fine of ten *krónur*: ten *krónur* at that time was the price of a yearling ram.

To come back to us boys on our journey – after great detours and many digressions and the usual boys' dawdling for much of the day, we eventually reached some hillocks to the south-east of the horse-moors. There were a few scattered farms around, some up on the hills and others in the grassy hollows or dales, and the lands belonging to these farms were festooned with barbed wire for their full length and breadth.

One of the farms there was called Hvammskot. We halted on the bank of a stream just outside the home-field, where a strong barbed-wire fence had been erected – quite at random, as far as one could see. And as we were standing there, out of sight behind a knoll, one of us volunteered the information that anyone who crossed a fence of this kind would be fined ten *krónur*.

We quickly agreed that it would be fun to risk a death-leap which was valued at such a high price. And because this crime had all the fascination that any kind of gambling has when there is money involved, we all set to and began jumping over the barbed wire. I will not say that the deed was done entirely without palpitations, and indeed we had a look-out posted to see if there were any spies about; but as we had really suspected all along, no one noticed the outrage we were committing, and no fines were imposed on us. Now, these lawful fines which were not exacted from us were in effect treasure-trove; so each and every one of us had profited by the equivalent of a yearling ram at the very first attempt. So it was little wonder that we tried again. We could not tear ourselves away from this lucrative work for hours, and it was still not nearly supper-time when each and all of us had become prosperous from unclaimed ten-*krónur* fines; and every time we performed another leap, another yearling ram was added to those we had already. In the end we were beginning to grow a little bored with all the sheep we had collected; and one of us worked it out that for all these sheep we could buy up all the chocolate there was in the country, even including caramels as well; and another said that our sheep would suffice to buy all the chocolate and caramels that had ever been imported into the country since the first settlement of Iceland. And then suddenly we were aware of a huge dun-coloured dog coming bounding towards us, barking fiercely and looking distinctly aggressive. We realized that this dog would scare away from us all the sheep we had accumulated that day, and we started to shout abuse and throw stones at him. At this the dog became twice as furious; indeed, as far as we could see he was undoubtedly a bloodhound and was sure to tear us to pieces, so we saw no other way but to take to our heels across hills and hollows as fast as our legs would carry us.

"We were beginning to wonder about you, my boy," said my grandfather and grandmother. "What happened to you?"

"We were up at the farms," I said.

"What were you all doing there?" they asked.

"We were making money," I said. "I have jumped two hundred times over the barbed wire at Hvammskot. That's two thousand *krónur*. And if a fierce dog hadn't arrived that wanted to kill us, we would have made another two thousand *krónur* as well."

"Tut tut!" said my grandfather. "Really!"

He was sitting on his hands on the wall of the vegetable garden, as he sometimes did of a fine evening, and he grimaced at my story as if he had the gripes; it was a habit he had when he heard something silly. "Tut tut! Really!" My grandmother stood at the door of the cottage and gazed at him for a long time. But nothing more was said that evening.

But a few days later my grandmother said to me out of the blue, "We have decided that I and not Björn should talk to you about the barbed-wire fence at Hvammskot, Álfgrímur dear."

"What barbed wire is that, grandmother?" I said, for I had forgotten all about that happy gambling enterprise.

"You should know by now, you young creatures, that it is against the law here in Iceland to climb barbed-wire fences," said my grandmother.

"It was only a game, grandmother," I said. "No one has to pay anything."

"You can be quite sure that Jón of Hvammskot saw you at it," said my grandmother. "Jón of Hvammskot is a good friend of Björn of Brekkukot here. Anything that displeases Jón of Hvammskot displeases Björn of Brekkukot. Anyone who climbs Jón of Hvammskot's barbed-wire fence climbs Björn of Brekkukot's barbed-wire fence."

I could not say anything – even though I knew full well that the day would never dawn when Björn of Brekkukot would buy barbed wire. I held my tongue. And besides, I knew all too well that every single misdeed a man could commit was first and foremost committed against my grandfather Björn of Brekkukot.

"What am I to do, grandmother?" I asked.

"I am going to give you some food and a new pair of shoes and send you up to Hvammskot today," she said. "I want you to ask to see the woman of the house there. Tell her where you come from and give her greetings from me, the old woman who stays with Björn of Brekkukot, and give her from me this loaf of bread."

My grandmother, in fact, was one of the greatest known artists at making pot-bread.

When my shoes had been made I set off for Hvammskot with this great loaf of pot-bread in a bag on my back, the two-thousand-*krónur* pot-bread, the two-hundred-sheep pot-bread:

this pot-bread that was worth more than all the chocolate which has been eaten in Iceland from the days of the first settlement down to the present day, even counting caramels as well.

My grandmother stood at the turnstile-gate and called out after me, "And be careful of the Soga Stream, Álfgrímur dear. Don't jump over it where it is narrow and deep. Wade over it instead, where it broadens out a bit."

"Yes, grandmother," I said.

But when I had gone a few paces farther she called out to me again:

"And if you meet the dog, Álfgrímur dear, then remember one thing: never abuse another man's dog. If you meet a dog, let him sniff the back of your hand, and he will quickly make friends with you."

8

THE MID-LOFT

It would drive one mad to try to tell about all the visitors who ever came to Brekkukot, and indeed such a book would burst all the printing-presses in Iceland; I intend to describe only a few of them here, not more than I can count on my fingers, and in particular those who concern my own story to some extent. And I will start by enumerating those who lived in the mid-loft.

A dilapidated, creaking stair with seven steps connected the passage with the mid-loft in our house. It was here that I and my fellow-residents lived. This mid-loft was the centre-space of the upper storey, partitioned off from the rooms on either side; we were in effect a sort of vestibule for those who lived in the east and west ends of the loft, as well as for anyone who went up or down the stair. When my grandfather did not give up his bed to a visitor, he slept in the part of the loft that faced south, but which was actually called the west end; otherwise he would lie on a pile of nets out in the store-shed, and would think nothing of it. Often our living-room was full, and people were tightly packed in at both ends of the loft; there were sleepers in the passage and sleepers in the doorway, and sometimes during the autumn trips, when we had the largest crowds, they would bed themselves down in the store-shed and the hayloft as well. But in the mid-loft slept only those who might be called the regular residents at Brekkukot. Apart from myself there were three other guests, if I can so call them, whose stay in the mid-loft was hardly brief – at least, I can remember them from as far back as I can remember myself. The four of us slept there two to a bed.

The beds were nailed to the wall under the eaves, and shared the same headboard; and above the headboard there was a window with a pane of glass about the size of a man's palm cut into the turf roof, and through this window could be seen one blade of grass and one star. Under the eaves on the other side was the trap-door to the loft, which gave a little additional floor space when it was closed, and a tiny partitioned-off cubicle or closet beside the stair-head, with a rickety door which seldom stayed on the latch. This cubicle had a bed, a bench, and a three-legged stool; it was sometimes used to accommodate married couples, or men who were particularly stout, as well as sick or mentally ill people, or else women who were giving birth or dying, or any others who for one reason or another needed to be alone. I was one of those brought into the world in that little cubicle, so I have been told.

I shall now tell you a little about the three resident guests, my companions there in the mid-loft. We mention first the celebrated Captain Hogensen, now deceased, otherwise known as Jón Hákonarson of Helgafell, a Breiðafjörður man. Captain Hogensen was up in years by then; the light of the world had more or less taken leave of this man, for he was almost blind. Like many others, he had heard away out west in Breiðafjörður what a popular and excellent place Brekkukot was to stay at; and when old age began to creep up on him, he came east with the sole purpose of taking a berth there. He was not only failing in sight but he suffered from rheumatism as well and no doubt many other ailments besides – which he never talked about, however. I am told that he surrendered a plot of land in return for becoming a pensioner in the mid-loft at Brekkukot.

Captain Hogensen was one of the most genuine saga-men I have ever known. He was descended from pastors, sheriffs, and poets. We shared a bed for as long as I can remember. He was grandiloquent in conversation; he never talked to me other than as one saga-man to another, and all the topics he discussed were above everyday trifles and incidents.

Captain Hogensen would sit on his bed and spin horsehair, which he used to procure for himself by all sorts of tricks and dodges. He teased the hair in his hands, combed it into a hank, fastened the hank with an awl to the post at the foot of the bed and then spun the hank on a spindle, and finally plaited ropes and girths from it by fastening the end round the bed-post. I had the job of collecting all the hairs that he let fall to the floor because of his failing sight.

This Jón Hákonarson was called Captain Hogensen because many many years ago it had been his job to pilot Danish survey ships in Breiðafjörður, where the navigational channels are difficult and hazardous for those who do not know the area.

Jón Hákonarson was certainly descended from good stock, and was a true-blue Icelandic chieftain in Breiðafjörður by nature and lineage, attitudes and ideals, even if there had been nothing else to commend him. But the King of Denmark himself had elevated him to a recognizable wordly rank that made genealogy, as well as attitudes and ideals, superfluous; and indeed he called himself by rights a Danish naval commander and His Danish Majesty's Pilot. He never parted with his blue, gilt-buttoned uniform nor the cap pertaining to His Danish Majesty's Pilot in Breiðafjörður. He always put on this uniform at Christmas and Easter, and also on New Year's Day and the first day of summer, and on these occasions he would sit on his bed with a dignified bearing all day without touching his horsehair. It was his custom to rise from his bunk on New Year's morning, put on his finery, and get someone to lead him into town in order to invoke God's blessing on the authorities and try to worm a little horsehair out of them.

Another of the guests in the mid-loft during my time there was our Superintendent, as we always called him, who I thought for a long time was the superintendent for the whole town. Apart from that, I think he was called Jón of Skagi.

This superintendent was a very distant relative of those two cousins, my grandmother and Kristín of Hríngjarabær. He was the sort of guest about whom one could never actually be sure whether he was staying there or not. Generally speaking, he never came to bed before everyone else was asleep, and he had finished his morning coffee with grandmother and gone off into the blue before anyone else was up and about.

Our superintendent was probably descended from the Hidden People; at least I never heard it suggested that he was descended from pastors, sheriffs, and poets. It was a real event if we who shared the nights with him ever managed to speak to him; for a long time I scarcely knew whether he was actually staying with us or not – and yet, his two pouches lay on a shelf over the bed when I was small, the one full of snuff and the other of gold. Whenever anyone happened to run into this superintendent he was invariably so clean and spruce that he shone. When a month or so had passed without anyone remembering that he existed, and someone then eventually came across him outside somewhere, he had no other news to offer than that it was splendid weather for mice that day; and when that was agreed, he would hasten to add, "Yes, and it's no worse for eagles."

I did not begin to inquire about who this man was until I was a little older; and I don't care if I anticipate my own story here: he was a philosopher. A certain bee had settled in his bonnet; he had left his farm in Akranes because he had come to the conclusion that he could be of greater use to mankind if he left off raising sheep for slaughter. He had sold his excellent salmon-river to the English for gold, and moved to the capital to become a superintendent. But in those two pouches that lay side by side on the shelf above his bed the chronicle that is recorded here came into being.

The superintendent's bed-fellow was the man whose job, in my younger days, was to spread manure for people in the capital, as well as on the home-fields of the farms in the nearby valleys and out on the Nesses. His name was Runólfur Jónsson. It would not be excessive praise to say of him that in the whole of Iceland there has never been a greater admirer of good cess-pools, not excepting the Icelandic Agricultural Society.

Runólfur Jónsson was also descended from pastors, sheriffs, and poets, but he was first and foremost related to one of the most excellent Chief Justices this country has ever known. He never discussed his distinguished antecedents in everyday conversation; but when he had a drink in him, which he called "acquiring a battleship", he would make his way down town and preach about the Chief Justice on the steps of the Theological Seminary or on the pavement in front of Gúðmúnsen's Store, although unfortunately the kind of audience he attracted there were least likely to be impressed by such distinguished antecedents. Runólfur Jónsson had worked on fishing-smacks, and had been on Gúðmúnsen's Store boats for more than thirty years, but now he had been put ashore once and for all because of salt-burn in his eyes; he had become what my grandfather called the retired dominie of Gúðmúnsen's Store. Most of Runólfur's earnings while he had been at sea had gone into paying fines for turning up late for his boat. On the other hand in his latter years, as I have already said, he took it upon himself to empty people's cess-pools in the town and its neighbourhood. From earliest times, cess-pools had always lain open and unprotected at people's doors in Iceland, as is still the custom on farms in France; and in these open cess-pools more Icelanders have drowned than in any other sea, the ocean excepted, and therefore it fell to Runólfur's lot to encounter more and more dangerous seas as he grew older.

But round about this time a symptom of the new age was appearing in the future capital city, as well as out at Seltjarnarnes, in that the pioneering elements in the farming community were building concrete pits on their farms to replace the cess-pools in front of their houses. Runólfur Jónsson admired these modern receptacles more than any other piece of contemporary crafts-manship in the world; he considered a good cess-pit to be a supernatural phenomenon, or a miracle. For him it was a pleasure not to be reckoned in money, and a compensation for much that he had had to do without during his life, to be allowed in his old age to spread manure from these matchless modern masterpieces.

Runólfur Jónsson usually got drunk four times a year, and then always for a few weeks at a time. In between times he was sober. It was more often than not the superintendent, his bed-mate, who enabled him to "acquire a battleship". It goes without saying that he invariably vanished from Brekkukot when The Drink called, and did not return until he had sobered up again; the spirit which prevailed at Brekkukot allowed that all people were considered human beings, not to say gentry, whether rich or poor, saint or criminal – all except drunkards. And besides, these crooked little turf cottages held up by a few rotting wooden spars would have been reduced to ruins long ago if they had housed drunkards. But no sooner had this Chief Justice's kinsman ended his battle-ship expedition than he came climbing up our stair again and began sleeping beside the superintendent once again.

I am not going to describe here Runólfur Jónsson's condition when he returned from these expeditions, except to say that the moment he turned up, the superintendent would cut his hair and beard and begin to clean him up carefully all over with soft-soap, creosote, and brimstone; the superintendent considered this service for Runólfur as axiomatic as giving him money for liquor.

But although Runólfur was always completely sober at home, he could never reconcile himself to the mental attitudes of those who live on this dry dung-heap they call land, and so his conver-sation with them was often rather weird. One of his conversational short-comings was that he could never remember the names of people or places, excepting only that of Björn of Brekkukot and that of Gúðmúnsen, when he was drunk. So he had to resort to the expedient of using long circumlocutions for personal names, and even his friends could find it difficult to fathom what he was saying. I shall not go right through his vocabulary here, but it must be admitted that it resembled in some ways Konráð Gíslason's Danish dictionary. He never called my grandmother anything other than "the woman who had the children"; his bed-mate he called "the man who owns the pouches", and Captain Hogensen he naturally never called anything but "the man who commands warships". Unfortunately, Runólfur Jónsson could not remember what the Saviour's name was either, and if it ever happened that he had to mention God he had to resort to the unfortunate expedient of referring to "the Man who is above Björn of Brekkukot". Nor did he know the name of the land he lived in, except that it was dry.

Before I end my description of Runólfur Jónsson's qualities, I must not forget the feat that is the most likely to immortalize his name in history: namely, that this worthy night-companion and foster-brother of mine was one of the first men to be run over by a motor car; he was then almost eighty years old. This came about because, when he was drinking, he invariably walked in the middle of the road, waving a bottle, singing, holding forth and laughing, all at the same time; and he was always followed by a motley collection of drinking companions, idlers, stray dogs, ponies, and cyclists (who were then just beginning to appear, and were Danish). He paid no more attention to motor-cars than to any other tin-cans rolling along the gutter.

So if by some ill chance it should happen that Runólfur Jónsson, that descendant of Chief Justices, should one fine day vanish from this book and that I forget to mark the moment of his disappearance, it is because my foster-brother has been run over by the first motor-car that ever came to Iceland.

9

THE AUTHORITIES

Visitors to Brekkukot sometimes talked about "the authorities" and "the gentry". But there was not much come and go, exactly, between Brekkukot and the doors of the authorities. "The authorities" – for long enough I had no idea what kind of foreign company this was. It is strange to have lived in the selfsame capital in which the authorities of the country sat (for that's what all authorities did – they *sat*), and yet not know with any certainty more about them than about the angels that flew upright with a garland of flowers in our picture. But when a man in a frock-coat with a velvet collar, a half-keg, a come-to-Jesus collar and lorgnettes came over to grandfather's wheelbarrow on a bright summer's day and raised his hat and asked with dignity and courtesy, "Did you have a good catch this morning, Björn?" while my grandfather laid a medium-sized cod on the scales for him and the man paid with a newly minted silver coin, and was given wire through the cod's head while others had to make do with sticking a forefinger through its gills, and then raised his hat again, and held the fish at arm's length as he walked away – that man was one of the authorities. But it happened more often that my grandfather would wheel his barrow to the kitchen doors of the authorities' houses and sell the fish to the maid. I myself, on the other hand, had no dealings with the authorities until I had grown important enough to enter their presence on New Year's Day with the late Captain Hogensen.

I am not actually going to describe all the New Year's Day expeditions I made to the authorities with Captain Hogensen in my childhood days, but only to touch lightly upon the first one we made, for it was somewhat the same as all the later expeditions on the same errand, and had the added interest of novelty.

I must have been about six when I was first appointed to guide Captain Hogensen into the presence of these gentlemen to wish them a good New Year. I want to make it clear that this expedition to the authorities was not memorable to me because of any reve-lation of the world's glory that occurred during the visit; rather, I am describing it because I believe it added an unexpected tone to the tale I am now telling.

I take up the story at the point when Captain Hogensen engaged a good man said to be skilled in such crafts to trim his hair and then shave the point of his chin to make him resemble King Kristian IX of Denmark as closely as possible. The Captain woke up about seven o'clock on New Year's Day, rose from his bed and began to dress himself, slowly and carefully, in the darkness the Saviour had bestowed on him, which neither candle-light, nor oil-lamp, nor the sunrise itself, nor any illumination other than the light of a dauntless heart, could conquer. Even though he was as purblind as one could reasonably expect of anyone, he invariably polished up the gilt buttons of his finery himself; and if these buttons were not genuine gold, then I have never seen it. By the time others were coming downstairs on New Year's morning, the Captain was sitting on the edge of his bed resplendent in his blue naval uniform with the gilt buttons, and waiting. The peak of his cap gleamed like a mirror. He would scarcely believe it when he was told that the grey of dawn was not yet showing at the window, and he asked his young attendant to stay beside him and tell him honestly whenever it was light enough for someone with sight to find his way into town.

When I was six, and indeed for some time afterwards, I was, like the eminent Candide, quite certain that the world we live in is best at home, and I therefore had no enthusiasm for anything beyond the turnstile-gate at Brekkukot; and as is common among primitive people, higher civilization was hardly likely to impress me.

"Well, well, may God give you all a good day and a blessed and prosperous New Year," said Captain Hogensen to the maid at the Minister's house when we went inside. "The Royal Naval Officer Jón Hogensen is here to pay his respects to the Minister."

The maid indicated a certain place in the vestibule where we could stand, but said that the public rooms were still being cleaned after the party the previous night and that the government officials were expected to present themselves just before noon, "but I can always try, I suppose, to tell the Minister that you are here, my dear."

When we had been waiting for a while in the vestibule, rather solemnly and in absolute silence, a man in shirt-sleeves and a fork-beard suddenly arrived, with his braces dangling behind him like twin tails. He was smoking a cigar.

"Well, well," he said, "a very good day to you, Hogensen, old chap, and welcome, we had better say, even though there is no more time to spare for the navy than usual. But we must look into it, as it were. May I offer you a cigar to puff?"

Captain Hogensen clicked his heels and turned towards the Minister with a salute:

"I wish the King of Denmark and you, his servant, good health and blessings in the New Year, at the same time as I express to you and His Majesty my wish and hope for improved political conditions for us Icelanders on land and sea in this coming year. And may I at the same time present to you this upright and gifted young lad who stands by my side, Álfgrímur Álfgrímsson, foster-son of that honourable and intelligent gentleman, Björn of Brekkukot."

"Quite so, my friend," said the King's Minister and came forward and offered us a finger; he even took me lightly by the nape of the neck and drew me across the floor to a double door which he half-opened, and showed me into an exceptionally beautiful room in which house-maids were at work; and then he pointed out to me on one wall a huge portrait which hung beside the portrait of King Kristian, and said to me, "Young man, do you know who that is?"

And my goodness, if it wasn't the portrait of that strange person with the Roman nose and the upturned face! And once again I asked myself, but this time at the door of the King's Minister's drawing-room: Did this man exist, or was he merely a picture? Or were we who lived at either end of the churchyard perhaps descended from angels when all was said and done? I was dumb-founded!

"That's the boy from Hríngjarabær," said the Minister. "He has carried Iceland's fame far and wide across the sea. You come from Brekkukot: so give a good account of yourself!"

It seemed to me that the Minister's face lit up at this, but Captain Hogensen, on the other hand, continued on his course with that single-mindedness which the blind have:

"And now," said Captain Hogensen, "that I have wished your Excellency and the Danish kingdom a good New Year, but particularly my friend King Kristian the Ninth who is a foreign official of the Danish State, just as I am, I should like to ask you to convey to His Majesty my hope that he take notice of the prophecy I expounded to you last year and the year before that and the year before that, here in this very vestibule, and I know that His Majesty will not be offended if I repeat it once again, namely, that ever since the English and the Faroese and Gúðmúnsen were permitted to use drag-nets and trawls right up to people's back doors, I am tempted to say right up into their vegetable gardens in the bays here, in Breiðafjörður Bay as well as Faxaflói, Iceland has been threatened with depopulation all the way from Rosmhvalanes to Látrabjarg. I request that this evil state of affairs should cease."

"Quite so," said the Danish King's Minister, and closed the door to the drawing-room with its famous picture. He took two cigars out of his pocket and thrust them into Hogensen's pocket.

"The matter demands closer consideration and investigation by the proper authorities," he said. "I shall try to keep it in mind. We are grateful to you, my good Hogensen. You are really the only navy we have. But as you will understand, I cannot promise anything about this at present. These are critical times, to say the least of it. If the navy is weak, the army is even weaker. All our hopes here in Iceland depend on young men who can make us famous as we were in the olden days – oh, er, give the boy a little chocolate please, my good girl. For the rest, my dear Hogensen, as you can see, I am not dressed yet. But as I say, if there is anything else I can do for you, I shall of course be only too willing to try."

"As His Majesty the King of Denmark knows," said Captain Hogensen, standing there on a Persian carpet in the King's Minister's vestibule – and every time he mentioned the King he would click his heels together and bring his fist up to his cap in a salute – "As His Majesty knows, it was the will of destiny that I should become the King of Denmark's man in my prime, and that is more than can be said about most of my countrymen. And although I have now been reduced in my old age to spinning horsehair, as was done in olden times to punish rogues in Bláturn and on Brimarholm, I do not consider myself any the less a man for that, and I have no regrets for the services I did the King and his warriors when they sailed the Breiðafjörður in their warships. But it is worth considering whether it would not redound even more to the honour of the Danish kingdom if His Majesty were to send his servant a trifling hank of horsehair from Denmark to supplement the rump-pluckings which I manage with the most painful difficulty to extract from these practically horseless crofters out here in Iceland."

The King's Minister stifled a yawn and replied, "I shall most certainly and sincerely keep this request in mind, my dear Hogensen. But as a matter of fact Iceland is, perhaps, as you yourself say, ahem, hardly the proper party in this matter. On the other hand I think it not unlikely that the proper authorities in this matter could be induced to consider, reflect, and examine whether or not to, ahem, to examine, reflect, and consider what could be done in such a case in these difficult times. And now we must try to get a move on, my dear Hogensen, for we are expecting visitors and to tell you the truth I am not awake yet."

"Yes, well, then it only remains to me to ask the Minister whether His Excellency himself could not see his way to manage a wisp of horsehair for me in the spring when the royal ministerial horses have their tails docked? I know full well that my good King Kristian the Ninth, who was once a German cottager in Holstein burdened with debts and a brood of children, understands what it is to be a foreign official in the Danish kingdom."

At this point in the conversation the Minister all but woke up, and he answered almost with force and conviction: "To tell you the truth, Hogensen, I myself am so short of rope that words cannot describe it. Quite frankly I have my hands full finding enough rope to bind the hay that is mown here in the Ministry's meadows. And it was only on Christmas Day that I decided, in agreement with the proper authorities, and gave orders to that effect, that this royal ministry should make every effort to supply itself with the necessary ropes from the horses it has been allotted, and I have taken steps to have the prisoners make these required ropes. On the other hand, here is a newly minted two-*krónur* piece I would like to offer you, and there's ten *aurar* for the boy. Goodbye."

In February, it so happened that Captain Hogensen was able to send me to see the Minister again and present him with a set of hay-ropes.

10

TALK AND WRITING AT BREKKUKOT

In certain ancient musical scales there are different intervals than those to which people are now attuned, and for that reason they seem to us to lack certain notes; and yet some of the loveliest melodies which are ever sung in Iceland have been written in these modes, such as *Iceland, Land of the Blest* and *Oh, my Beautiful Bottle.*

At home in Brekkukot we did not acknowledge all the concepts which are now all the rage, and indeed had no words for them. All sorts of talk that was in common currency outside the turnstile-gate at Brekkukot struck us as mental illness; words which were commonplace elsewhere sounded not only strange to our ears but were downright embarrassing to us, like smut or other shameless chatter.

For instance, if someone used in conversation the word "charity", we thought of it as some sort of frivolous, irrelevant, or untimely quotation from the *Book of Sermons.* "Charity" was called "kind-heartedness" in our house, and a charitable person, as one would say in spiritual language, was simply called "kind-hearted", or "good". The word "love" was never heard in our house either, except if some inebriate or a particularly stupid maidservant from the country happened to recite a verse by a modern poet; and moreover, the vocabulary of poems like these was such that if ever we heard them, cold shivers ran down our spines, and my grandfather would seat himself on his hands, sometimes out on the garden wall, and would grimace and jerk his shoulders and writhe as if he had lice and say, "Tut tut!" and "Really!" On the whole, modern poetry had the same effect on us as canvas being scratched.

"Falling in love" did not exist with us; instead it was said that someone "liked the look of" a girl, or that a boy and a girl were "becoming close". "Courtship" could be mentioned, but that was as far as one could go. I can swear on oath that while I was growing up I never heard the word "happiness" except on the lips of a crazy woman who lodged in the mid-loft with us for a time and who is not mentioned in this book; I never came across the word again until I was almost grown up and beginning to do translation at school. Even after I was fully grown I still believed that the word "weeping" was borrowed from Danish. On the other hand I can remember that when my grandfather was once asked, sympathetically, how the people at Akurgerði who had lost their breadwinners at sea the previous year were keeping, he answered at once, "They have plenty of salt-fish." In the same way, if someone asked how anyone was, we invariably replied: "Oh, he's fat enough" – which meant that he was well, or, as they would say in Denmark, that he was happy. If someone was not well, one said: "Oh, you can see it on him"; and if the person under discussion was more dead than alive, one said: "Oh, he's a bit low." If someone was dying of old age, one said: "Yes, he's off his food these days." About someone who was on his deathbed, it was said: "Yes, he's packing his bags now, poor fellow." Of a mortally ill youngster it was said that it did not look as if he would ever have grey hairs to comb. When a married couple separated, one used the phrase: "Yes, there's something wrong there, I believe." At Brekkukot every word was precious, even the little words.

My grandmother had a habit of answering people with sayings and proverbs. Often there was good-natured humour in the reply, but almost absent-minded, somehow, or as if she were talking out of an open window to someone standing behind her: the rather tuneless drawling chant she used carried a hint of compassion, almost of resignation, but never bitterness. But it was not just proverbs that she had at her command; she knew a couplet or a scrap of verse, some sort of mixture of adage and nursery rhyme, for every occasion, or else she would quote a bit of a psalm or rigmarole or folk-ballad or some other obscure old poetry. She was such a well of knowledge, in her own quiet way, that if one pressed her and tried to find out just how much she knew, one never reached the bottom. She knew whole ballads off by heart from beginning to end. For the benefit of those who no longer know what Icelandic ballads (*rímur*) are, I shall interpolate here that they are a form of poetry about heroes of olden times and mighty deeds from the days of the epic; this poetry is composed of intricately rhymed quatrains, sometimes so intricate that each strophe is a rhyme-riddle. A medium-sized ballad, that is to say one ballad-cycle, can be thirty poems, each one of them consisting of at least a hundred quatrains. There are hundreds of *rímur* in Iceland, some say thousands. My grandmother also knew whole books of psalmody. She sometimes mumbled this stuff to herself while she was knitting, but not for anyone who was listening, and really not for herself either, for she was often quite obviously thinking about other matters. If there was something in the psalm which prompted my curiosity, such as for instance what kind of dripping one put on the Bread of Heaven, and I started to ask questions, it was as if I had roused her from a dream, and she would say that she did not really know what she had been reciting; and then she could not pick up the thread again.

I was never really aware that she preferred any one poem to another, any more than a printer does who sets the type for good and bad books alike. One could undoubtedly have recorded whole volumes from her, if anyone had bothered to write it all down. I do not believe that many universities have at their disposal teachers with any more literature at their fingertips; and yet I have met few people who were further than this woman from being what is sometimes called "literary" and is used as a term of praise for the gentry.

As is known, the ability to read and write was almost as common in Iceland before the days of printing as it has been since; and actually I think that my grandmother was closer to the people who lived before the days of Caxton. Spelling-books were never used in Iceland. My grandmother said she had learned to recognize the letters of the alphabet from an old man who scratched them for her on the ice when she had to watch over sheep during the winter. She learned writing from an old woman by making letters with a knitting needle on a piece of smoky glass; they used to tinker unobtrusively with this in the evenings sometimes, by moonlight. When she was ninety, my grandmother wrote me a letter when I was abroad; it was fourteen lines long, like a sonnet. I lost this letter a long time ago but it still exists nonetheless; I can remember her handwriting vividly even now. She wrote not only all the more important nouns with an initial capital but all the more significant adjectives as well; and that is the very style used by Fitzgerald in the poem called *The Rubaiyat* which he re-wrote from Omar Khayyam, and which is considered by some to be one of the most adroit poems ever written in that part of the world which turns towards the bright side of the moon: "Oh, Moon of My Delight". When I read that poem I said to myself, "This man writes like my grandmother."

I was five years old when my grandmother took out a book from her little chest and said, "Today we shall start to learn to read, Álfgrímur dear."

This book began with a rigmarole that goes like this:

"Abraham begat Isaac and Isaac begat Jacob and Jacob begat Judah and Judah begat Pharez with Tamar and Pharez begat Hezron and Hezron begat Ram and Ram begat Amminadab and Amminadab begat Nahshon and Nahshon begat Salma and Salma begat Boaz with Rahab and Boaz begat Obed with Ruth and Obed begat Jesse . . ."

We spent nearly all winter struggling with this rigmarole.

"What a terribly tedious rigmarole this is, grandmother," I said. Then my grandmother recited this verse:

"The Bible sticks in my throat like an old piece of fish-skin;
I gulped it as quick as I could,
And it hasn't done me much good."

When it was nearly Christmas, I said: "Why is this rigmarole so tedious, grandmother?"

"It's in Hebrew," said my grandmother.

But by the end of the winter I had learned to spell my way through this dreadful rigmarole, and from then on I could read any book whatsoever.

11

THE ICELANDERS' UNIVERSITY

From time immemorial it has been the custom in all sizeable farms in Iceland to have a good reader available to read sagas aloud or recite *rímur* for the household in the evenings; this was the national pastime. These evening sessions have been called the Icelanders' University. Old people who had attended this university for eighty years or more came to know the curriculum pretty well, not surprisingly. Saga-readings and *rímur*-recitations at Brekkukot were for the most part performed by visitors who stayed with us from time to time, or even just overnight, for my grandfather Björn of Brekkukot, as I have said already, was no more of a bookman than he had to be. Visitors from distant parts of the country often proved to be excellent entertainers. The best were those from the north, particularly from Skagafjörður; they were heroic-looking men who wore thigh-boots, whereas the people from the south contented themselves with thin-shoes. They were bursting with all sorts of poetry, good and bad alike, and their speech was much more vigorous than ours; and when someone from Skagafjörður was settled comfortably against our gable-wall and was launched on to the Úlfar-*rímur* set to a Skagafjörður chant, with that obligatory opening about King Cyrus, there opened up before us the whole wide world of heroic poetry all the way to the Orient, fitfully lit by strange flashes of illumination.

The sprinkling of books we had at Brekkukot was mostly a motley collection of strays, as I said earlier. And yet it was easier than one might think to arrange them into literary order. It bore witness above all to the nature of our visitors, in particular to the fact that there had been more of those who were fond of champions, knights, and sea-epics than of those who preferred Danish novels – this was the name which was applied in our house to modern literature in general, but particularly anything to do with hysteria.

When we talked about Danish novels, it was as if we had in mind a vague impression of Dostoyevsky and those other story-tellers who appear to have spilled a great mass of tar which then, obeying only the laws of gravity, somehow oozes along formlessly into every crack and crevice.

Many of those who came to visit us were not only good readers but also masters in the art of telling stories. The stories we heard most often were of disasters at sea and on land, or of Herculean feats; also, tales about great gluttons and other peculiar people – not forgetting stories about ghosts and the Hidden Folk . . .

A weatherbeaten man from some far-off place sitting under the lamp at the door-post of the mid-loft, reading aloud from a book or telling a story; my grandfather with a net fixed to one of the rafters, silently mending mesh after mesh; and likewise Captain Hogensen's rope growing longer and longer, and the bed-post creaking at his every pull; Runólfur sitting with his fingers in his toothless gums like a baby, and the tears trickling down his cheeks not because he was crying, but because he had been so long at sea that the salt-burn never left the corners of his eyes now; a few others sitting on the beds and on other seats; the trap-door over the stairs lying open, with my grandmother sitting knitting on the bottom step, for she was expecting more visitors. And the story slowly unfolding.

What story can it have been?

The stories were innumerable, but most of them had this in common, that the method of telling them was diametrically opposite to the method we associated with Danish novels: the story-teller's own life never came into the story, let alone his opinions. The subject-matter was allowed to speak for itself.

They never hurried the story, these men. Whenever they came to anything that the audience found desperately exciting, they would often start reciting genealogies at great length, and then they would launch into some digression, also in great detail. The story itself had a life of its own, cool and remote and independent of the telling, free of all odour of man – rather like Nature itself, where the elements alone reign over everything. What was one little shrivelled person in some fortuitous lodging compared with the wide world of the heroic age, the world of epic with its great events that happened once and for all time?

The Lives of Great Icelanders – sometimes I dream that I have this book in my hands once again. What can have become of this book? I remember it so clearly at home in Brekkukot. I have run my eye over various catalogues, but cannot find it listed anywhere. Is my memory deceiving me in thinking that it ever existed at all? Or did it just come to exist inside me, somehow? How can it be that I know so many stories from it? Since I myself am now engaged in composing a book, I would just like to have written up a few stories from *The Lives of Great Icelanders.*

If I were now to write from memory, without a book, a story about a Great Icelander, like one of those we used to hear at home in between sagas and *rímur,* I think that one of the first to come to mind would be the story of Pastor Snorri of Húsafell. Perhaps I ought to try to recall it here; but I would point out that I am not telling it as it stands in the book, because the book is lost, but rather according to its essence, and what I feel were its main features when I heard it told at home in Brekkukot. It may well be that I confuse incidents from the Lives of other Great Icelanders with the Life of Pastor Snorri, but what does that matter? It is only because I feel, deep down, that all Great Icelanders ought to be the way Pastor Snorri was.

Pastor Snorri was a huge man, powerfully built and manly in every respect. Even in his old age he never lost his agility and strength, as can be seen from the fact that when he was in his seventieth year he leapt over the Hvítá at the lava outcrop below Húsafell. When he was working as a seaman off Snæfells Glacier in his youth, most men found him an overpowering partner to be rowing beside; and such was his fishing luck that even when he put out his line where others found nothing and called the sea barren, he would haul in fish after fish.

Pastor Snorri was immensely quick at composing verses, even when he was very young. When he went to school at Skálholt, he made such rapid progress that many teachers and hoary old

Latin scholars had to watch their step. It has never been forgotten that about the time he graduated from school, a distinguished Frenchman arrived at Skálholt bringing with him an enormous book in Latin, and this Latin was so difficult, particularly towards the end of the book, that not one of the teachers there could translate such a text. Then Snorri of Húsafell was called in. Snorri looked at the book and smiled, and then he set to, translating into Icelandic every word that was printed in the book just as if it were another native tongue to him; and around him stood pastors, teachers, and Frenchmen, all agape with amazement at such learning. Many years later, when someone asked Snorri what sort of Latin it had been that had so baffled the pastors of Skálholt, he gave a little laugh and said that this had not been so surprising, since the first half of the book had been in Greek and the second half in Hebrew.

Pastor Snorri of Húsafell was so good at Icelandic wrestling that it is believed that for more than fifty years there was no clergyman in the whole synod who could stand up against him. He was also uncannily skilled at fighting with bulls. There are many stories of how on his travels he would often rush up to vicious bulls, seize hold of them in a wrestling hold, and throw them to the ground.

It is also said that he once laid low a giant negro with a hip-throw on board a merchant-ship at Stapi. And it has been reliably reported that he once threw an ogress on Holtavörðuheidi; he felled her with a special crutch-throw known as the ogress throw.

Pastor Snorri was so skilful a smith that people in Borgarfjörður believed that he could do cold-welding. He was also such a prodigious snuff-taker that when he went over to the parish-of-ease at Kalmanstunga to sing Mass there, only a day's journey from Húsafell, he would take with him for the night two ram's-scrotum pouches crammed full of snuff. He was also a very fine singer of the Mass.

Of Pastor Snorri's versifying, it is commonly held (and this is supported by many learned men) that there are perhaps a few master-rhymesters who at their best could compose verses as intricate as those of Snorri, but none more intricate. He composed a great number of *rímur*, of which *The Ordeals of Jóhanna* is the largest cycle.

And now a word about Pastor Snorri's strength of faith. It is said that there were more Christians in Iceland in his time than ever before or since; and this was thanks to the influence of the Danish kings here in Iceland, who issued an edict about church attendance, that people were to be birched if they fell asleep in church. It is the general opinion that although there were many men in Iceland at that time who could give a good account of themselves in this question of faith, there were few of his countrymen who were any match for Pastor Snorri in a trial of religious conviction. It is also said that there was scarcely a disputant in the land whom Pastor Snorri could not convert; nor was there any blasphemer alive in Iceland in those days, learned or lay, who dared to debate with Pastor Snorri.

At that time, Magnús Stephensen, the Chief Justice, lived at Leirá. He was considered the greatest expert in French humanism of all his countrymen and he even wrote books on those matters with discriminating intelligence.

The story goes that Magnús Stephensen took a horse one summer's day and rode over to the Borgarfjarðardalir with a few attendants, and did not pause until he reached Húsafell. He asked to see Pastor Snorri, and when they met and fell to talking, Magnús the Chief Justice let it be known that he had come for the express purpose of holding a disputation with Pastor Snorri about Hell. Pastor Snorri accepted the challenge and invited Stephensen to enter his home and accept his hospitality; he proposed that after they had eaten they should go to bed, and begin their disputation the next morning. This they did.

In addition to his skill in French learning, Magnús Stephensen is reckoned by men of wisdom to have been one of the most erudite of Icelanders both in antiquities and in dialectics, and not least in those studies which derive from Latin and Greek; he always had at his fingertips weighty references to fundamental sources and to those Latin sorcerers known as *auctores*; and it is said that the man sufficiently adept at citing these *auctores* can refute most people's arguments.

For most of the day the two of them, Pastor Snorri and
Chief Justice Magnús, wrestled over the matter in hand, using
every hold in learning and logic and matching one another's
rhetoric; the aforementioned *auctores* were cited with greater zeal
than had ever been heard before in any one room in Iceland, and
indeed they drank so much whey during the disputation that four
serving-women had their hands full fetching and carrying away
for them. They cited evidence from *auctores* from Ireland, France,
and the Roman Empire, all the way east to Muscovy and even a
few from China, some say. Such uncommon sages as Avicenna
and Averroës were brought forth there, and for a long time it was
uncertain which of the disputants would gain the upper hand.

But it is generally believed that towards evening the contest
was beginning to turn against Pastor Snorri, until he was in
danger of being completely overthrown; and that was because
Chief Justice Stephensen managed to bring up some rather
rare thesis by the hellhound Abracadabra, who lived in Persia
seven centuries before the birth of Christ. Pastor Snorri
had never heard of this cleric before, and was left completely
defenceless against the potent and evil heresy contained therein;
it made little difference when Snorri remonstrated with Magnús
that this Abracadabra must certainly have been a child of the
devil. Pastor Snorri now fell silent for a while, and the lobes
of his ears were like two large blisters, swollen because of the
seething in his blood at the arguments against Hell that Magnús
Stephensen the Chief Justice had managed to dredge up from
Abracadabra. But after Pastor Snorri had been silent for a
while, he summoned up all his reserves and said to the Chief
Justice: "Would you walk up the hill behind the farm here with
me for a spell, Magnús?" Stephensen consented to this. So
they walked up the hill. And after they had been walking for a
while, Pastor Snorri led his visitor into a ravine and pointed
down into a fissure there, from which there arose smoke and
fumes that smelled horribly. And after Snorri had lured the Chief
Justice into peering down into this fissure for a while, it is
said that certain exceptionally rare sights appeared in the depths
before the eyes of this erudite official and renowned rationalist,

some of them so loathsome and abominable that scholars have shrunk from committing such things to writing. And Magnús the Chief Justice was so terrified at this sight that he took to his heels and ran back to the farm as fast as he could. He called on his attendants to have the horses ready at once, saying that he had just seen Hell itself before his very eyes in that place; and he rode away from Húsafell that same evening.

Another example of Pastor Snorri's strength of faith and spiritual power was when he gathered together most of the ghosts and goblins and demons which were then at large in the upper part of Borgarfjörður, including an assortment of lesser sprites which always infest a farm, imps and boggarts and byre-bogles and various other fiends, some of which had been conjured up against Pastor Snorri himself by those who envied him. Pastor Snorri brought all this assembly to Húsafell and made an appointment with them for sunrise on Whitsun morning at the Big Stone right at the corner of the sheep-pen at the far end of the home-field at Húsafell; there were twenty-one of these visitors in all. The pretext that Snorri used was that he was inviting this rabble to attend Black Mass, in which the Benediction, Lord's Prayer, and Amen are reversed. But here the miscreants miscalculated badly; for no sooner had Pastor Snorri started on the *introitum* than he changed direction completely and poured over this congregation a torrent of searing and high-flown exorcisms in which the names of Jesus, as of the Virgin Mary and Mary Magdalene, were so inextricably interlocked, so balefully entwined and bound together, that in the face of such conjurations all this host shrivelled up and turned into toads; and then the whole assemblage crawled under the Big Stone at the corner of the sheep-pen at Húsafell and has never come out since; nor have any particular manifestations been noted around Borgarfjörður from that day to this. The great boulder that swallowed up all that ghostly crew is still to be seen at the corner of the Húsafell sheep-pen, and is sometimes called the Ghost Stone; and it will never open again until the last Trump sounds on Doomsday.

Pastor Snorri of Húsafell had many descendants in

Borgarfjörður; he was the progenitor of the younger Húsafell kin. Most men of understanding are agreed that there has never been a cleric in Borgarfjörður who was a better seaman, a more passionate champion of the faith, a greater snuff-taker, singer, poet and smith than he. His two daughters, Engilfríður and Mikilfríður, were also good smiths; but there are no reports that they could do cold-welding.

And that is the end of the story of Snorri, the pastor of Húsafell.

12

A GOOD FUNERAL

Have I not mentioned somewhere already the copper bell outside, which sometimes answered the silver bell in the living-room clock in our house?

"Someone is being buried today," said the visitors, when the sound of the copper bell carried into our living-room from the churchyard. A short while afterwards one could also hear the strains of *Just as the One True Flower* floating over in the breeze.

"Yes," said my grandfather, "it's amazing how they are all dying off, these people. They are always dying. There were hordes of them dying last week, I can't remember how many. Two funerals a day, sometimes."

"Yes, they have plenty to do, these pastors," said someone.

"Poor old Pastor Jóhann, he's getting so shaky in the legs these days," said my grandmother. "Many of these people are from other parts of the country and die in the hospital here, and it's remarkable how he manages to keep up with them all, the old soul."

"Will it not be getting too crowded in the churchyard, if they are going to bury the whole country there?" someone asked.

"Ah well, I've got my eye on a place for us two old bodies, and I hope we'll be allowed to keep it."

I always found it so agreeable and comfortable, when I was a boy, to hear my grandfather and grandmother talking to people about death; and to see the funeral processions moving slowly through the churchyard and then start singing. The cathedral pastor's black silken gown gleamed in the sunshine so that it looked almost blue; and the black horses which drew the hearse seemed almost green across the loins. I hope that famous critics will not class me with certain devotees of death and doom if I say here that I think that funerals in our churchyard gave me more entertainment than most other things when I was a little boy.

Suddenly and without any warning, so to speak, when one least expected it, in the middle of the day and the middle of the week, one would hear a single stroke of the clapper. Then a long, long time, almost a whole eternity, would elapse before it tolled a second time. When the first note sounded in the bell-tower over the mortuary in the churchyard, the funeral procession would just be setting off from a house somewhere up in Laugavegur, perhaps. Gradually the strokes of the bell would quicken, and the chiming would grow louder. I would sit a little distance away and wait for the black horses. Perhaps there had been rain that morning, there was such a fine scent from the tansies. I cannot have been more than about five years old. Soon the singing started. The birds and the flies sang too. The sound of *Just as the One True Flower* eddied in the breeze, *vox humana* and *vox celeste* by turns, and sometimes a spurt of panic-stricken tremolo in the gusting wind.

How very peaceful and comfortable it was to know that people went into the ground like this to the accompaniment of singing and the sound of bells when they had finished living. But I have to admit that there was one type of dead I felt a little sorry for: people who were washed ashore drowned, and others who had died forsaken among strangers and knowing no one, on a journey, for instance, or were simply foreigners here in Iceland. Old Jónas the policeman and another man sometimes brought these corpses up from town on a hand-cart and put them on a board which was laid across the seats in the mortuary, sometimes without any covering. I often kept watch at the mortuary window and peeped at the corpses; sometimes they were just stumps of people, without head or limbs, sometimes they were women with long hair, and it looked as if their hair were pouring off the bier on to the floor. And now I shall shortly be telling you more fully about one particular funeral.

I was not very old by the time the breeze had wafted the funeral psalm *Just as the One True Flower* so often to my ears that I got to know it, and the melody as well. I recited for my grandmother the snatches I had managed to pick up from the psalm, and she filled in the gaps for me. Sometimes I was lucky enough to find a sea-scorpion which I first of all baptized and named after some man of note and then buried with great ceremony in a corner of the vegetable garden at Brekkukot, playing all the parts myself – pastor, procession, and black horse; then I would sing *Just as the One True Flower* at the top of my voice from beginning to end over this ugly fish.

One quiet summer's day I was sitting up in the churchyard playing on the bench-shaped tombstone of the late Archangel Gabriel, which was so called because there was a marble angel kneeling on the top of it. I looked up all of a sudden and saw, not far off, a funeral procession approaching, if it could be called a funeral procession. There were no horses. Nor were there any singers. Four men were carrying a short, broad coffin out of the mortuary; I am sure it can only have been a stump of a corpse they were burying. Two of the coffin-bearers were the old men who often did odd jobs in the churchyard for the municipality, the third was the lame man who always drove the hearse-horses, and the fourth was the late Jónas the policeman with the gilt buttons on his tunic. Behind them came the funeral procession itself, which consisted of Pastor Jóhann, the old cathedral pastor, in his gown, and old Eyvindur the carpenter, who made the coffins; and that was all.

There was a wonderfully stimulating air about the churchyard that day, and indeed the old men were in excellent spirits. They caught sight of a little urchin not far off; his head only just reached over the top of the tombstones, and he was watching their movements with rapt attention.

"Come over here and talk to us, little boy," said Pastor Jóhann. "We need a third man."

I scampered over to them out on the path and shook hands with them, and Pastor Jóhann and Eyvindur the carpenter placed me between themselves and led me along behind the coffin as the third man in the funeral procession: everything comes in threes.

"I have seen you here in the churchyard when we have been officiating at funerals, little boy. You must be the foster-child of Björn of Brekkukot; I must have baptized you once, didn't I?" said Pastor Jóhann.

"I can't remember who baptized me," I said. "But my name is Álfgrímur. Er – is there a man in the coffin?"

"You might call him that, my child," said Pastor Jóhann. "On the other hand we don't know for sure who baptized him, or whether he has any name at all."

"I always baptize the sea-scorpions before I bury them," I said.

"Indeed," said Pastor Jóhann, "we are not burying him because we know who he is, but because we know that God loves all men equally; He feels the same love for me and you and Eyvindur the carpenter there who is holding your other hand as He does for the man who is lying in that coffin."

"Is it perhaps the man who was lying in the mortuary the other day and whose face is gone?" I asked.

"Yes, I'm afraid so," said Pastor Jóhann. "His face is missing, so to speak, and that is why we do not know who he is. We think we know he may be a certain person; but it could just as well be someone else. We know only one thing: that God created all men equal, and the Saviour saves all men alike."

The coffin was lowered into the grave and Pastor Jóhann went over to the edge of the grave and took some earth on his spade (which I think was called a trowel) and said a few words; then he took my hand again and led me to the edge of the grave and said:

"And now, Álfgrímur, we shall sing the psalm that Hallgrímur Pétursson wrote on his little daughter's death for all men who live and die in Iceland."

Pastor Jóhann then began to sing in his brittle old man's voice, weary and tuneless.

> "Just as the one true flower
> Grows in the barren ground . . ."

and I held his hand and joined in the psalm in my clear childish voice; and thus I began to sing for the whole world. It was not without pride that I felt myself somehow to have been chosen to sing both for the living and the dead. Jónas the policeman also sang, and Eyvindur the carpenter too. The lame man who owned the hearse-horses was also trying to sing. And the birds sang.

When we had finished singing we stepped back from the grave. Pastor Jóhann was still holding me by the hand. His gown was longer at the front than the back because he now walked with a stoop.

"That, when all is said and done, was a fine funeral," said Pastor Jóhann. "A lovely funeral. May God grant us all such a fine funeral."

I said nothing as I trotted along beside him and he led me by the hand. I could not really understand why it was that Pastor Jóhann thought it such a fine funeral, when there were not even any horses.

The old cathedral pastor bade me farewell at the lych-gate.

"Goodbye, little boy," he said. "And if you are ever playing in the churchyard here when we are officiating at a funeral, and you see a procession that is not very large, I mean a rather small, good procession like the one today, for example, you are welcome to join in and sing with us. I am not very good at singing, I'm afraid. But even though I'm not very good at singing, I know that there is one note and it is pure. Here are ten *aurar* for you. Give my greetings to Brekkukot, give my greetings to your grandfather and your grandmother. I thank them also for the singing."

How very old and worn his purse was! But the ten-*aurar* piece he gave me was beautiful. At that time, caramels cost only half an *eyrir* each.

13

A WOMAN FROM LANDBROT

One fine day it so happened that an elderly woman swathed in dark shawls was sitting on the horse-stone across from the cottage-door at Brekkukot, trying to summon up enough courage to knock on the door. Then my grandfather arrived and greeted this woman and raised his hat.

"You must be Björn of Brekkukot, surely," said the woman. "God give you good day."

She was pale, with bulging eyes and protruding teeth. She was wearing thin-shoes, and her skirts came down to her ankles. She looked very thin and frail inside all these skirts and shawls.

"Who are your people, if I may ask, and where do you come from?" asked my grandfather.

"I am from Landbrot, out east," she said.

"That's a good step, if I may say so," said my grandfather. "Are you visiting someone here in the south?"

"No, nothing like that," said the woman, and smiled. "I have come here to die."

"Just so," said my grandfather. "Won't you come in and have something warm?"

"Oh, there's no need for that," said the woman. "But I must confess that I have heard many good things about you people here in Brekkukot. And if you want to do an unknown woman from the east a favour, then I want to ask you to be so kind as to allow me to die here with you."

"Well, you are not asking much," said my grandfather. "But we are not so well equipped for that sort of thing here as the hospitals."

"I have just come from the hospital," said the woman. "I travelled here to the south early this spring in search of a cure, but they say it's too late. I have only a few weeks left, I'm told."

"Yes, as I say, even though the odd person has been glad to creep in here in order to kick the bucket," said my grandfather, "there is not much nursing we can give the sick. There is no room here except for a couch in the mid-loft with old Jón the pilot, who calls himself Hogensen, and Runólfur, who spreads manure."

"Oh, there's no need for anything fancy with me," said the woman. "But there's always a snag to everything. There is one small thing I have promised my family."

"Your affairs are your own to decide, my dear," said my grandfather.

"Well, it's like this, Björn," said the woman. "I have to be sent back east when I am dead."

"Ah, so that's it," said my grandfather. "A seven or eight days' journey, no less! Don't you know that we have a churchyard right under our noses here, so to speak, my good woman?"

"Yes," said the woman, "but it's your churchyard."

"We'll cross that bridge when we come to it," said my grandfather. "And don't sit out here on that stone any longer."

"I would rather not come into the house," said the woman, "until this matter is settled. I promised my children before I left that I would have myself sent back east when the time came. They are alone. And they are only youngsters. And our Lykla is calving in September."

"I don't have anyone to send all the way east to Skaftafell District," said my grandfather.

"I have been thinking of having myself sent back east as freight," said the woman. "But someone would have to look after me on the way."

"I have always understood that people don't need very much looking after once they are dead," said my grandfather.

"We have to prevent them from burying me west of Skaftafell District," said the woman. "I flatly refuse to lie west of Skaftafell District. I have always lain in Landbrot; and that is where I am going to lie."

"Then do you not want to set off with the postman while you are still on your feet?" asked my grandfather.

"I have always wanted to die with strangers," said the woman.

But however long or little they argued about it, the outcome was that the woman came inside, and my grandfather uttered the phrase he always used when making visitors welcome:

"Have a seat and show us some cheer, my good woman."

She was certainly a woman of foresight, but rather cold in her manner and not particularly attractive. A bed was made up for her without a word in the cubicle beside us in the mid-loft, even though my grandfather would not take upon himself any obligations concerning her after she was dead.

"Who are you?" said Captain Hogensen.

"I am called Thórarna, and I come from Landbrot."

"Have you come to town on a pleasure-trip?" asked Captain Hogensen.

"One could doubtless call it that," said the woman.

"Quite so," said Hogensen, and cleared his throat before adding, "Well, I am called Captain Hogensen, of the Hogensen family out west at Helgafell. I served under the Danish kings in my time, and piloted them all over Breiðafjörður. That's the way of it, my good woman."

"Fancy that," said the woman.

"By the way, who are the local magistrates and the main people of note out there in Landbrot?" said Hogensen.

My grandmother interrupted: "You must not tire the woman, Hogensen dear, she is ill. She just wants to lie in there until she gets better."

"Oh, I can't feel very sorry for people so long as they still have their sight," said Hogensen. "And it's not worth while shutting that bit of door between us, my good woman, because even though I myself might be a little tedious these days, we sometimes have some entertaining people to talk to up here, like Runólfur Jónsson. And at night when everyone is asleep, up comes our philosopher, who is a commandant in the municipality. That's the way of it. And which are the most important farms out there in Landbrot, my good woman?"

"My own plot of land, I suppose," said the woman.

"Precisely," said Hogensen. "Owns one plot of land. And isn't that quite enough, my good woman? My forefathers owned lands all over the place – and here I lie. It is just as it says in the memorial ode that Sigurður Breiðfjörð composed about the late Jón Hákonarson, my grandfather:

> 'At Helgafell, where is poor Jón
> Hákonarson now? Alas, he's gone.'

I suppose the only things that count are the things a man gets for himself, my good woman. Would you care to see my peaked cap? Álfgrímur! There's a good lad, find my cap and show it to the woman. And if there's any fluff on the peak, blow it off."

While the woman was examining the cap, Runólfur came up into the loft. Captain Hogensen recognized our room-mate by his breathing even though he could not see him.

"Be careful, Runólfur," said Captain Hogensen, "we have got a land-owning woman in the cubicle. She is from the east."

"You'll be all right here with the man who commands warships," said Runólfur. "Where are you from, if I may ask?"

"I am from Landbrot," said the woman.

"What kind of fish do you have there?" asked Runólfur.

"We live for the most part off torsk," said the woman. "And we had a little ling when I left home."

"Torsk, indeed? Well, well," said Runólfur. "And did you say ling? What happens to all the proper codfish, woman?"

"You never see proper codfish on the inland farms," said the woman.

"Tcha, the sort of fish you mentioned, we just use that for fertilizer down here in the south," said Runólfur. "By the way, since you are getting out and about again, you ought to take a little pleasure-trip out to Ness to see the parish clerk's marvel; and you should not underestimate the miracle at Grótta, either – my goodness, what cess-pools, heavens above! That would be something to put in your letters home, woman. There has been nothing to equal them in the whole world since the great peat-pits were dug in Vatnsmýri many years ago."

14

LIGHT OVER HRÍNGJARABÆR

In a book by a major author it says about a certain place that the air in the city was pregnant with the name of a certain lady. I have sometimes thought that something like that could be said about our air round the churchyard and the name of Garðar Hólm. His portrait was always hanging there, both in our living-room and the living-room at Hríngjarabær, as well as in the drawing-room of the King's Minister; and although one never heard him mentioned spontaneously in our house, I soon realized that his name was closely connected with the workings in our old clock. If a visitor brought up his name, as if by accident, the question was evaded; at the very most they might say something to the effect that little Georg had been a nice boy when he was growing up in the church-yard here; but these evasive replies were not least what made him so exciting in my eyes. It was strange that this man who performed in concert halls all over the world and had become such an Ariel that we scarcely dared mention his name aloud, should once have been a little boy here in the churchyard just like myself. I always felt sure that whenever my grandmother and Kristín of Hríngjarabær were talking together in private with pious expressions on their faces, they were talking about this supernatural creature.

I do not know whether it was the awareness of this world singer, who had once been a boy here like myself, that was responsible for the fact that from my earliest childhood I began to take notice of singing and everything connected with singing, and had now begun to sing at small funerals for Pastor Jóhann; but it was not because I was taking Garðar Hólm as a model, at least not deliberately – his portrait was too remote from me even though it hung in people's living-rooms.

Perhaps it was just that the same sound had awakened us both, except that for him it had been a quarter of a century earlier.

But one thing was certain: I can scarcely remember the time when he was not the distant murmur behind the blue mountain beyond the sea in my own life.

By this time, I had been taught to read by my grandmother. The reading-matter that took over where the Saviour's genealogy in Hebrew ended consisted of advertisements in the newspapers; the *Ísafold* came to us twice a week, four pages each issue. At that time it was the custom to advertise in verse if one wanted to sell stockfish or needed a girl for spring work. We learned these verses by heart. Even to this day there is scarcely any poetry I find so memorable as advertisements celebrating frozen haddock and other stockfish, paying tribute to a foreign pastry called Fluff, and a Chinese all-purpose medicine from Denmark discovered by a man called Valdimar Pedersen. I shall permit myself to quote here for the purpose of preservation a poem by a lively saddler in Laugavegur about saddles and bridles and other leather goods:

> "Gentle clients, I invite you,
> Come and look around my store;
> Whips and saddles to delight you,
> Leatherwork galore.
> Straps and girths that never, never wear;
> Accoutrements of copperwork that gleam with loving care;
> Bits and bridles made of silver rare;
> Bring your lady-friend – she would love this treasure-horde
>   to share!
> My livery's the best in town,
> The Bishop does his shopping here;
> Travel-goods of high renown,
> All made by me – and not too dear."

"Yes, reason can make rhyme out of anything," said my grandmother, as I tried to spell my way through these advertisements for her.

But there were other texts, in prose to be sure, which quickly attracted my attention after I had learned to read, and these were the articles about the fame of our world singer, Garðar Hólm. I do not think that any paper was ever published in Iceland in those days which did not carry at least a brief notice about his fame as a singer, and sometimes even more than one article in each issue. The headlines always went something like this: "ICELANDIC SONG ABROAD"; "ICELAND'S ART WINS FAME AFAR"; "ICELANDIC MUSIC IN OTHER LANDS"; "THE WORLD LISTENS TO ICELAND"; "IMPORTANT CONCERT IN CAPITAL CITY"; or, "ICELAND APPLAUDED IN INTERNATIONAL PAPER LE TEMPS". The subject of the articles was always the same: Garðar Hólm had yet again earned fame for Iceland abroad. In the town of Küssnacht he had sung the following songs: *How Beautifully that Bird did Sing*, *The Sheep are Bleating in the Pen*, and *The East Wind Coldly on Us Blew*; and the newspaper *Küssnachter Nachrichten* had said such and such. A little later, Garðar Hólm had sung in all the major cities of France, all of which I somehow seemed to feel started with a "Q" and ended with a "q". Then all at once it turned out that he had set off on a concert tour to London, Paris, Rome and Cairo, New York, Buenos Aires and onwards. Soon afterwards snippets would appear from *La Stampa* and *The Times* of London, as well as some lavish words of praise from Mohammed ben Ali in Cairo; in all these cities, people had been breathless with admiration for the artistry that had come from Iceland. The late Kristín of Hríngjarabær now appeared in a very special light. Strangers would come up to me in the street and pat me on the head and say they knew that I was related to him in some way. And when I was sent to the Store to buy oil, the shopkeeper would give me a fistful of raisins as a mark of respect. Yes, many were the free hand-outs I got in Gúðmúnsen's Store on the strength of Garðar Hólm's name.

Every single summer for as long as I can remember, the return of the world singer was awaited with due taciturnity but infinitely more eloquent glances on both sides of the churchyard, until this tension had lasted for so long that I began to think it natural and inevitable that Garðar Hólm was not arriving that summer, and perhaps even never; for there are so many cities in the world. And just when I had finally reconciled myself to the idea that Garðar Hólm was just an idle rumour, like most other events that were reported from abroad, and had prepared myself to believe that he would never, ever, arrive – suddenly he came.

One midsummer morning, when the soft clouds were disinte-grating over Mount Esja, Kristín of Hríngjarabær had just risen from her bed and was going outside to feed the hens as she always did first thing in the morning; and what did she see but a gentleman in an overcoat standing on the paving at the door of Hríngjarabær and having a good look all around? At first the old woman thought that this was a foreigner who had arrived to take pictures of the funny life led by people in Iceland, where one could still see, in among the timber-houses with their corru-gated-iron covering, turf cottages with dandelions and buttercups on the roof, and horse-daisies growing between the stones in the paving, and where people still wore the same kind of home-made moccasins which peasants in Europe used to wear a thousand years ago when towns did not exist and therefore not cobblers either. But this was not one of the lesser gentry, judging by his overcoat, which could scarcely have cost less than the price of a cow; and a hat like that must have reached the best part of a suckling lamb.

"*Godmorgen*," said Kristín of Hríngjarabær in Danish.

And at that this great and distinguished person turned to the woman and took her in his arms. It was her son.

I would point out that although this is how Garðar Hólm's return was described to me, I did not hear the story in our house. I have said it often, and I say it again, that regardless of what I myself may have thought from the beginning, and regardless of what other people in Brekkukot may have thought, Garðar Hólm and his travels and fame and anything else that concerned him were simply not considered news in our house. It may well be that the two old women needed to slip across to see one another for a private chat round about this time, but scarcely more often than usual. But I have no doubt at all that they found it a complicated problem, I am tempted to say an insoluble social problem, to have in the family someone so at odds with his environment in size and shape as Garðar Hólm.

I was accustomed to having strangers who came to the capital staying with us overnight, and so it came as rather a surprise to

me that Garðar Hólm did not ask to stay the night with us at
Brekkukot. I mentioned this to my grandmother.

She replied, "How could you ever imagine that Kristín of
Hríngjarabær's son would stay at our house?"

I understood this to mean that obviously Garðar Hólm would
be staying with his own mother. And one day soon afterwards,
when I was sent over to Hríngjarabær with some milk for Kristín,
I began to peer all around me to see if I could spy any evidence
of the presence of a visitor.

"What are you looking for, child?" said Kristín.

"I thought perhaps there was someone here," I said.

"Who did you think was here?" she asked.

"I thought perhaps that Garðar Hólm was here," I said.

"Who has taught you to mention him?" she asked.

"Everyone is talking about it," I said.

"Talking about what?" said the woman. "And who is everyone?
Certainly not Björn of Brekkukot."

"There's something about him in the *Ísafold*," I said.

"In the *Ísafold*!" said the woman. "God help the child, he's
started to read newspapers. Here's a lump of candy for you, and
off you go home. And don't go dawdling on Archangel Gabriel's
tombstone, in case your grandmother needs you for a message.
Garðar Hólm! The very idea! The things the child says! If he were
not living in the Governor's house, my boy, he would obviously
be staying at the Hotel Iceland where it costs a suckling lamb to
sleep for a night and a cow to sleep for a week."

A reply like that was not exactly calculated to add haste to the
steps of a thoughtful chap on his way through the churchyard.
It was a mathematical problem, really. If it cost a suckling lamb to
sleep for a night and a cow to sleep for a week, what an unimag-
inable host of sheep and cattle we must own at Brekkukot! On
the other hand, if it ever occurred to my grandfather to move
house with us all from Brekkukot down to the Hotel Iceland
(which actually was called "Hotel d'Islande" in print), including
Runólfur and Captain Hogensen and even the superintendent as
well, and we all then began to sleep there, and slept for perhaps
a month, then things would begin to get tricky. And yet despite

all this, the Hotel d'Islande was not grand enough for Garðar Hólm; it was beneath his dignity to stay with a lesser man than the Danish King's Chief Minister in Iceland, the one whom Kristín called the Governor, the man who had no horsehair.

15

WHITE RAVENS

"White ravens are rare," said Björn of Brekkukot one morning when the sun glistened on the fish-scales in the mire round our house and two important-looking visitors were edging their way through our turnstile-gate.

"Hullo, my dear Georg, and welcome home. And hullo to you, little Gúðmúnsen. Well, well, it's enough to make the lice drop dead from my head! Condescend to enter the house."

The man my grandfather called "little Gúðmúnsen" was in fact none other than Gúðmúnsen the merchant himself, the owner of Gúðmúnsen's Store where I had got all the raisins on the strength of a dubious family relationship with a great man; and "my dear Georg", this foreigner with the broad-brimmed hat and the eyes, nose, and mouth of an eagle – this was the great man himself. It was no wonder that I was too tongue-tied to say hullo.

"Who are you, young man?" said the world singer.

"Álfgrímur," I said.

He gazed at me abstractedly and repeated my name to himself: "Álfgrímur – he who stays one night with the elves. Álfgrímur – that's what we should all have been called."

Gúðmúnsen the merchant put his hand into his pocket for a ten-*aurar* piece for me.

"*Le petit garçon*," he said.

Like all the gentry he wore a black overcoat with a velvet collar, even in the middle of the summer, and he had a thick gold chain across that broad paunch which only men of standing ever have, but he was cheerful and smiling as a country girl, or rather, as was said of the Apostle Peter in one of my grandmother's rhymes: "Ruddy and sweet as a plum". To me, who was only a boy myself, he seemed more like a boy who had grown a moustache before he had grown up.

"I have been meaning to come and see you for a long rime now, my dear Björn," said Gúðmúnsen the merchant, and kissed Björn of Brekkukot. "But I've always lacked company. Now at last I have come to you in the right company."

"You are welcome," said my grandfather. "But let us not kiss too much to start with."

Garðar Hólm stepped over the threshold into the fish-shed and kissed a few bunches of hung lumpfish which were dangling from a spar, and inhaled their smell at the same time.

"God be praised," he said. "Long live Iceland."

"You are always yourself, thank goodness, my dear Georg," said my grandfather.

"I have often pictured to myself at home the romance of Brekkukot," said the merchant, "how the lumpfish hangs from the spars in the fish-shed, pair by pair. *Madame la baronne est chez elle.* As Georg here says, I am absolutely certain that here dwells the true Iceland: the national soul, the national anthem, *Oh, God of Our Land.* It is good to have one's thoughts supported by world-famous people. No lumpfish is so good as hung lumpfish. My father always keeps hung lumpfish in the room where he sleeps. I sometimes sneak down to the cellar for a bite of it. To tell you the truth, I don't think there is any other food than hung lumpfish."

"Yes, my dear fellow," said Garðar Hólm. "At least there is no need to tie a ribbon round such food before it is eaten."

"Well, as you know, Georg, my wife comes of that Danish merchant nobility that became Icelandic fish-businessmen here in the south," said Gúðmúnsen. "*Monsieur Gaston est sorti.* She is what is called a fine lady, and we know what that is – and what it costs. No lumpfish, at least not in the kitchen; and certainly not in the living-room; and least of all in the bedroom. But true romance – that's what my heart has yearned for all my life, as you know perfectly well, my friend; for otherwise I would not have been shovelling gold and silver into your pocket for ten years."

"We know that your wife's toasted white bread is the best you can find anywhere," said that world-famous man, Garðar Hólm.

"Yes, you're great lads," said my grandfather. "Dammit, but you're great lads. Do come in. I hope the old woman has something warm. At least we can always find a lumpfish-head for you."

When the gentry came into the living-room, my grandfather said, "Well, have a seat and show us some cheer."

And when they were seated – "What news about the fishing, lads?"

It was Garðar Hólm who answered: "Plenty of skate in Paris this spring, my dear Björn; I ate it to whet my appetite in the Hotel Trianon every night for a month. Choice shark there in Paris, too. *Raie* and *requin*, you might say, to throw in a little French *à la Guðmundur*."

My grandfather seated himself on his hands but did not begin to grimace yet, nor did he jerk his shoulders; but as always when laughter or other unbecoming behaviour was in the wind he began to say "Tut tut!" and "Really!" And he added, "It is good to hear that you have been having fish, my boy. I know it would have pleased your mother. It is good to have fish."

If one looked out of our tiny living-room window one could see the horse-daisies sprouting between the stones of the paving; the swedes and potatoes were coming up in the garden; the low rotting fence between the home-field and the vegetable garden lay smothered in tansies, dockens, and angelica; the home-field sloped down towards the end of the Lake, where the buttercups grew; beyond that, Vatnsmýri where the terns nested and where, according to Runólfur Jónsson, the greatest peat-pits in the world were to be found; then Skerjafjörður, where the lumpfish lived, then Bessastaðir, and finally the mountains on the moon.

"Should I not just buy all this whole damned caboodle from you just as it stands, my dear Björn?" said Gúðmúnsen the merchant.

"Eh?" said Björn of Brekkukot. "What's that?"

"All the romance here, just as it stands," said the merchant.

"Romance?" said my grandfather. "What sort of a beast might that be?"

"Here are two *aurar* for you, Guðmundur," said Garðar Hólm with a grimace. "Out you go now."

"I want to buy this cottage," said Gúðmúnsen in all seriousness. "They will soon be building palaces in Iceland. What do you say, Björn? I shall let you have a first-class basement up in Laugavegur. And gold in your hand like dirt, to last you the rest of your life."

"Tut tut!" said my grandfather as he sat there on his hands. "Really! We have been having poor weather this spring, lads."

"What do you say?" said the merchant.

Then my grandfather turned to me and said, "Will you tell the man that I and all of us at Brekkukot here are beginning to grow a little deaf."

"He is going to give you gold, grandfather," I said.

"Will you tell them that if they were thinking of talking to me about fish, then I shall sell little Gúðmúnsen half a dozen pairs of hung lumpfish on account."

Gúðmúnsen the merchant now raised his voice. "I want to buy this plot of land off you, my dear Björn," he said to my grandfather. "I want to build a fine mansion-house here. I'll pay whatever you ask."

"I'll give you a pair of smoked lumpfish, little Gúðmúnsen, so that you can have something to chew on while you're walking home," said my grandfather.

"Remember what I have said, Björn," said Gúðmúnsen. "My offer stands. Any day at all, I shall pay out whatever amount you decide."

"It is not very pleasant to be so deaf that one can no longer argue with people because one cannot hear what they are saying – not to mention when one cannot even understand the little one does happen to hear."

And now suddenly there was a tight, sour look on Gúðmúnsen's face. The plum had lost its sweetness. He fished his gold watch out of his pocket and saw that he unfortunately could not stay any longer, he had urgent business to attend to: "*Allons, enfants de la patrie*," he said. "Goodbye everyone."

"That wasn't much of a visit," said my grandfather. "You haven't had anything to eat – and there must be some fish in the pot, and some chicory-brew at least. But there's nothing to be done when people are itching to move. You will be better treated next time. And now I shall see you to the door."

They closed the door as they went out.

The famous man who had sung for the whole world and Mohammed ben Ali stayed behind in the living-room. All the tomfoolery dropped from his manner the moment the door closed behind his companion. Now he was lost in thought. And when I compared him with his portrait on the wall, I saw to my surprise that in the portrait his reverie was bright and angelic, whereas in the flesh, as he sat there in the little living-room at Brekkukot, his brooding look had become dark and touched with pain, as if the gold carriage which had been driving across the heavens was now out of sight. He kept crossing and recrossing his legs, one over the other. He was wearing a suit of blue material with a red pinstripe – and was brushing a scrap of moss off one of his trouser-legs with his fingers; or was it a wisp of hay?

Then he looked at me.

"What is your name, dear friend?" he said.

"Álfgrímur," I replied.

"Ach, what am I thinking of?" he said. "Of course, you're called Álfgrímur. By the way, what do you think of the world, Álfgrímur?"

"I don't think anything," I said. "I just live here in Brekkukot."

At these simple words, which I had thought the most straight-forward words in the world, it was as if the visitor suddenly woke up. He discovered me. He gazed at me for a long time – me who had been wishing I did not exist even though I was, as you might say, squatting there in the corner.

"Remarkable," he said. "Most remarkable."

He stood up and stared out of the window in our low-ceilinged living-room; it had four panes of coarse glass, slightly blue in colour, with air-bubbles and other flaws in it, rather like the glass in old bottles. The world singer looked out on the world through our window; and I am sure I heard him murmur to himself, "So the room with that window exists after all."

At that moment our clock struck two, I think, or perhaps three, with that clear, sharp tone that silver bells always have.

"And that clock still strikes," he said.

He turned to the clock and stood in front of it for a long time and listened to its old familiar ticking which one could always hear so clearly when there was silence in the room. He looked at the hands moving and studied the ornamentation on the face and read the name "James Cowan" to himself over and over again with the kind of reverence one owes to the names of those who rule the course of history. Finally he began to stroke the clock with his fingers, like a blind man feeling a living creature to find out its nature; and as far as I could see, the tears were streaming down the cheeks of this famous man.

16

SUPERINTENDENT AND VISITOR

The man who owned the pouches, as Runólfur Jónsson called him, or the commandant with the municipality, as Captain Hogensen called him, that is to say, the town's superintendent, as I thought he was – he was the one member of our fellowship who chiefly graced our company by his absence. I had lived with him ever since I was born; but that summer I discovered him at last by a complete and utter accident: there was a man there. It was like catching sight of a cairn that stands on a knoll to the south of the house; it has always been there, and that is why one never notices it. A generation passes, and then it suddenly comes to light that the cairn one saw so long ago must have been the noon-cairn.

I woke up with a start in the middle of the night at the beginning of the hay-harvest; not really in terror, that would be saying too much, but certainly more than a little startled to hear the voice of the superintendent, and particularly on discovering that he was talking about something other than eagles and mice. I am sure that if he had been confiding to my grandmother that a little mouse had had a litter under the threshold of his establishment that day, or even if he had been bellowing this information into Captain Hogensen's leather eardrums, nothing would have happened. I woke up because this phantom person was whispering confidentially with one of his friends; and because the subject of their conversation was the world and time, as well as mankind and the purpose of human achievements on earth; and the discussion was accompanied by the chink of that metal which many people regard more highly than silver and copper, and only a very few value lower than dirt.

I understood instinctively that secrets were being discussed here, and so took care not to open my eyes, so as not to become involved. I lay even more still than a sleeping person ever can. My grandmother and Kristín sometimes used to talk together in private, as I have said already; and both of them, but particularly the late Kristín, had impressed on me that it was a sacrilege to eavesdrop on a private conversation, and that if a decent person was unlucky enough to be a witness to such confidences, they then became his or her secrets too.

Naturally, I had no idea what had already passed between these two friends by the time I woke up in the middle of their conversation, still less what passed between them after the host had accompanied his visitor to the door and all was silent again. Nor did I ever see the visitor – nothing was further from my mind than to sit up in bed behind Captain Hogensen to have a look. Curiosity can be called a virtue or a vice, depending on what kind of elementary ethics one reads; in our house at Brekkukot, curiosity was considered on a par with thievishness. But now, when all the parties to these confidences are gone elsewhere and that world is no more, and I am the only one left, the spirits rise up from the well of oblivion. People and pictures from a vanished world are reincarnated and assume a significance which was hidden at the time.

That is what happened over this segment of a discussion that woke me up from my sleep here many years ago, this nocturnal meeting which I witnessed against my will. It does not occur to me for a moment that the words which were spoken then are exactly the same or in the same order as here; but I am absolutely sure that the very same line of argument which comes out in the conversation as it has been recreated in my mind determined the decisions that were taken that night.

"Yes, you are quite right, my friend: we are certainly related. And even though I may not understand as clearly as geneticists or chemists what a relationship is, I know something that matters far more: we are much more related than other people, as you are the best known of all Icelanders and I am the least known."

"My dear kinsman," came the whispered reply. "You know that I am not worthy of tying your shoelaces. I know it is downright laughable when I say 'kinsman', even though I call you that. 'Maestro' is the only word that befits you. If you lived in India, you would be made to live in a gilded palace on top of a mountain. Men and women from distant lands would come and walk up the mountain to you on their knees. And these people would lay their foreheads in the dust before you."

"It's funny," said the superintendent. "I have always felt that the man who makes a pilgrimage on his knees all the way up the mountain, and the man who lives in the gilded palace on the mountain-top, are one and the same person."

"Do you never feel that you are throwing this one life of yours away, kinsman?"

"It is said that a cat has nine lives – until it is hanged."

"I mean, do you never think it improper that a gifted man like you should be living your life in degradation, as the lowest of the low?"

"High and low, my friend," said the superintendent, and tittered slightly, but almost inaudibly. "I don't know what that is."

"I'm referring to a man's position in the world; the amount of influence he wields; the importance of your work. Pardon me."

"That's quite right," said the superintendent. "In the Sagas a distinction is made between people and events. There are heroes and little men. There are great events and small trifles. Or rather, little men and small trifles aren't admitted to the Sagas at all, preferably. On the other hand, life has taught me to make no distinction between a hero and a little man, between great events and small trifles. From my point of view, men and events are all more or less the same size."

"But if you were in some other position, kinsman; or even in no position; I mean, if you were so placed that you could see the

thing as it really is – *in re vera*, as we used to say in Class I?" asked
the visitor.

"I'm afraid I'm not very good at Latin," said the superintendent. "On the other hand I sometimes think about arithmetic;
and in particular about one number – the number One. But I
will admit that it is also the most incomprehensible number in
the world. Beyond this particular dimension I know only one
thing which is supernatural, even though it may well be the reality
that affects mortal men most deeply; and that is Time. And when
one comes to think about this strange place I was telling you
about, the world that is only One, and its connection with the
only supernatural thing we know, Time, then everything ceases
to be higher or lower than anything else, larger or smaller.".

"Yes, but are you content?" asked the visitor bluntly and perhaps
a little impatiently.

"If I can do something for a person who comes to me, then
I am content," said the superintendent. "I am not saying that I
am always utterly content. I am always unhappy, for instance,
when a thief is being hanged. But I was also very pleased when
I heard that the Prince of Montenegro got married the other
day. I know perfectly well that I am nothing to anyone. But the
middle finger is no longer than the pinkie if one measures both
against infinity; or if one clenches one's fist. People on horseback
often come to me and dismount at my door; they are perhaps
setting off on a long journey, perhaps ten days or more. What I
can do for them is to hold the stirrup for them while they mount.
I reckon that the source of well-being lies in not troubling oneself
about where other people are going; I feel well to the extent that
I consider it a matter of course to help each and every person to
get to wherever he wants to go."

"By the way, kinsman, to come back to the assistance which I
mentioned to you: how do you know that you are not helping me
to become a criminal? Would you want to help me to do that?"

The superintendent replied, "I would rather not help you to
do other people an injury, my friend; or to do yourself any other
injury than the one you feel to be your paradise. The mouse lives
in a hole. It is extremely difficult to live in a hole; at least, birds

would think it a bad paradise. On the other hand, the eagle feels
at home in the mountain peaks and calls itself king in the hall
of the winds. Ah, what absolute nonsense, my friend! And our
poor little moorland birds, they come flying here to Iceland every
spring and go back again every autumn on those useless little
wings over that fearful ocean. But you must not think that they
do this accidentally or at random. No, they have their philosophy,
even though one can cite authorities to prove that it is a piece
of folly. I never cite authorities. Many people think it right to
shoot birds because they are so stupid. I would not do that. I
reckon one should help all creatures to live as they want to live.
Even if a mouse came to me and said that it was going to fly
over the ocean, and an eagle said it was thinking of digging itself
a hole in the ground, I would say, 'Go ahead'. One should at
least allow everyone to live as he himself wants to live, as long
as he does not prevent others from living as they want to live. I
know it is possible to prove that it would be best if we were all
worms in the same vegetable garden; but the eagle simply does
not believe the truth, neither does the mouse. I am as much on
the side of the eagle that adheres to a patently false doctrine, as
of the mouse which is so humble in its way of thinking that it
makes itself a hole in the ground. I am a friend of the migrant
birds even though, to put it mildly, they adhere to dubious
philosophies – perhaps even wrong ones. And even though it is
stupid and dangerous and indeed downright criminal to fly across
the ocean on those useless little wings, the golden plover has a
lovely song in spring, and Jónas Hallgrímsson has written a poem
about it."

"And it never occurs to you, kinsman, that it is a humiliation for
you to work at such a disgusting job?" asked the visitor.

"Well, that's just the way of it," said the superintendent, and
thought for a while. "I shall tell you a story now. As you know,
the only insult that can really rile an Icelander is to be called a
Dane. When I was a farmer up at Skagi, I came here to Reykjavík
on a visit once. I went to two places; these places have this in
common, that country people have to visit them for the good
of their health. One of them was the place where I am now the

superintendent, or as old Jón Hogensen sleeping over there
would say – the commandant. I had been to many indifferent
places before; but in this one there was even less cleanliness than
in most of those I had visited. Unfortunately, it was Icelanders
who were in charge at this place. But I also had to pay a call of
nature at Mikael Lund's chemist shop, and he is, begging your
pardon, a Dane. To put it briefly, I had never before visited any
place where one felt one could see one's own reflection not just
on the ceiling and walls, but on the floor as well. And every single
object smelled not just of disinfectant but of soap and perfume
as well. That very day, I got a vocation."

"A vocation?" asked the visitor. "From whom?"

"From God," said the superintendent.

"Which god?" asked the visitor. "I thought you didn't believe in
any god."

"Now you just be careful what you say, my friend," said the
superintendent. "Who knows, I may believe in more gods than
you do. At least I got a vocation. I got a vocation from a good god
to make that establishment down there by the harbour as nice and
clean and fragrant in its own way as the one in the chemist shop
owned by Mikael Lund the Dane. I sold up all my possessions in
order to pursue this vocation. I know you will understand, when
you start to think about it, that I cannot find it disgusting work to
pursue a vocation from a good god. The only disgusting work
there is, is badly done work. The world is One, and mankind
is One, and therefore work too is only One; there can be a difference in workmanship, but not in work."

"Since you have now half-promised to give me some assistance,
kinsman," said the visitor, "would it alter anything if I could
give you in return some assistance which I doubt if anyone else
could give you quite so easily? I am well in with most of the
more important people in this town, and on familiar terms with
the leading men in the land. It would be the easiest thing in the
world for me, any time at all, to get you a job with many times
the remuneration you have in your present one; a position which
would enable you to perform a much nobler service for your
fellow-citizens than you do at present, a man of your abilities."

The superintendent replied, "I know perfectly well that my position is not considered high. But it will never be low for as long as man himself is conceived and born."

Like the man who discovered that it must have been the noon-cairn he had seen so many years previously, it was not until many years later that I, Álfgrímur, realized that here, one night in my youth, I had overheard an absolute friend of mankind speaking in the language of the Fathers of the Church and the Saints – but actually with directly opposite connotations from them, for they spoke with absolute disgust about mankind's creation: *homo inter faeces et urinam conceptus est.*

I did not know whether the visitor had given up all hope that his efforts to persuade the superintendent would bear fruit, because he said no more. The latter carried on from the point where they had left off, and wound up that part of the conversation which took place in the mid-loft, and after that they both went out:

"No, my friend," he said. "I have no desire for any other job than the one I have already. Even though I were the Governor himself, I would not think I could serve other people, and least of all myself, better than now. I hold the stirrup for people while they mount. I know that what I can do for you is only a trifle; and that is because the world is only One, and it is in Time; and Time is supernatural and the invincible overlord of everything. On the other hand, I am prepared to take a little extra upon myself in order to assist you. I have two pouches. In one of them there is snuff, in the other there is gold. I have often thought how grateful I would be to Providence if I were given the occasion to give up taking snuff. And now I have found that welcome opportunity; and you shall have the whole of my monthly pay. On the other hand, I do not dare to give you more than twenty or thirty of the gold coins I got for my land; because someone else might come to me when I least expected it, and I might perhaps find it my duty to hold his stirrup for him too while he is trying to mount."

17

PEPPER FOR THREE *AURAR*

If one glances at the newspapers of that period, for example the *Ísafold*, it comes to light that life was not entirely uneventful in this little fishing-station, even though some people might think that it lies beyond the edge of the world. At just about this time the news was spread round the country that our famous singer had now written a letter to the exalted Althing itself. In this letter he took leave to inform the nation's legislators that, because of his fame throughout the world (which was due much more to God's mercy than his own merits), there was now no longer any need for the horny-handed sons of toil in Iceland to be burdened further with taxes on his behalf; with this letter he was renouncing the funds he had been granted by the Treasury; the time had now come, the letter said, for the roles to be changed: it was now up to him to start kneading the golden dough for those fishermen and farmers from this day onwards. At the same time he thanked the Althing for the sums it had up to now granted him out of public moneys in Iceland in order to promote culture abroad. The Government's magnanimity was eloquent evidence of the fact that the nation which lived here was still determined to hold aloft the banner of its great past. Above this letter there was printed a picture of Garðar Hólm, one of the first portraits to appear in Icelandic newspapers and the largest to be printed in those columns until the day the Danish king came to Iceland a few years later.

In the newspapers of those days one can read innumerable eulogies about this young genius, who was already acknowledged as the nation's favourite son. Among other things, it was freely asserted in praise of Garðar Hólm that he was an example to every young student in the respect one should show to the Treasury.

He was regarded as one of the foremost of the intellectuals because of the consideration he showed for the farmers and fishermen. In one paper it was said that no artist could achieve greater distinction in his career than to deny himself the privilege of grabbing the gold which was scraped from under the nails of these poverty-stricken people; nor could there be any doubt that the farmers and fishermen knew how to appreciate the moral strength that shone so brightly in the famous man's letter. In a brief news-paragraph elsewhere in the paper one could then read that the singer had presented to the nation ten thousand picture-postcards of himself to be sold for the benefit of tuberculosis patients. In the next issue there appeared a further effusion from Garðar Hólm, again headed by the huge picture: "I wish to express my fervent and most heartfelt gratitude to ship-owner and shopkeeper Mr Jón Guðmundsson, Knight of the Danish Order of Dannebrog, as well as to his son G. Gúðmúnsen, wholesale merchant and Commander of the Danish Order of Dannebrog, for the money which those enlightened progressives, patriots, and compatriots disbursed so freely when a young Icelander timorously and apprehensively set foot upon the steep path never before trodden by anyone from this country, with little in his knapsack except the courage of hope. I thank these two good men and true Icelanders and Knights of the Danish Order of Dannebrog for their sympathy towards the endeavours of a little boy who from the very beginning believed in the voice of Iceland in the choir of the world: it is my hope that Icelanders will get the singing that their country deserves. Respectfully, Garðar Hólm."

Yet another article was headlined in large type as follows: *DER ERLKÖNIG* AT AUSTURVÖLLUR. This report stated that Garðar Hólm the opera singer was intending to entertain the public with a concert from the balcony of the Althing building on the following Sunday, weather permitting. The famous singer was going to sing a few songs from the programme he had presented abroad, particularly those which had earned the greatest acclaim in the Teatro Colon in Buenos Aires and on the balcony of the Sultan's palace in Algiers, such as *The Sheep are Bleating in the Pen*, *How Beautifully that Bird did Sing*, and *The East Wind Coldly on Us Blew*.

To these Icelandic songs countless thousands of people throughout the world, adherents of the Pope and Mohammed alike, had bowed their heads. In addition, he was intending to entertain his fellow-countrymen here with a few songs of the type that had originated under the warm golden skies of the Mediterranean but had never before been heard in the cold blue realms of Iceland's mountains – the famous so-called arias. Finally, he would be singing *Der Erlkönig*.

"Why do you never read the *Ísafold*, grandmother?" I asked.

She replied, "I have always been thought stupid."

"It says in the papers that Garðar Hólm is going to sing at Austurvöllur on Sunday."

"That doesn't surprise me," she said. "'Sweetly sings the swan all the summer long'."

"Should we not go down to Austurvöllur on Sunday, grandmother?" I asked.

"Oh, I don't think we'll be going down to Austurvöllur to hear a song we cannot hear at Brekkukot, my child," said my grandmother.

"In that case I'll go by myself," I said.

"Do that," she said. "In any case I have already heard my own song. Yes indeed. But you have yet to hear your song. On you go. And attend to God, as my grandmother used to say."

All the same, I had a suspicion that there were few things that preoccupied people more on both sides of the churchyard. I do not think it is putting it too strongly if I say that everyone and everything, town and nation, earth and sky, were waiting for this singing. The churchyard and all its fantasies disappeared beyond my horizon of those days, the two bells ceased to sound, the clock stopped ticking.

On one of those days of expectancy just before the concert at Austurvöllur I was sent to town on an errand for my grandmother, and was walking down Löngustétt, as the main street in Reykjavík used to be called in those days, where Gúðmúnsen's Store and the Theological Seminary and the Hotel d'Islande stood. It was just after midday. The weather was dry. I was watching a train of pack-ponies loaded with stockfish moving off; in those days, farmers bought dried cods'-heads and transported them on ponies out to the eastern districts on journeys as long, measured in days, as a journey from Paris to Peking, through countless districts, over mountains and moors and across rocky deserts and rushing rivers. It was a most impressive sight to see such a train setting off; there was about it an atmosphere of distant eastern places. Suddenly I felt a hand under my chin.

"I thought it was myself," said Garðar Hólm; he was out taking a stroll with his cane like all fashionable people.

I gaped at him at first, tongue-tied, and finally replied, "No, it's me."

"What are you doing?" he asked.

"I'm buying pepper for three *aurar*," I replied.

"Just like me," he said. "Can't I offer you something?"

"No," I said.

"Not even a five-*aurar* cake?" he said.

"There's no need at all," I said.

A cream cake little bigger than a five-*aurar* piece cost at that time as much as enough fish for ten people. It happened all too seldom in those days, unfortunately, when I had the taste for sweet cakes, that I was well enough off to invest in business of that kind. These delicacies had another drawback as well, for it was impossible to hold them in the mouth for more than a fraction of a second; the cake melted away on the tongue like snow in sunshine and slid unbidden down one's throat just when the good taste was beginning to make itself felt. And one never had the money to buy another one. It was no trifling matter to be invited to a party where a treat like that was in store.

He made me walk beside him down Löngustétt. Everybody who was anybody raised his hat, and ladies of standing inclined their heads. Some people stopped and turned and stared after him as he went by.

"Now what's your name again, old chap?" Garðar Hólm asked me.

"I'm called Álfgrímur," I said.

"Ach, what am I thinking of!" he said. "It's just so difficult to believe it. What I meant to say – have you set your heart on anything?"

I said, "I'm thinking of going down to Austurvöllur on Sunday."

"What do you want to go there for?" he asked.

"I'm going to hear you sing."

"Why?" he asked.

I thought for a moment, and replied, "There's something I want to hear."

"Something?" he said. "What do you mean?"

"I want so much to hear that one pure note."

Garðar Hólm woke up suddenly like a sleepwalker in the middle of the road, stopped, and stared at me.

"What are you saying, child?" he said at last. "What kind of talk is that?"

Suddenly my shyness left me and I looked at him directly; and then, as if nothing could be more natural, there in the middle of Lõngustétt I put to him the question that had been troubling me for three years, ever since Pastor Jóhann had talked to me in the churchyard:

"Is it true," I asked, "that there is only the one pure note?"

"Certainly it's true," said the singer. "I almost said – unfortunately."

"But if one should perhaps achieve this note?" I said.

"Ha, did I not suspect it was myself I was meeting here in Lõngustétt buying pepper! So you too have started talking to Pastor Jóhann, then?"

When I was growing up, it was only beautiful belles and fine ladies who were entrusted with the task of looking after those indescribable treasuries of confectionery art which filled our baker's shops in Reykjavík, richly arrayed on every tray and counter and every shelf on every wall. A baker's shop like Friðriksen's, for instance, could only really be compared with Persia itself, plus half of Syria and a part of Constantinople, as these places are described in the Úlfar-rímur. And indeed, no sooner were we inside the door of Friðriksen's basement shop than the world singer tore off his hat and bowed low, I might almost say right down to the ground, and reverently uttered this one word: "Madonna!"

Here at last was a man who knew how to conduct himself fittingly towards shop-girls at a baker's. And the one who stood behind the counter here, wearing the national costume with silver filigree on the bodice, smiled too in the correct style and blushed suitably; but she did not swoon; perhaps the singer had been there before.

In front of the counter stood a plump little girl, a full year or so older than I, who was buying two French loaves. When the singer entered the baker's shop and started taking off his hat, and the madonna started blushing, this little dumpling was also thrown into a dither, and she dropped a curtsey with a look of ecstatic alarm in her eyes. At this the singer caught sight of the girl, and recognized her. He went over to her and kissed her on the forehead and caressed her crimson cheek and asked her what she had to say for herself.

"Nothing," said the dumpling, beginning to recover herself a little. "Except that Daddy and Mummy are always saying that you never come to see us."

"I am coming at once to have some toasted white bread," he said. "But first I want to introduce you to this young lad who will soon be as big as you are; he is myself, you see, as I actually am, what's my name again?"

He looked at me and no doubt expected me to answer, but I did not dare to speak my name in such a strange environment. Since I made no reply he went on, "This is little Miss Gúðmúnsen. Her mother toasts white bread better than any other lady in Iceland."

It was as if a cloud passed across the young girl's face, and she said haltingly, "Is – that one with you?"

"We are all with one another, my children. Do help yourselves to a five-*aurar* cake."

"No thanks," said the girl, and went on measuring me up and down, uncomprehendingly. "I have to hurry back home."

"There's no hurry, little Miss," he said. "Madonna, could I possibly ask you to fetch me that broad white tray standing over there?"

The madonna laid a tray filled with cream cakes on the counter before us. It nearly made one's heart ache with spiritual and physical joy to look at these delicious works of art.

"Help yourselves, dear children," said Garðar Hólm.

I took a cake and was going to eat it nicely, as I had been taught to do; I was moreover trying to pick out the cake which was the least spectacular in colour and shape, because my grandmother had firmly impressed on me that when I was visiting I should always choose the plainest-looking piece. But if one takes such a cake and tries to bite it politely, one is left with very little more than a tiny smear on the fingers. But then I caught sight of the singer himself tackling the cakes. It is not too much to say that he dealt with them like a man of authority. Never had I seen a performance like it; there was certainly no question now of choosing the ugliest cake first. Little Miss Gúðmúnsen looked on as well, and the madonna smiled at every cake that disappeared into the singer; for they disappeared, or to be more accurate, they flowed into him in rapid streams, one after another, sometimes two or three at a time. And while he ate he never paused in his promptings to us dear children to help ourselves. I was so thoroughly unnerved that I cannot properly recall whether I ever ventured upon cake number two; I seem to remember that I contented myself with standing there like an idiot with the smear from number one on my fingers.

"Jesus!" said little Miss Gúðmúnsen.

"It's vital to put them away before they turn sour," said Garðar Hólm, and indeed the tray was quickly empty. "Shall we ask Madonna for another tray?"

"Yes," said little Miss Gúðmúnsen with a gasp. "I wish Daddy could see this, he always says that well-hung fish is the best; or Mummy, who always says it should be toasted white bread."

Garðar Hólm wiped his mouth with his handkerchief, and laughed at us.

"How much, Madonna?" he said.

He put his hand in his pocket and made something jingle, then brought out a handful of gold coins. He threw one gold coin down on the empty tray and said, "There you are, Madonna."

"Jesus!" said little Miss Gúðmúnsen. "Is that a genuine gold coin?"

"Genuine gold does not exist, children," he said. "Gold is by its nature not genuine."

"Jesus!" said little Miss Gúðmúnsen.

"I'm afraid I haven't got change," said the madonna, and

examined the coin on both sides. "There has never been so much money in my till since I came here. You will have to speak to Friðriksen himself."

"We'll let that wait until next time," said Garðar Hólm. "Adieu, Madonna."

"No," said the madonna, "I can't have that. I scarcely dare touch it, even. I wouldn't have a moment's peace of mind so long as I knew it was somewhere near me."

Garðar Hólm was halfway up the basement steps, with his arms around my shoulders and Miss Gúðmúnsen's as if he owned us both equally. The madonna came running after us with the gold coin.

"I beseech you, Garðar Hólm, take your gold coin from me," she said.

"Give it to this young lad, Madonna," said the singer. "He is nearer to being myself than Garðar Hólm is."

The madonna put the gold coin in my hand and pressed my fingers round it.

"Here is the coin," I said when we were out in the street. "And now I must go. I had almost forgotten that grandmother sent me out to buy pepper."

"Just like me," said Garðar Hólm. "My mother once sent me out to buy pepper, and I have not returned home yet."

"Here is the gold coin," I said again.

"Oh, just put it in your pocket, old chap," he said.

"Jesus!" said little Miss Gúðmúnsen. "I wish Daddy could see this. And Mummy."

He left me standing, in the street outside Friðriksen's baker's shop with the gold coin in my hand. He himself strolled off in the other direction with his cane in one hand and leading little Miss Gúðmúnsen and her two loaves with the other. But when he had gone a short distance he suddenly remembered something and turned on his heel and called out to me as I stood there with the gold coin still in my hand:

"I clean forgot," he shouted, "to ask you to give my greetings to your grandmother. And also to Pastor Jóhann. Tell him that he was quite right: there is only the one note – and it is pure."

18

WHEN OUR LYKLA CALVES

I have forgotten all about the woman from Landbrot in the excitement over this great concert at Austurvöllur – which never came to anything, of course. The visitor who had come to see the rest of us had to sail away the day before he was due to sing, naturally, because he was committed to the wider world for greater things which could not wait. But the visitor who had come to see the woman from Landbrot, he stayed.

"Learn never to look forward to anything," said the woman. "It is the beginning of knowing how to endure everything."

"What would your children say if they knew of you lying in the midst of this noisy company here in the mid-loft at Brekkukot?" said my grandmother.

"I like hearing their voices," said the woman. "I always dread it when someone goes out."

"Well, we have nothing but chatter to offer you, either," said my grandmother.

Then the woman said, "My little boy, who could never bear to be away from his mother, and my little girl, who now owns twelve sheep – I know that they would never expect me to be so unkind as to die before their eyes just when our Lykla is at last about to start giving milk – we who haven't owned a cow for seven whole years."

"I see that you have hung up your tunic, Commandant," said Captain Hogenson. "Tell us the latest lies before you go to sleep."

"I have lost the wretched cat which has been wandering around my place down by the harbour for a month," said the superintendent. "I wouldn't be surprised if the authorities have hanged it. Developments are so rapid nowadays. Excuse me, but whose is that gold coin lying on the shelf above you, Captain Hogensen?"

"It is Álfgrímur's gold coin," said Captain Hogensen. "People are beginning to give even gold coins away nowadays. One doesn't dare give a child anything less than half a cow's worth now. Come on now, make up a few real sensations."

"No sensations," said the superintendent. "Not yet. It's only here in the mid-loft that anything happens. Anything new with you in the cubicle there?"

"I suppose I'm rather like the cat," the woman called out from her cubby hole. "It gets lost in between times and then turns up when it has been given up."

"That's right," said the superintendent; he was taking off his socks on the edge of Runólfur Jónsson's bed. "Cats have nine lives. Time enough to mourn when we have seen Pussy hanged. The real sensation, Hogensen, would be if it were now to be proved that there was a life after the lives of the cat. But I haven't heard that yet. Not today, my friend. But perhaps tomorrow, my friend."

Runólfur Jónsson, whom everyone had thought to be asleep, turned on his other side and spoke up: "The woman who eats the ling," he said, "ought to take a trip out to Ness to see the miracles."

"Well, I don't give a rap for the cat," said Captain Hogensen. "I only care about ticks, my good men – poli-ticks. Ha-ha-ha-ha. I don't call anything news if it isn't about politics."

"I understand, my friend," said the superintendent. "We understand. We know you are on board warships. That's very important. But I too have my place, my dear Hogensen. Creation is incomparable as far as it goes."

"And I could never hold with grumblers when I was navigating," said Captain Hogensen. "They cursed every day except Sundays. Because they got soup every week-day. *Den helvedes suppe*, they used to say. But on Sundays there was a bit of pork in it; and then they said, *Lovet være Herren den Almægtige.*"

"Precisely," said the superintendent. "*Lovet være Herren den Almægtige.* Except that I would say these beautiful words every day except Sundays; and that is because I have never been able to eat pork. I have only to smell pork and I am done for. And now I'm going to bed. May God give you all a good night. And remember to tell little Álfgrímur when he wakes up tomorrow morning that I have put the gold coin aside so that it does not get lost."

And the woman who ate ling went on living. For a long time she would reach out for the door and pull it to while she was having her attacks, because she did not want her groans and cries to disturb the man who commanded warships. When the attack had passed she would push the door open again. But if any visitors arrived with news about great events, or if someone was telling an episode from *The Lives of Great Icelanders*, or if some cheerful fellow started reciting verses about seafaring, or horses, the woman would throw her door wide open. She always said something to me whenever I walked past; she invariably asked about the weather, about the direction of the wind that day, or whether I thought it would manage to stay dry. But it was a tricky business answering her on these matters.

Once I said to her, "The rain has set in."

"What absolute nonsense!" said the woman. "To the best of my knowledge it was dry this morning."

"Look out of the window," I said.

"I know," said the woman. "It's pouring at present. But no one says that the rain has set in unless the stones haven't dried for a week."

Late one evening she asked me the same question; I was at pains to be accurate and said, "It was coming down this morning."

"It's terrible, the way you talk!" said the woman. "And the sheep already gathered for the autumn! You never say it's coming down unless it rains while the hay is still being dried."

So it was little wonder that I suspected that something lay behind it when this philological woman asked me one day, "Tell me, my boy, can you read and write?"

I could not bring myself to deny it, but on the other hand did not dare to make much of it.

To be able to read and write has never really been considered education in Iceland, any more than taking dried cods'-heads apart; not even among the lowest of the low. In my time, children were not generally sent to school until after they had read all the Icelandic Sagas at home, about forty books in all; but though I had often heard visitors reading aloud parts of the Icelandic Sagas, I myself had read no others than those which happened to be in our house because someone had left them behind.

Even though I tried because of this to make as little as possible of my reading and writing ability, nonetheless the woman decided there and then to ask me to go down town for her and buy her a pen for half an *eyrir* and stationery for two *aurar*. No sooner had I returned with these implements than she began to dictate a letter. I should make it clear that I had not managed to achieve any great familiarity with orthography, and therefore my spelling was not unlike that of learned men in Iceland round about the year 1100. This woman's letter was my very first attempt at calligraphy; I am thus one of the people who invented orthography in Iceland. I shall not reproduce this orthography here, but the substance of what I wrote down to the woman's dictation was something like this:

"To Nonni and Gunna, they are my children, you see. Our Lykla will be calving in autumn; we have always longed for a cow, you see. When she calves, I want to ask you to be kind to her. I know she has been getting ready for a long time. I think now, since the hay-harvest was so good, that we should have the courage to add another head to our stock. If it's a heifer, we should call her Rose. But it's not easy to rear a heifer, Gunna dear. When our Lykla has calved . . ."

It was going to be a long-drawn-out business to compose this document. The woman was so fastidious in her choice of words that she made me cross it all out as fast as I wrote it down.

"We'll tear up this awful rubbish," she would say. And the few lines we had been struggling to compose for most of the day were consigned to oblivion. We went on like that for days on end. We never succeeded in expressing meticulously enough the kind of slops the calf was to be fed. By nightfall we were so exhausted that we were almost in a coma; and then we tore up the whole day's output. This woman must surely have been descended from Snorri Sturluson. One thing is certain, that she never deviated from the most stringent standards of Icelandic prose style. Often when I myself am writing something, this woman comes to my mind again. Unfortunately, she failed to realize that one can set one's literary standards so high that it becomes impossible to utter a single word or groan except at the very most to say *A-a-a*. Often these letter-writing sessions would end with the woman taking a fit. I would leave the cubicle, defeated, with the pen and stationery, and close the door. Captain Hogensen would take a pinch of snuff from the medicine bottle he kept under his pillow and say, "I think the time is coming for me to brush my coat."

October passed, and there was no change inside the cubicle; except that the woman only became paler and more lifeless. Until finally the time came when she became transparent; she underwent that transformation, that transfiguration of countenance that sometimes comes to sufferers when the last of their strength ebbs away.

One day after the frost had come, this woman from Landbrot asked to see Björn of Brekkukot; she wanted to give him some money she kept in her skirt pocket, so that he could buy some wood to make a coffin for her.

He said, "Well, I have never nailed a box together except perhaps for fish. But I can perhaps get hold of a handyman."

Not to make a long story of it, they found someone handy with a hammer, and work on the coffin started in the store-shed. My grandfather and the handyman he had got hold of measured the woman with a ruler. I took part in this work in various ways, handing them nails and other small things and finally holding the little jar of lamp-black which was applied to the wood as a sign of mourning. The woman asked incessantly how the work on the coffin was going; she had somehow got the notion that the coffin would be too short, and there were times, when the pain left her, that she was distinctly worried about this. She made me measure her with a length of twine and then sent me out to the store-shed with the twine to compare it with the coffin. But by that time the coffin was finished and the handyman would answer:

"Tell the old crone from me, my lad, that if she is too long for the coffin we'll cut her down to size. Stranger things happened in the Sagas."

"When our Lykla calves," said the woman –

"When our Lykla calves;

Yes, when our Lykla calves:

If it's a bull,
If it's a little bull-calf,
Then Nonni must grind peat for his bedding.
Each morning and night: dry peat.
But if it is a heifer, as we all hope,
She is to be called Rose.
We shall give her a pint of fresh milk every feed;
No, wait, let's make that two. We must not be mean to her.
It will pay dividends in the long run, dear children.
It's good to put some groats in too.
And boilings from the fish-pot do no harm.
Some people put coffee-dregs
Into the calf's slops; that's said to be wholesome,
But more for cud-chewing than nourishment.
Have I written that she should be called Rose?
Oh, how messy all this is,
There isn't the slightest trace of order in it;
We'll tear it up and try again:
When our Lykla calves.
When our Lykla calves.
When our Lykla calves:
Yes."

At this point the woman suddenly began to fail rapidly. I sat on the cobbler's-stool with the half-written letter on my knee. Just then, Runólfur Jónsson arrived home and began to talk miracles and phenomena.

"Not so loud, Runólfur," said Captain Hogensen. "She is near the end."

Runólfur looked into the cubicle and saw how things were.

"So that's the way of it, well, well," said Runólfur. "As far as I can see we should be sending for Björn of Brekkukot."

"I don't see that there is much point in sending for anyone," said Captain Hogensen. "Can't you understand that it's nearly over, man?"

"Well, then I see no other course than to have a word with the Man who is above Björn of Brekkukot," said Runólfur Jónsson.

Frost and snow had set in. The woman was taken out the

following day. Old Jónas the policeman had arrived, along with a workman from out east at Kolviðarhóll who had agreed to take the corpse with him the first stage of the journey; the plan then was to keep the corpse at Kolviðarhóll until the opportunity arose of giving it to some reliable man who was travelling east over the mountains. In those days it was considered a seven-day journey on horseback from Reykjavík east to Landbrot. But people thought it much more likely that it would take the corpse all winter to travel alone in stormy weather such a long way through vast districts, over moors and mountains and sands such as one meets on the way east to Landbrot, not forgetting some formidable and fast-flowing rivers.

The laying in the coffin and the house-service were combined into the one ceremony, but without Pastor or religious devotions, except that I was made to sing the long coffin-laying psalm because I was by then so accustomed to funerals.

I was told to start the singing as soon as my grandmother had dressed the corpse. I stood singing at the edge of the stairhatch like a bird on a branch while the coffin was being manoeuvred down the steps. Runólfur Jónsson sat on his bed with salt-burn in his eyes and his fingers in his mouth like a little boy. The ceremony was given an exceptionally dignified air by Captain Hogensen, who had got up and dressed to represent the navy. His uniform was carefully brushed, not to mention the gilt buttons and the peak of his cap. He stood like an admiral by the bed-post at the head of his bed, and one could see the coiled blue veins under the parchment skin of his temples. This foreign official of the Danish State, who looked so exactly like His Majesty King Kristian IX, raised his gnarled workman's hand to the peak of his cap when the coffin was carried past him, and remained standing in that position without blinking while I sang the psalm right through to the last Amen.

19

MORNING OF ETERNITY: AND END

Late in the winter, my grandfather Björn started calling me at six o'clock every morning so that I could help him see to the lumpfish-nets in Skerjafjörður. These mornings have always remained fresh in my memory.

What happened? Nothing really happened, except that the sun was getting ready to rise. The stars are seldom as bright as they are in the morning, either because one's eyesight is clearest just after waking, or because the Virgin Mary has been busy polishing them all night. Sometimes there was also a moon. A tiny light had been lit in a cottage on Álftanes; probably someone was going out fishing. Often there was frost and frozen snow, and the ice creaked in the night. Somewhere out in the infinite distance lay the spring, at least in God's mind, like the babies that are not yet conceived in the mother's womb.

My grandfather had a large boat, and a small one. The small boat was used for the lumpfishing; it was beached at the high-water mark in front of a shed in which we kept our gear. The boat was easy to launch; it went practically of its own accord if the rollers were placed correctly. And so we rowed out among the rocks and skerries to where the nets lay. Sometimes the gulls followed us in the moonlight. Lumpfish-nets are not normally hauled in; you row alongside them and gaff the fish, or else just grab them by hand, wearing mittens. I kept one oar out and held the boat in position while grandfather used the gaff.

My grandfather was always in a good humour and always reasonably cheerful, but never exactly jolly. He could be mischievous in an innocent sort of way, and enjoyed trying to out-row me. He also laughed if some of his snuff were blown into my eyes when he was taking a pinch, probably because he did not think it was manly to show it if one's eyes watered. I never knew what he was thinking about, because he talked mostly in stylized phrases, both about the weather and the fish. But I somehow felt that in this man's presence, nothing untoward could happen. I often thought to myself how good the Saviour had been to send me to this man for protection and help, and I made up my mind to stay with him for as long as he lived and always to catch lumpfish with him at the end of the winter. And I hoped to God that he would not go from me before I myself was well on the way to being as old as he; and then I would find myself a little boy somewhere and have him row out with me to the nets early in the morning when the stars were still bright at the end of the winter. In the moonlight, the gulls seemed to have golden breasts. If you looked down over the gunwale you could see the lumpfish gliding among the seaweed, feeding; occasionally they would even turn their pink-shaded bellies upwards in the water.

Sometimes we would fill both the hand-cart and the wheelbarrow with this fat fish. And just when the stars were really beginning to pale, we would cart our catch homewards straight across the Sands. Grandmother would give us coffee, and then we would go down town to sell the catch just as people were getting up. Grandfather would stop with his hand-cart somewhere in the square, and people would come along with money to buy lumpfish while others just came to greet him and discuss the weather. I was often sent with a string of lumpfish to the regular customers; usually the maid came to the door with the money and took the fish, but sometimes the lady of the house herself would be there, or else, for some incomprehensible reason, the daughter of the house.

"Aren't you the one who's related to Garðar Hólm?" said the slip of a girl who unexpectedly came to the back door of one of the houses to take the string of lumpfish from me.

"No," I said.

"Yes, of course you're related to him," said the girl. "It was you he gave the gold coin to. Well, I'll be absolutely blowed! Fancy selling lumpfish! Don't you know that it's a vulgar fish?"

I said nothing.

"Don't you want to be anything, then, when you grow up?" she asked.

"I'm going to be a fisherman, if it's any of your business," I replied.

"A lumpfisherman!" she said. "Aren't you ashamed of yourself? And you related to such a great man! Put the lumpfish down on the doorstep there, I'm not going to touch it. Ugh, it's just like a sea-scorpion. And you related to a world-famous man!"

"I am to get money for the fish," I said.

"I haven't any money," said the girl. "The maid's left."

"I am to get money nonetheless," I said.

She replied. "You can jolly well use the gold coin you got last year, you beastly pig!"

With that she went inside and slammed the door shut, but immediately opened it again and spat out, "And I only hope it was counterfeit!"

Then she slammed the door again for good. The fish lay on the doorstep. I took them back and put them on grandfather's barrow and said that I had not got the money. To be honest I was a little annoyed that such fine fish should have been abused.

These mornings when we were seeing to the lumpfish in Skerjafjörður (and they were really all one and the same morning) – suddenly they were over. Their stars faded: your Chinese idyll ended.

My grandfather had given me a sign to ship the oars. The boat came to rest with its bows on a shelf of rock, and the red clusters of seaweed eddied round the prow in the calm sea as the sun rose. It was almost spring. Grandfather took a careful pinch from his snuff-horn, and then said,

"Your grandmother has been talking to me."

I kept silent, and waited.

"As you know, my boy," he said, "we are not really your grandfather and grandmother. We are nobody's grandfather and grandmother; we are not even married. We are just two old bodies. But I knew your grandmother's sister here a long time ago."

"I didn't know grandmother ever had a sister," I said.

"Your grandmother's sister died more than fifty years ago," said grandfather. "But it is partly because of her that your grandmother is with me. I was fond of your grandmother's late sister."

"Did grandmother maybe come to you when her sister died?" I asked.

He replied, "Your grandmother's sister was never with me. And your grandmother was married and living away in the east."

Then I suddenly remembered that my grandmother had told me that she had once travelled all the way from the east over the mountains to the south here.

"Indeed!" he said. "Tut tut! She lost her husband in the spring fishing season. He drowned in Thorlákshöfn one Easter. And then there was no one left."

"Eh?" I said, "no one left? Why was there no one left? Where were – the others?"

"There was nothing left," said my grandfather. "She had had three sons, and lost them all. The last of her sons was on his bier when his father perished. She had given them all the same name; she was always a little obstinate. They were all called Grímur, after her grandfather. Most children here in Iceland died in those days; if it was not something else, it was the diphtheria. But when the youngest son was dead, and she had lost the father as well, the same Easter, well, it was obvious that she had to give up her home. Since her husband was gone too, naturally there was nothing else to be done. So I invited her to come here to Reykjavík, if she wanted to, because I had known her sister a little. And so she left there and came here."

"I thought that grandmother had never known anything more dangerous than the Soga Stream," I said.

"When your poor mother wanted to christen you Álfur, years ago, your grandmother insisted that you were also to be called Grímur. That is how obstinate she is. And for that reason she does not want you not to drown in the Soga Stream when you go to fetch Gráni home."

"I shall try to be careful, grandfather," I said.

Then he started again: "As I was saying, your grandmother has been talking to me. She says that according to Helgesen, the teacher, you can learn. We want you to have an education."

"Why?" I asked.

"Her people in the past were all educated men," he said.

"Then what will I be made to do?" I said. "Will I not be allowed to come out fishing with you again?"

"We were thinking of sending you to school, my boy, and making you learn what they call Latin. The idea is that you start in the autumn, if you are accepted. I went to see Pastor Jóhann; we have got a University student from Copenhagen to prepare you. There was some talk of you starting tomorrow."

I asked, "Are you then not going to wake me tomorrow morning to go fishing?"

He replied, "Your grandmother wishes you well, my boy. And so do I, even though I am ignorant."

And with these words he put out his oar and we pushed off from the rock and rowed ashore.

In Stephan G. Stephansson's biography it says that when the poet was a foster-child up north in Skagafjörður he saw some young men riding over the mountains on their way to school in the south one autumn. He was so deeply distressed by his own misery at not being able to go to school himself and become an educated man that he threw himself down on the heather out there on the moor and wept for a whole day. I have always found it difficult to understand that story. The thought of becoming a Latin scholar had never once occurred to me. I had never been impressed by seeing schoolboys walking around with their tattered books under their arm, nor had I ever wanted to be in their shoes. And now that I had been informed that I was to go and start learning Latin, I inwardly felt as if my grandfather had told me to become an organ-grinder or a scissors-sharpener – the sort of riffraff that sometimes came over from Denmark during the summer.

It came like a thunderclap out of a clear blue sky. All my plans for eternal life at Brekkukot were destroyed. My joy in existence was shattered. The Great Wall of China, within which I was the Son of Heaven himself, was breached – and not at the blast of a trumpet, but at a word. How bitter that it should have been my grandfather who spoke the word that ruined for me our turnstile-gate at Brekkukot. I broke down. I had not cried since I was small, because we did not cry at Brekkukot. I felt that nothing could ever console me again. I rowed and rowed with all my strength to keep pace with my grandfather, and cried and cried. When we reached the shore, he said:

"Bear in mind, my boy, that you have to take the place of your mother's Álfur and the three Grímurs of your grandmother."

20

LATIN

I wonder what my grandfather Björn of Brekkukot really thought that Latin was? Did he think it was the magic Sesame which opened all cliffs in Iceland? If so, I am not at all sure that he was all that far from the truth. Where fish leaves off in Iceland, Latin takes over.

In the old days there were more Latin-educated men in Iceland, relatively speaking, than in most other countries. Latin was the badge of nobility in Iceland. A beggar who could lard his speech with Latin was always considered a better man than the one who gave him alms. No one was considered really and truly literate in Iceland unless he knew Latin.

Until this day, the world that I lived in had seemed so sufficient to me that I had never wanted any other. I had everything. Everything in our world was in its own way perfect and complete in my eyes. It had never crossed my mind that Captain Hogensen or Runólfur Jónsson or the superintendent lacked anything in fullness of stature. Hitherto I had believed that my grandmother had never had any Grímurs except me, Álfgrímur. And I had thought that just as she was everything to me, so I had been sufficient for her just as I was; but now I suddenly learned that she had had three Grímurs, in the hope, as far as I could see, of bringing up at least one who would know Latin like her forefathers; and because that had come to nothing she had travelled all the way over Hellisheiði and found me here in the south and reared me in the hope that I would learn Latin in place of her own Grímurs. I could scarcely help feeling that I had rather been tricked.

But I cried only on that one morning, and then silently began my education. And little by little I somehow became reconciled to those three Grímurs who had more or less been wished on to me during a fishing-trip. But on that selfsame day a new course was set, as it were; and a new poem. I took my leave of the cod and the lumpfish, the cow and the horse, the bluebottle and the hen, the low fence that was drowning in tansies, and the horse-daisy; and the harmony of silver and copper – that too faded into the distance.

But when it came to the point, it was not just Latin that I needed instruction in; I had to buy all sorts of other books as well, some of them in languages whose names I did not even know. In Danish, there was the book that told you how many bones there are in a dog. There was also the famous book by Geir Zoëga which starts, "I have a book, you have a pen, there is no ink in the inkstand". These languages, however, were scarcely considered a formal part of education; I was ordered to learn them for myself while having my meals. The only thing that mattered at all in education was to know how to decline and conjugate, that is to say to inflect Latin nouns according to their cases, and conjugate Latin verbs. These declensions and conjugations were not unlike the magic Sesames I mentioned earlier. In addition I had to learn a piece called The Greater Multiplication Table, which the poet Benedikt Gröndal in his autobiography called the Muck-Rigmarole.

By the time midsummer approached, these rigmaroles came pouring out of me of their own accord at the sight of the blue-faced student who was instructing me at the instigation of Pastor Jóhann. When Pastor Jóhann came to see us at the start of the hay-making, I declined for him all the classes of nouns in three genders, all the way from *mensa* to *dies*, and recited four different subjunctives of verbs in all *temporibus* into the bargain. Pastor Jóhann was so delighted with all this that he said that anyone who could decline correctly could also think correctly; and anyone who could think correctly could live correctly – with God's help. I was now to try for entry into the second class of the Grammar School that autumn.

I want to make it clear that although I was reconciled to do all this to please my grandmother, for many years thereafter I harboured a resentment over the slow severing of my roots that my schooling brought about; for a long time, half of me went on trying to shelter in this maternal lap, full of mistrust and fear towards everything outside: other smells, other people, other fish. A certain apathy settled over me during this period of my life, a dull lethargy that no joy of youth could dispel. Strangers went past me like ghosts which try to take shape but only become tufts of wool. People's talk became in my ears merely sound wafted in through the window at dusk, of which you can only distinguish a word here and there. I liked nothing better than to sit on grandmother's hearthstones while she was cooking, just to talk to her about the weather, or to hear her mutter some ancient ballad or recite a psalm into her knitting.

I have been told that at school I was the sort of simpleton who suffered from dux-disease. It is reckoned in Iceland that those who are afflicted by this disease can never become anything other than drunkards, journalists, or junior clerks. For my own part, since I was not allowed to become a lumpfisherman I did not care in the slightest what I became; I was not interested in anything particular, I wanted nothing. It could well be that my mental inertia during this period was a help to my capacity for memorizing. I learned every conceivable thing by rote quite automatically and without caring. I was spiritually as well as physically in a state of suspended adolescence. Lessons came welling up out of me as if I were talking in my sleep. I could reel off the bones in a dog at the drop of a hat, any time at all, just as if I had them in my pockets; if I had been woken up at three o'clock in the morning, I would have detailed each and every one of them, just as if I had been lying on them.

This spiritual defect used to be considered intelligence. But it also led to my becoming popular with my instructors, and this "intelligence" undoubtedly saved me from the embarrassments I think I would otherwise have brought upon myself wherever I showed my face during my adolescence. Photographs taken of me during these school years made me look like a fugitive from a home for mental defectives. I grew much too tall very quickly from all the liver and fish-roes at Brekkukot – and the succulent fat lumpfish did not make things any better. I was one of the

tallest boys in the school when I entered the second class, in my
confirmation year; for instance, my legs were so long that they
always got in my way when I walked, and my arms hung on me like
some tatty pieces of luggage that I did not know how to get rid
of. My face showed no trace whatever of a smile, just as if the soul
had been drained from it leaving nothing behind except the
anxiety it felt about its own emptiness: a life-prisoner peering
out through the bars. Two hundred hairs round the crown of my
head invariably stood straight up like a broom, and no power on
earth could quell them or sleek them down until Time itself took
a hand and I began to grow bald.

I shall try not to bore everyone with too much talk about the
appearance of this boy who came from a turf cottage and was
now to start stalking the varnished floors of the Grammar School
with the sons of merchants, civil servants, and landowners; but
nevertheless I feel I cannot completely ignore my boots, and
anyway they come into the story again to a certain extent later on.

I was provided with a pair of boots which some peasant had left
behind in our house when he set off for America twenty-five years
earlier. I was told to wear them out that winter, since my grandmother and grandfather had at long last given up all hope that
the man would return to fetch them. But it was easier said than
done to wear out these boots. I am not going to say whether these
boots were ugly or handsome, for people's taste in footwear is very
varied; shoes of all sorts of shapes and sizes have been considered
beautiful in this world, each in turn; once upon a time a shoe was
considered the more beautiful the longer a toe it had, until the
toe stood straight up like a spike as high as a man's knee; but at
other times the world will hear of nothing but open-toed shoes.

It may well be that the boots I wore in my confirmation year
will come into fashion sometime, for they were good boots, and
seldom has anyone been as delighted with his shoes as I was, at
least to begin with; truth to tell I was relieved to be able to discard
these flimsy moccasins of raw hide which were called cowskin-
shoes in Reykjavík in my youth. If I had any fault to find with
my boots, it would perhaps be that they had rather a lot of nails
in the soles, in fact rather like a bed of nails.

Every time I wore these boots into town a nail would emerge, sometimes many nails at once, and I would tread them into my foot. It really was not practicable to go for a walk in these boots unless one took a pair of pliers along too; I had not yet become such a dandy in those days that I would think twice about sitting down in the gutter to haul a few nails out of my boots if the need arose.

On the other hand there was never a live mouse inside the heel of my boot as is now said to be the fashion in Paris, I understand; yet there is nothing I remember so well about these boots as the din and racket they made in polite homes, and most particularly in the Grammar School. The thickness and toughness of the soles, as well as the iron with which the boots were shod, ensured that most people began to feel uneasy when I was heard approaching in the distance.

21

CONVERTING THE CHINESE

I developed a neutral expression which caused people more or less not to see me at all; it was as if a cocoon formed around me. I never looked miserable enough to tempt people to make fun of me for any length of time; I was just a little odd, in a rather uninteresting way. But it may well be that people made fun of me more than I realized; I was so unaware as a youth that I did not understand teasing until it became malice or downright mischief – and scarcely even then.

The man is not born, they say, who cannot find his equal. I found Grandpa Jón on my first day in the second class, and he me. He was twice as old as I was and had to shave every day to avoid having a long beard. He came from the Dalir, out west. Through some society which published Christian pamphlets in Norway he had received a higher calling – to convert the Chinese. Grandpa Jón was a constant target for the malicious; people were always telling him obscenities and trying to distress him with them. This broad-shouldered, fair-haired man was convinced that people would be improved by reading Christian pamphlets in Norwegian, and that it would benefit the Chinese to study enormous illustrated volumes of Biblical stories printed in Kristiania. People never tired of ridiculing his ideas, on the ingrained assumption of Icelanders that all believers must be out of their minds. Because of his age, Grandpa Jón was rather slow at his lessons; but his slowness of comprehension was as nothing compared to his total inability to remember anything. He thought Latin a ridiculous and unnecessary invention, particularly the subjunctive; he believed that it was the prince of darkness who had so arranged it that one verb could have different forms by the score in Latin and by the hundred in Greek; and yet he did not hesitate to tackle all these rigmaroles, for the sake of his calling.

And since all this drivel came pouring out of me in a constant, effortless stream right from the very first day, the teacher suggested to me that I should give Grandpa Jón a helping hand as far as his Latin was concerned.

Often I toiled late into the night trying to force some Latin into him, then hurried home to Brekkukot to sleep and got up again at the crack of dawn to make him repeat it. Grandpa Jón had long been accustomed to getting up very early to see to the cows, and he was always in the best of spirits when I came to see him in the morning, except that he had usually forgotten all the Latin of the previous evening. He wanted us to pray for the Chinese in New Norwegian, and naturally I had nothing against that, except that I thought it would be more to the point to pray to the Saviour to help Jón to learn Latin. New Norwegian was the ideal language for Grandpa Jón, for it is so truncated that it does not have any cases at all apart from a tiny vestige of a German peasant genitive: *the man his dog.* In this preposterous language we would beseech the Saviour to convert the Chinese. Our schoolmates called us Long-Loony and Broad-Loony and people stared at us wherever we went, and drunks pestered us in the street.

But there was one other thing which bound us together more than all the Latin and New Norwegian and salvation of the

Chinese, and that was music. No obstacles were so forbidding that Grandpa Jón would not attempt to overcome them, if the salvation of the Chinese were at stake: and that is why he also embarked on studying music. He had somehow got hold of a little harmonium and was trying to play it; but he was not doing very well, which he blamed on the fact that the keys were too narrow. He did not really care much for music; but he had heard that when one was instructing the Chinese in Biblical stories, one had to play the harmonium as an accompaniment. Finally he decided to seek tuition in organ-playing.

This was during the period of my life when all singing seemed to have died out in me. I never knew what kind of sound would come out of me if I opened my mouth. I had ceased to hear the music that once had filled the air all around me. I contented myself with reading the news which the papers published about Garðar Hólm's never-diminishing fame as a singer abroad; it was now being said that he had taken up residence in a baronial castle.

A girl dressed in Danish style halted on the other side of the street to stare at us. There was nothing that Jón and I were less inclined to do than pay any attention to women. I did not even look across the street; but I had the vague impression that she was wearing red gloves. We were so accustomed to being gaped at in the street that we ignored it. Then I noticed that she turned and changed direction, and crossed the street to meet us. She looked at me. This was just before spring, and I was soon to sit an examination for the third class and be confirmed by Pastor Jóhann. Her complexion was like summer butter. Her gloves were red, just as I had suspected, and had tassels. I had an idea I knew her. Was I seeing right?

"Don't you know me?" she said.

"No," I said.

"Why don't you know me?"

"Raise your cap," said Grandpa Jón.

"Why?" I said.

"Are you such a boor as all that?" she asked.

When I looked at her more closely I saw that she was scarcely a woman except in name only, even though she was wearing those red gloves; perhaps not more than a couple of years older than I.

"Why is there never a card from Garðar Hólm?" she asked.

"What sort of a card?" I said.

"What a fool you are," she said. "And who is that fool who's with you?"

"Why are you concerning yourself with us?" I asked.

"Tell me absolutely truly" – and she lowered her voice and came a little closer to me: "Wasn't it quite definitely a gold coin?"

"Yes," I said, "of course it was a gold coin."

"Jesus, how glad I am to hear you say that!" she said. "Daddy says it must have been brass."

"What does he know about it?" I said.

She said, "Yes, that's just what I always say. Thank you very much. I see you're at school. What are you going to be?"

"A lumpfisherman," I said.

"When are you going to stop behaving like a fool?" she said.

A little later I said to Grandpa Jón, "Listen, Jón, I'm beginning to want to learn to play the harmonium."

"I would not advise any man to do that," said Jón. "It is both a tedious and a trivial exercise. I would never have let myself in for it had it not been essential for China."

Music had not been an educational subject in Iceland since the Middle Ages – indeed, it was considered an affectation or an aberration, especially among the educated – until Garðar Hólm won for Iceland musical fame abroad; and then a few people began to think more highly of it. But for a long time afterwards it was still generally considered rather odd to be famous for singing. So it was practically unthinkable in my younger days for people to let themselves in for the tedium that music involved, except in the cause of salvation; music was good when people had to be put into the ground.

What surprised me most was that the precentor in the Cathedral should recognize me when I went to him with Grandpa Jón to learn to play the organ.

He said, "Was it not you whom Pastor Jóhann sometimes led by the hand into the churchyard to sing for him?"

"Only for very minor funerals," I said apologetically, for I knew that the precentor himself had the honour and responsibility of all the major funerals.

"That doesn't matter, I recognized you all the same," said the precentor. "You are related in some way to our Garðar Hólm. Are you perhaps thinking of playing before the Sultan in Algiers? Or for the Chinese, like our friend Jón here?"

This was the first time that I had encountered the phenomenon of a "dwelling-house" in the sense which has existed in one part of this world since the year 1000: dining-room and drawing-room; not just an open hearth, but a kitchen; furniture with French names, *chiffonier*, *buffet*, *canapé*; and a Danish wife. For the first time I sat on a plush chair with tassels. The harmonium stood in the precentor's study next to the vestibule. But the gleaming grand piano in the drawing-room seemed to me to be the crowning glory of the house. I thought at first that an instrument with such a broad keyboard must contain all the notes that can be heard in the universe, and was astonished when I learned that its characteristic feature lay in the fact that each note had its fixed position, so long as it was not out of tune, and that even the violin encompassed more notes although it only had four strings.

"Have you ever heard any music?" asked the precentor.

"Not since I was small," I replied.

"Oh well," he said, "that's something at least, if you heard some music when you were small."

I did not explain it further, for truth to tell I had been thinking of the bluebottle, which even in winter sometimes still buzzed in my inner ear when I was falling asleep.

"Blær!" he called out. "Come and play the piano!"

In the doorway there appeared a vision which struck me dumb for a long time. Every ray of light had been gathered into one point, and there stood this transfigured shape. The sun shone into and out of her hair. She looked at me with eyes in which blue blended with green. Then she sat down at the piano.

I can no longer recall with any certainty what it was she played, but I have the impression that it was something by Gade or Lumbye; or was it Hartmann? Perhaps it was just *The Snowdrop*.

Did she play well? She had large blue hands. I regard them as being above all other hands. The movements of her body were like the leisurely tail-movements of the lumpfish, and the soul in her face had the fragrance of strawberries. Seldom has anyone ever listened to piano-playing with such a devout lack of spirituality: I was hoping and praying that this could be life itself and that it would last as long as the melody.

Then the melody ended. She stood up and smiled. The music had warmed her eyes, and her cheeks were flushed. I could feel everything going black, as if I were about to faint. But when she had looked me over, she stopped smiling. Then she went out. I was sure she had not thought it worth her while, playing in front of such a person.

Under the sloping roof in Hríngjarabær there stood a harmonium with four and a half octaves, and every second key silent: Garðar Hólm's legacy.

"What a mess your instrument is in, Kristín dear," I said.

"What do you mean, child?" she replied. "I'll have you know that I wash it in soap and water every spring and autumn."

"You can only hear every second note," I said.

"It sounds perfectly all right to me," said the woman. "If any more sound came out of it I would get a fright. You only need to touch a single note in it and then I see everything before me just as it was here in the churchyard in the old days."

Nonetheless she gave me permission to let Grandpa Jón help me to repair it. Neither of us had ever repaired a harmonium before, but we prayed to the Saviour in New Norwegian before we started, and by the time we finished we had succeeded in making most of the keys produce a sound. And that evening, when I began to practise my scales, the old woman came in and sat down in her easy-chair and listened. Life's morning visited her again, the morning of eternity, the churchyard as it used to be. Before long she was asleep in her chair.

22

SCHUBERT

I came once a week or more for tuition with this kindly man with the long face and brown eyes and the huge Adam's apple in which dwelt the gentle bass voice I had sometimes heard trembling in the breeze from the churchyard when I was small; there was a cleft in his collar for the Adam's apple, like those pictures of Danish composers; and his good wife gave me coffee with bread and cheese. I was so entranced by the study of music that if I started on the harmonium under Kristín's sloping roof at bedtime, I would often sit there throughout the night until it was time to go and meet Grandpa Jón next morning. The precentor's instruction had little form and bore no relation to actual music lessons; it was like an extension of casual gossip about this and that, or as if we were amusing ourselves with an innocent pastime because we had nothing else to do. There was never any suggestion that this musician, who was then the finest musician in Iceland, thought it a waste of his time to be teaching such a lout the scales. We had one thing in common, teacher and pupil: neither of us ever mentioned payment. I never realized until many years later that the actual time of this composer – the only Icelander who could compose music in those days, who was the Cathedral organist as well – could be reckoned in money; yet perhaps it was not so after all.

But though this house of sunshine was so far beyond me, it nevertheless drew me so irresistibly that the Grammar School faded away into the twilight even though I was attending it. Most other things paled beside music. I would much rather have gone to that house every single day.

Sometimes, late at night, a strange thing would happen to me; suddenly I would get up from my studies for no apparent reason at all and go out; and before I knew what I was doing, I would be standing in front of a red-painted house of timber and corrugated iron with white window-frames, or else I would be seated on the stone dyke round a little cottage across from it, staring at the windows. Sometimes there was music and singing to be heard from within the house; sometimes the shadow of what I was sure was a girl would be thrown on to the curtains. And although I am doing my utmost to avoid any exaggeration, I do not hesitate to say that no other sight has ever had such an effect on me. I thought at first that my heart had stopped, and then it started beating furiously; and at that I would take to my heels like a thief and scurry away out of sight. The night watchmen would give me a very strange look, to put it mildly. I find it hard to believe that any thief suffered more agonies of conscience than I, for having stolen with my eyes a glimpse of that shadow. Sometimes I felt that the only thing that could save me would be if it had been the shadow of someone else.

I was always aware of whether she was at home in the house or not. I always felt much better if I saw that her coat was not hanging in the vestibule. If I became aware of her presence in the house from some muffled sound, like a creak on the staircase or a door slamming upstairs or certain footsteps in the kitchen, I would become distracted and confused, and even start wondering if my boots were not too large.

"What's wrong?" asked the precentor. "Have you been up all night with Jón again, praying for the Chinese?"

If I was lucky, and she was out of the house throughout the whole music lesson, the precentor would say, "I really do think you could learn to play this instrument. By the way, what are you thinking of doing with yourself when you leave school?"

I said that I had always thought of going in for fishing although I could not bring myself to mention lumpfish specifically; apart from that I had no definite plans, I would say.

"You're not, I suppose, thinking of becoming a world figure, like Garðar Hólm?" said the precentor.

"Oh, I don't know about that," I said, and thought for a bit; then I added, "But it would be good to hear Garðar sing a song like *Der Erlkönig*."

"Ah," said the precentor. "That's what we are all waiting for."

"He must be the greatest singer in the world, isn't he?" I asked.

"I don't know," said the precentor. "He was working behind the counter of old Jón Guðmundsson's Store when I knew him. If I remember right, the old man had even started paying for him to go to school at that time; but that didn't last long. People who want to become world-famous never stick in a classroom for long."

"Is it not then absolutely certain that he is a world-famous person?" I insisted.

"He is at least so famous that both of us have heard about him," said the precentor. "And that's something."

"Have you never heard him sing, then?" I asked.

"No," said the precentor. "But neither was I present when Christ redeemed the world."

I must have been considerably taken aback to have found at last, in this precentor, the only person outside the turnstile-gate at Brekkukot who seemed reluctant to commit himself about the genuine fame and excellence of Garðar Hólm, the singer. And I do not remember, in the period covered by this book, ever again having mentioned my former neighbour at Hríngjarabær to anyone else – this man whom people called my kinsman, and who had said that he too had been sent out to buy pepper for three *aurar*, just like me.

Did I mention that the precentor often lent me music-books with finger-exercises in them? Once, some real music got in among them by mistake, a book of Schubert's songs, and from this I had learned *Der Erlkönig*.

I began leafing through this volume on the old harmonium at Hríngjarabær, and quickly came to the conclusion that it was for much more advanced pupils: solo songs with accompaniment, with German lyrics. Nevertheless, I started working my way through it, and since I had no voice at all at this time, I had to pick out the melody with my fingers. Since Latin had come before German, as far as I was concerned, I had to look up every second word in order to understand the poetry. The extraordinary corporation of poets who provided Schubert with his texts aroused both my wonder and my curiosity so overwhelmingly that I find it difficult to imagine that a tribe of pygmies in darkest

Africa could have been more astounded than I was. Naturally I could not manage the accompaniment except for brief passages here and there, nor was the instrument suitable for it; but there I found the harmonies which laid a spell upon my heart. The harmony of water and wind, often with the sound of some kind of drum – this for a time was the accompaniment to my life. It was no small adventure in the middle of one's formative years to find oneself right at the heart of the German worship of romanticism. On the other hand, the iron discipline that was applied to words in Brekkukot retained its influence over me; the eloquence of that German corporation was worthless coinage in our house. In Brekkukot, words were too precious to use – because they meant something; our conversation was like pristine money before inflation; experience was too profound to be capable of expression; only the bluebottle was free. The over-luxuriant German poetry actually told me very little, and sometimes nothing at all; I was merely astonished. But one note, if it were played in correct relationship to other notes, could tell me much; and sometimes everything.

> *Ja spanne nur den Bogen mich zu töten,*
> *du himmlisch Weib.*

If people adhere to the doctrine that words are spoken in order to hide one's thoughts, that words mean something entirely different, sometimes even directly opposite to what they are saying, it is possible, occasionally at least, to reconcile oneself to them and to forgive the poet; not to mention if the words in all their strangeness have the task of indicating the truth in music; one is forced to acknowledge them then to a certain extent – for the music's sake.

One day when it was nearly spring I arrived as usual for my lesson with the precentor. And as usual when I was clumping up the steps to the front door, I was probably wondering whether I was really wearing the right shoes. Be that as it may, I had no sooner knocked on the door than it was opened, and there on the threshold stood Blær.

I am not going to try to describe this woman; what she actually looked like does not concern this story, and anyway I have forgotten it long ago. Her appearance was as far removed from telling the truth about her as any words would be. In my eyes she was not only the beautiful miller-girl and the fisher-girl and the sad little maiden in the grove, the furious huntress Diana and the virgin nun; she was also the trout and the lime-tree, the song of the water and the litany; in a word, Schubert.

She looked at me. "Daddy is not at home," she said. "He asked me to take the lesson with you."

I said nothing. I stood rooted to the threshold. She went on looking at me. Everything began to go black.

"Come," she said, and took me by the hand when I did not move. She took me inside and made me sit down at the harmonium. I felt that I was dying, and perhaps I did die a little, or rather began to die in the way that the cocoon of the chrysalis cracks at the end of winter; but unfortunately I did not die so thoroughly that I achieved new life like a butterfly.

"What were you to practise?" she asked.

"I can't remember," I said.

She opened the exercise book and said, "Then play something you have practised already."

"I've forgotten it all," I said.

"Then just play the scale," she said. "You can't have forgotten that."

"Yes," I said. "I've forgotten the scale."

"That's impossible," she said. "No one can forget the scale, because it's only the note sequence."

But on my oath, I could not even remember the note sequence any longer. And then she started laughing. I got up from the harmonium and went to the door. I walked across the room in my boots, with the pliers in my pocket and the tuft of hair which refused to lie down; and she followed me with her eyes.

I never went there again. I stopped learning to play the harmonium. Spring came. I had my confirmation, and passed my exams. Grandpa Jón went back west to the Dalir. I did not dare even let myself be seen anywhere near the house, scarcely even dared look in its direction. Sometimes it occurred to me that I might steal over there some night when the days began to shorten again. But then I remembered the night watchmen.

23

GARÐAR HÓLM'S SECOND HOMECOMING

I was in my eighteenth year when Garðar Hólm returned to
Iceland for the second time. By then the superintendent's snuff
had all been used up long ago, and the pouch lay shrivelled
and dusty on the shelf; but there was still something left in the
gold-pouch.

Articles began to appear in the newspapers saying that the
singer was expected soon, but no one knew when. At last it was
announced that he would be coming on the mail-boat *North Star*
in the first week of August. He had been living on the other side
of the world, giving concerts in Australia and Japan. Now the
invitations were pouring in from opera-houses all over Europe
and America, but he did not choose to tie himself to any one
opera-house while the whole world was his oyster.

At the start of the hay-making, everyone started talking about
preparations to welcome Garðar Hólm: the nation had to put
its best foot forward when the world singer was swept home on
the crest of his fame, back to the lowly home-town that foreign
travellers always described as huddled up against the North Pole.
A meeting was held of the various captains of the ship of state,
such as the town council, the fire brigade, the literary society, the
brass band, and the women's society The Bracelet. At this meeting
it was decided to erect across the pier a triumphal archway
garlanded with flowers, and then to have four powerful stalwarts
at hand to carry the singer shoulder-high through the archway;
trumpeters were to be there, to play the Björneborgernes March,
and gaily-dressed girls were to come forward to present bouquets.
It was intended that the sheriff of Reykjavík would make a little
speech, and furthermore it was taken for granted that one or
other of the nation's epic poets, presumably the editor of the
Ísafold, would compose an ode. It was expected that Garðar Hólm

would greet his home-town with a song when he stepped ashore, but no agreement could be reached about which balcony he was to sing from.

During the days before the *North Star* arrived there was a rush to give buildings a coat of paint; Gúðmúnsen's Store, for instance, was painted grey-green, as was the office of the *Ísafold*, and the Theological Seminary also availed itself of the opportunity to be painted the same colour. Shops in the side streets like Veltusund and Fischersund refused to be outdone, and displayed enlarged portraits of the great man in their windows among all the soap and hemp and match-boxes and saucepans. Lapel-badges with pictures of the artist were on sale, yet another image of the man who gazed entranced at the golden carriage wheeling across the skies.

If ever it happened that a few weeks passed without any mention of Garðar Hólm in the newspapers, someone at home in Brekkukot would perhaps say something like – "Yes, he was a nice boy, Kristín's little Georg, when he was growing up here in the churchyard." It goes without saying that the silence about him at Brekkukot deepened the more fuss there was made about him outside. The wave of fame associated with his name was never less likely to burst through our turnstile-gate than when it was beating most strongly against it from outside.

Somehow or other I could never really and truly believe that this ceremonial reception would ever take place; and I shall make no bones about it now – it never did take place. It seemed to me that people were always being duped by Garðar Hólm, whether he was coming or going; but he never let himself be duped, not even with a triumphal arch and a brass band – indeed, his upbringing in the churchyard would have been wasted on him otherwise. Nor was he ever likely to conform to the expectations of others.

I can remember the day the *North Star* arrived as if it were yesterday. Naturally it was raining and blowing half a gale – who would have expected anything else? The eight or ten little girls stood soaked and freezing at the quayside, and their knees shook and the rain beat down on their bouquets. A handful of weary workmen carrying their wind-instruments, among them the crippled shoemaker from Brunnhús, were almost perished with cold; and it rained into their instruments. They decided to play the Björneborgernes March before there was any sign of the ship's boat, just to thaw out their mouths and fingers. The word went round that the sheriff was about to put his coat on and had his goloshes on already. And then, in the middle of the March, someone arrived with a message from the deck of the *North Star* to say that Garðar Hólm was not among the passengers, it was all some sort of misunderstanding, he was in Paris right then giving a concert. The bandsmen stopped playing, emptied the water out of their instruments, and dispersed. The sheriff was reported to have taken his goloshes off again. The little girls ran home in the rain with their flowers. And the garlanded triumphal archway was taken down.

This was what I had always suspected.

On the other hand, about a week later I was completely taken by surprise in Suðurgata one day. I was on my way into town. When I came to the corner where the path to the churchyard branches off up the hill, I suddenly ran into a gentleman who was out for a stroll with his cane. I was not, in point of fact, accustomed to looking people in the face when I passed them, but one was always aware from a long way off what was coming towards one in the street. This time I happened to look at this man's face by accident; it was none other than Garðar Hólm.

At first I really was not sure that I had not made a mistake, for truth to tell this person seemed to me a little down at heel. Five years is a huge span of a man's lifetime, of course, and indeed he had aged appreciably, in the face at least, the features hardened, the lines deepened. He was not merely sunburnt, but downright weather-beaten; and there was now a suggestion of squinting in the expression of his eyes.

To be sure, this was the man who gazed at the heavenly light, as it said in the Latin book about the eagle, *adspicit lucem caelestem,* so there was little hope that such a person would recognize Álfgrímur; but as he strolled along pensively, heedless of time and place, he nevertheless threw me a glance with that sidelong squint he had now developed. How did it happen that in the instant that I drank in the man's face and appearance with my eyes and

compared it with the image I retained in my childhood memory
of the heaven-gazer, and also the picture of him you could get in
the shops on postcards and badges – how was it that I suddenly
could scarcely help feeling that he had become a little ordinary?
At least, he did not have the same dash as before. And unless
I was very much mistaken, he was wearing the same hat as he had
been previously. On the other hand he was wearing new shoes,
and that was a rare enough sight in my youth; to be honest I
could not remember ever having seen a person in new shoes
before – they shone from afar. There was not a stain or wrinkle
on his clothes, any more than there had been five years ago; but
I was not absolutely sure that he had got himself a new suit since
then; at any rate, this suit was of the same kind of blue cloth with
red pinstripe as the old one.

I stopped as soon as he passed. I could not help it. I turned
round and stared after him. And for some reason or other, he too
looked back over his shoulder and paused.

"Do you know me?" he asked.

"Yes," I said.

"Who are you?" he asked.

"Álfgrímur," I said.

"Ah, so it wasn't a lie after all?" he said, and smiled at me out
of his dark brooding. I stood nailed to the road. Finally he walked
up to me very simply and stretched out his hand:

"So you really exist after all. I thought I had dreamed it. Was it
not you who ate the five-*aurar* cakes?"

"Well, yes; I was offered them; bu-but I never ate more than
one," I said.

Garðar Hólm threw off the burden of his world fame and
laughed. "At all events it was you who was sent to buy the pepper.
Did you buy it? Have you ever delivered it?"

I did not trust myself to answer this question, and changed the
subject.

"We thought you had decided against coming," I said. "The
triumphal arch was taken down."

"How like them!" he said, and laughed with an affected gaiety
I did not really like very much. "Come and see me some time.

We shall go and buy five-*aurar* cakes."

"Hmm," I said. "Thank you very much, sir."

"There is no need to be so formal with me," he said. "It is like being formal with oneself. But if there is anything I can do for you, then let me know. Think about it."

He was ready to say goodbye and hurry away, obviously not expecting that I had a wish ready-made. But that was just what I had. For years and years I had had this wish; and now the time had come to make it:

"I want so much to ask you to sing *Der Erlkönig* for me."

"*Der Erlkönig*?" he said in amazement. "What *Erlkönig*?"

"*Wer reitet so spät durch Nacht und Wind*," I said.

"What's all this about?" he said. "What business is this of yours?"

"I have been having a look at Schubert," I said.

"Schubert?" he said. "What for?"

"It was just by chance," I replied.

"We'll have a talk about this later on," he said. "Come and see me one day. Hotel d'Islande. I shall try to do what I can for you."

He shook my hand in farewell – and I noticed that his hand was hard and rough.

24

DER ERLKÖNIG

That summer, things began to look up a little for me. For many years I had not dared to open my mouth to sing within earshot of anyone else for fear of the sound that might come out. But when I was away on errands far from any company, either down at Skerjafjörður or at Sogin, the pressure of the melodies building up inside me forced me to utter bursts of sound; and that summer, my throat began to produce noises something like the note I was trying to achieve. After that I seized every possible opportunity of exercising my voice whenever I found solitude.

It so happened one day that I caught sight of our Pastor

Jóhann, now in his eighties, hobbling up to the churchyard, almost bent double now, behind the coffin of some stranger. So I joined him, as I had done when I was small. Unbidden, I sang *Just as the One True Flower* over the coffin, nearly the whole psalm, if I remember rightly. When I had finished singing and Pastor Jóhann had scattered earth over the coffin, he came over to me, much moved, and took me by the hand and said:

"You are now such a big, tall man, my dear Álfgrímur, that I cannot bring myself to give you ten *aurar*. Instead, I am going to pray to God to be with you, always."

"Thank you," I said, although I would really much rather have had the ten *aurar*. "But I can hardly believe that I deserve God's presence for that caterwauling. Actually I was beginning to think that I would never be able to croak another note again."

Then Pastor Jóhann said, "Some voices never manage to break properly. But in all good men there lurks a true note, I won't say like a mouse in a trap, but rather like a mouse between wall and wainscoting. But it is a special grace if God allows them to sing the note that they hear. I am old now, and my voice has never recovered from breaking; I have never had the good fortune to sing the note I hear inside me. But that note is just as true for all that."

It was little wonder that I was thinking about singing that summer, when my voice was coming back; and very understandable that I was so elated at knowing that the great singer himself was now in the country. And on his friendly invitation, and in the hope of hearing *Der Erlkönig* at least, perhaps, I was not long in taking advantage of the kindness. I smeared sheep-leg grease on my footwear and tried to subdue with water the tuft of hair on the top of my head, and set off for town. I did not stop until I reached the lobby of the Hotel d'Islande; I went over to the hotel-keeper, who was sitting behind the reception desk, and bade him good day.

After a long pause he looked up and glanced at me over his spectacles, but he went on leafing through his papers and did not reply to my greeting. There were some canaries in a cage behind him. This was all very Danish. I cleared my throat.

"Who are you?" I was asked, in half-Danish.

"My name is Álfgrímur."

"Yes, and what's wrong with you?" said the man.

"Nothing," I said. "I just wanted to see someone."

"Someone?" said the hotel-keeper, and looked me up and down. "There is no someone here."

"Excuse me, but doesn't Garðar stay here?"

"I don't understand," said the man.

"I have business with Garðar Hólm."

The man stood up and took off his spectacles with great ceremony to look at me: "Are you referring to the opera singer?"

I said yes.

"What do you want with him?"

"He asked me to come and see him."

"My dear young man," said the hotel-keeper, coming right forward to the counter: "You must be from the provinces."

"I live at Brekkukot in Reykjavík here," I said

"You come from old Björn of Brekkukot?" said the hotel-keeper. "What makes you think that you can talk to the opera singer?"

"I am mo-more or less related to him," I said.

"One never knows here," said the hotel-keeper. "What can I do for you?"

I told him once again what I wanted.

"If you know Garðar Hólm, then you ought to know that it is not just anyone who can come and talk to opera singers," said the hotel-keeper, and he was now speaking entirely in Danish. "If one were allowed to see him, the whole town would follow. They think they own him. You claim to be related to him, and I have no ready way of disproving that, I have to take your word for it; but I give myself leave to doubt whether the kinship is matched by close friendship, if you seriously think you can burst in on your kinsman as casually as ordering a ham sandwich. Certainly, this is his address while he is staying in Iceland. I have the honour of receiving his letters on his behalf and saying that he is not in; and now and then he gives me a genuine gold coin. But naturally no letter ever arrives, because he has no friends who hold him in such low esteem as to think that he actually stays at the Hotel d'Islande. He calls us a *pension de famille*. If he ever happens to come in here on some urgent errand he runs away again as fast as he can whenever he hears the canaries singing."

"Could you not please tell me, then, where he is living," I said.

"Living!" echoed the hotel-keeper. "Garðar Hólm is not living anywhere. Obviously he is staying out on the French warship that brought him to Iceland two nights ago; it's anchored just off the islands. But during the day when he's ashore, he is naturally at the Governor's house."

A few days later, yet another vagrant was being buried; or perhaps just a sea-scorpion. Anyway, I received a message from Pastor Jóhann asking whether I could be persuaded to sing at the graveside for thirty *aurar* or so.

I went up to the churchyard at the appointed time. Pastor Jóhann and the coffin and the policeman were there, and the usual municipal grave-diggers leaning on their shovels. As always, sorrow manifested itself chiefly in the lamp-black. Pastor Jóhann sprinkled the earth and promised the deceased due resurrection on Doomsday according to the manual, and after that a signal was given and I began to sing. But whether it was because I was becoming bored with Hallgrímur Pétursson's psalm *Just as the One True Flower* and wanted a change in the churchyard, or because I thought to myself that it was better to do for oneself than ask of one's brother, I took my courage in both hands and sang Schubert's *Der Erlkönig* – "Who rides so late through night and wind . . ."

As everyone knows, *Der Erlkönig* is really only *Ólafur rode beneath the cliffs*, except that the elf-maidens in the German poem do the enticing of Ólafur through the mouth of a third person, and a man at that, namely the Elf-king himself, whereas in our folk-song, death comes in the guise of the last elf-maiden. But even though it is a non Icelandic idea, and irreconcilable with life in Brekkukot, that a man should want to tear a boy from the arms of another man, this ballad nevertheless touched some hidden chord within me. Was it perhaps these triolets from a terror-stricken tambourine that had been hidden somewhere deep in the night over Álftanes when grandfather and I were out catching lumpfish?

"I have never been against the new tunes," said Pastor Jóhann, when I had finished singing *Der Erlkönig* in German over the vagrant's grave. "And that is because the old tunes do not become any worse simply because the new ones are good. Here are twenty-five *aurar*, but that isn't enough."

"I wanted to try this tune," I said. "I knew anyway that there would not be very many listening to it."

"Quite right," said Pastor Jóhann. "Everyone here in the churchyard is deaf, except God. And God thinks the new tunes just as good as the old tunes. I really think my purse must be beginning to leak. But here we are, here are two *aurar* at last."

"Thank you very much indeed, Pastor Jóhann," I said. "And now you must not pay me any more. I know that you yourself get nothing for burying destitute people like these."

"I could naturally get something for burying them, just like the others," said Pastor Jóhann, "if I claimed it from the authorities. But to be honest it has always given me greater satisfaction to bury the poor than the rich. And that stems from the fact that the more humble they are, the larger the place they have in the Saviour's heart. And now here's another stray two-*aurar* piece at last. I really must be getting myself a decent purse. I am not even going to manage to scrape together these thirty *aurar* I more or less promised you. I must ask you to let me owe you one *eyrir*."

I sat down on the tombstone of the late Archangel Gabriel with my funeral-song fee in my palm, after Pastor Jóhann had gone. All was quiet again, apart from the grave-diggers who were hastily shovelling earth on to the stranger, not far away. And then, before I knew it, a man sat down beside me. He took off his hat, for the weather was warm, and smoothed his hair out from the parting with the palms of his hands. He had greyed considerably, and there were deep furrows across his brow. Then he looked at me hard.

"How have you found that note?" said Garðar Hólm.

"What note?" I said.

"You have a note," he said.

"I sometimes try to sing a little for Pastor Jóhann," I said.

"You had better be careful," he said.

"I went to see you the other day," I said. "But you were out on the French warship."

"Why did you stand so close to the edge of the grave while you were singing? Do you think that the singer should push himself forward past the widow?" he asked.

"There was no widow," I said. "I am never asked to sing for people who have widows."

"One should not sing for one's own enjoyment," he said.

"If I had seen you, I would have called on you to sing," I said.

He stood up as if he were almost annoyed. Was he angry at me? Or was this aloofness of behaviour something which fame thrust on people?

"There is the one note," he said, almost like a continuation of Pastor Jóhann's words. "But he who has heard it, never sings again."

While I was contemplating his clothes and shoes, which were as spotless and uncreased as ever, I suddenly caught sight of a wisp of hay clinging to one of his trouser-legs just behind the knee. Now, he had not really been particularly pleasant to me on this occasion, even though he had paid me these rather ambiguous compliments; but nevertheless I thought it would be little less than a disaster if any speck were to be seen on such a man, to say the least of it. I stood up and brushed the wisp of hay off him.

"What's wrong?" he said, rather irritably, when I started to brush him.

"It was a wisp of hay," I said.

"Ah, I've been sitting on the ground," he said, and smiled at me in gratitude, albeit condescendingly, shook hands, bade me farewell, and disappeared among the tombstones.

25

A MAN IN THE CHURCHYARD?

In Löngustétt one could see signs that something was afoot, this time at the *Ísafold* offices. The editor was not going to rest content with a mere coat of paint; he had also hired a carpenter to spruce up his balcony with a lathe-turned balustrade. At this time the editor of the *Ísafold* was considered to be the most likely person to become the King's Minister after the next elections. Now the rumour spread that this leader of men was going to give a banquet on Saturday evening, to which were invited all the more important shopkeepers and the most distinguished consuls in the country, as well as the officers of any Danish naval vessels in Icelandic waters at the time; but the special guest of honour was to be the man who had come to Iceland in a French warship, Garðar Hólm the opera singer. On this occasion nothing was printed in the newspapers in advance, for people had learned by experience that it was best to be on the safe side when talking about celebrities. But although there were no advertisements or articles this time, the populace of the town guessed that the balcony had been balustraded so that Garðar Hólm might be able to step out on to it and greet the country with song when he had eaten.

It was a late-summer morning in Suðurgata. The sea-breeze had not yet started to breathe over the Nesses; the Lake was calm and beautiful apart from an occasional ripple. As usual I was up and about at first light to let the cow nibble the tufts of grass between the paving-slabs. I had her on a halter so as to keep her away from the rotting fence round the vegetable garden. I sat on the stone dyke at the roadside and listened to the cow grazing in the stillness of the dawn as my grandmother's chimney was beginning to smoke.

There was no one stirring except for a few red-bearded peat-cutters who sat on their frame-carts as solemn as Biblical pictures, whipping their lazy hacks on the way south to Vatnsmýri where there were once the greatest peat-pits in the whole world. The clucking of the hens was just about reaching its climax, with all the dedicated lack of humour which is the chief characteristic of the hen-run.

Then suddenly I heard the iron gate at the footpath into the churchyard being opened; the hinges squeaked. When I looked round I saw a woman come out of the churchyard and pull the gate shut behind her, a plump and glowing girl wearing Danish clothes with her coat flapping open; and in one hand she held her hat by the elastic as if she were carrying a bucket. At first she looked at me without seeing me; she was deep in thought, and I imagined that she had got up early to go to the churchyard to mourn a lost friend. She set off in the direction of town. Somehow I got the impression from her walk that she was rather depressed; at least she was taking no particular care over the way she walked, and her hair was dishevelled by a breeze that was not there at all.

When she had gone about a couple of hundred yards in the direction of the town she suddenly stopped and looked back. She looked at me and gave me a nod, away in the distance. Perhaps it had taken her as long as that to call to mind this boy who was sitting on the wall looking after a cow; but then she turned right round and walked back towards me. She was in every way a big girl, even bigger from the front than behind; perhaps she had been eating too much white bread. I began to feel a little uncomfortable; I was not used to seeing women, and always found it a little embarrassing. I wished she had taken off her coat. When I realized that she was heading towards me, I looked away and was staring at something entirely different when she came up to me. The cow continued to graze.

"Good morning," said the girl.

"Good morning," I replied, rather reluctantly, and stared into the blue.

"It's lovely weather today," said the girl, trying to be affable.

"Yes, tolerably so," I replied.

"I'm just having a stroll to amuse myself," she said. "The doctor says I'm too fat."

When she came close I could not help noticing that her face was a little drawn and her eyes lustreless, with dark blue shadows under them; and there were wisps of hay in her hair.

"Don't you recognize me?" she said. "At least I know you. What's your name again?"

"Long-Loony," I said.

"Long what? Why are you telling me fibs? Do you think I'm as stupid as that?"

"You've got some rubbish in your hair," I said.

She put her hand up to her hair and pulled out the wisps of hay.

"There's a bit of moss left," I said.

"Oh, I'm so glad you've told me about it – will you remove it for me, I haven't got a mirror?"

When I had pulled the rest of it from her hair, she said, "Can I ask you something?"

She took a photograph out of her coat pocket and handed it to me. It showed a woman, not quite middle-aged, and two children, a boy and a girl. At first I thought it was an American photograph, because the women in the pictures we sometimes got from America had the same backwoods-farmer's expression as this one had, the same hands disfigured by digging-tools or by grappling with boulders and tree-stumps, or else boiled by endless wash-days; and clothes and hairstyles in some out-moded foreign fashion.

The children's clothes were too big, as if they had been made for them in a hurry for the sake of the photographer. The little girl's hair was plaited into two pigtails that stuck out like bristles, and her eyes were wide with fear and curiosity; but the boy was beginning to look around in a self-possessed sort of way. But what surprised me most was that the name of the photographer was quite obviously Danish, and underneath it was printed the name of a town in Jutland.

"Who are the people in this picture?" asked little Miss Gúðmúnsen.

"How should I know?" I replied. "Where did you get it?"

"I found it up in the churchyard," said the girl.

"How extraordinary," I said, and looked at her in surprise.

"It was lying on a tombstone," said the girl. "Are you quite sure you don't recognize it?"

I said it was out of the question.

"I'm sorry," she said. "And goodbye. Listen, how far are you on at school, by the way?"

I told her, more or less.

She asked, "What are you going to be?"

"I am going to be a lumpfisherman," I said.

"Oh, do stop teasing me always," she said. "Well, I'm off home now for some sleep. Don't you think I'm beginning to get thinner? Listen, talking about something completely different – exactly how are you related to Garðar Hólm?"

"I don't know," I replied.

"Of course you're related," she said. "Do come along with him some time when he comes."

"Thanks," I said.

She had walked away a few steps when she turned on her heel again, or rather on the pointed toes of her fashionable little shoes – "Oh, what's the name of Garðar Hólm's wife again? And what's her nationality? And where is she now?"

"Garðar Hólm's wife?" I said. "Are you in your right mind?"

"No, of course I'm not in my right mind," she said. "And anyway one couldn't possibly imagine a greater shame if he were married, a world-famous man like that, and not tell anyone about it! By the way, could I leave this photograph with you?"

"What on earth am I to do with it?" I said.

"Perhaps you would be kind enough to return it for me – to the churchyard."

"This photograph doesn't concern me in the slightest," I said.

"But won't you in that case just do me one tiny little favour?" she said. "Who knows, I might be able to do you a favour some-time."

"Oh, I suppose I can throw it over the churchyard wall for you, if you like," I said.

"No, don't throw it," she said. "Give it to the man who is sleeping in there in the churchyard. You see, there's a man sleeping on a tombstone; a foreigner."

"You surely haven't been going through the pockets of a sleeping foreigner?" I said.

"How can you be such a beastly pig!" she said. "But even though you think such horrid things about me, I hope with all my heart that you don't talk about it to anyone. Perhaps I'll do you a favour another time. Goodbye."

And with that the girl set off homewards once again, and this time she did not turn back. I sat on the wall with the photograph in my hand, and stared after her. The cow went on grazing. There was a wonderful smell of peat-smoke coming from my grand-mother's chimney. When the girl was out of sight I went into the churchyard to look for the foreigner whose pockets I thought little Miss Gúðmúnsen had searched to steal a photograph of his wife while he slept on a tombstone. But no matter how I searched, I found no one sleeping on a tombstone in the churchyard.

26

THE NOTE

Guests in their party best went streaming into the home of the editor of the *Ísafold* at twilight that late-summer evening, and all over the house the lights were fairly blazing. As the evening wore on, the townspeople began to gather in the street outside; they were the sort of people who neither had the worry of preparing for parties nor the bother of attending them, dockers and sea-men with jackets over their jerseys, the kind of men who in my young days used to be called "landless men" because they had a house full of children but no cow; and there were the bakers and artisans who were establishing urban culture in Iceland by acquiring hard hats and stiff collars and canes, the kind of people who live in constant risk of being mistaken for one another – and their wives; there were fishwives who had lost their employment salting down fish on the shore because of old age – this was about the time when Iceland had just become the first country in the world to pass a law relating to old-age pensions, even though that pension scarcely covered the cost of a rusk; here and there one could see pretty young girls in national dress, some from out in the country, others from Hafnarfjörður in the south; a few young louts just about as tedious as myself were slouching around; and there was no shortage of the kind of cynical mocking-birds who have always peopled town squares as a matter of course ever since the days of the Greek Comedies.

Did I happen to mention that it was raining?

Time passed, and we stood outside in the late-summer rain. Occasionally a face would peer out of a window, or a shadow would pass across a curtain, and something like a swift gust went through the crowd waiting in the street: It's Him.

But always it turned out not to be Him.

What were we expecting of this singer? Were we perhaps some singer-race which had been shipwrecked here on a silent shore long ages ago and had been waiting ever since for this one thing, generation after generation?

But I shall not keep the reader waiting any longer for the story. Very late that evening, when most of the people were wet and some soaked through and the town was in darkness, the balcony doors of the *Ísafold* were thrown open and a shaft of light streamed out, thick with the fumes of guests, steaks, and tobacco; and then out stepped an elegantly clad gentleman, and many of the people started clapping. It was the owner of the house. He signalled for silence, and then started speaking. The burden of his speech was that he urged everyone to go home, because the invited guest of honour had not turned up, they had been waiting for him all evening; but a letter from him had just arrived, saying that the French warship, the vessel on which he was the guest of the commander, was putting out to sea at that very moment. Garðar Hólm was gone, and sent his greetings; he sent his greetings to all Icelanders, both high and low, and wished that the Icelandic nation might live, thrive, and flourish.

And now the expectant throng of people who had long been waiting for the singing, tortured by silence, began to disperse in the rain with an air of patient resignation that suggested that this was

not by any means the first time that they had suffered disappoint-
ment. I turned my cap round so that the peak faced backwards,
to prevent the rain from pouring straight down the back of my
neck, and began to plod home after the fiasco of the evening. As
I said earlier, this was so early in the autumn that the street-lamps
were not yet lit, although here and there light spilled from a
window. When I had reached Suðurgata, just below the Melsted
building, I could just make out a woman keeping well out of my
way, wrapped up in dark shawls almost the colour of the night.

She was very unsteady on her feet, this woman, and she was
almost criss-crossing the street like a helpless drunk. Finally I saw
her wander right off the edge of the road and tumble into the
ditch in a heap. I made haste to go and help her if I could and
then I saw that it was our Kristín of Hríngjarabær.

"Did you hurt yourself, Kristín dear?" I said and lifted her to
her feet and helped her back on to the road; she was obviously
rather wet and muddy from the ditch.

"I've become so terribly night-blind, somehow," she said apologetically, as if we did not all know how badly her eyesight was
failing. But even though I had lifted her to her feet she was still
stooping down and feeling around her on the ground. At last we
found what she was looking for. It was her basket.

"I just popped out to Friðriksen's," she said.

That was certainly true, because a powerful aroma of cloves
and cinnamon and other bakery confections was coming from her
basket. I offered to guide her home and she accepted this and
took my arm. I soon realized that she was soaked through and must
have been standing out in the rain at least as long as I had been.

"My goodness, how wet it is," she said. "Fancy getting soaked
just from popping out to Friðriksen's bakery!"

I helped her up the slope all the way home to Hríngjarabær.
The windows were in darkness, of course, and there was no sign
of life about the house, for the bell-ringer had been dead for
twenty-five years, and the cow too.

"Bless you for letting me lean on you, my child," said the
woman – she never noticed how tall I had grown, except that
she had stopped giving me the customary ten *aurar* as she used

to, worse luck. "Come inside now and have a sip of coffee."

Hríngjarabær lay in the farthest north corner of the church-yard, right at its highest point. It was a tarred wooden cottage, jointed or ribbed, as it was called; it had a living-room and a small kitchen with a range downstairs, and two rooms in the loft upstairs. The old bell-ringer had lived here for several genera-tions, and Kristín had benefited from that by being allowed to stay on there after his death. The patch of grass round the house had for the last few years been mown by the town council for hay for the hearse-horses. But behind the cottage still stood the late bell-ringer's cow-shed, now used by the churchyard authorities for storing their junk; and the hay from the grass-patch, these ten or twenty trusses, was hauled up through the hatch of the hayloft and stored there until late winter, when it would be fetched by the man who looked after the town council's horses.

"There is no point in offering you milk," the woman said. "It's your own milk from Brekkukot, anyway. But I've got a little cold coffee here, that's always refreshing; and you can have something with it."

She lit the little lamp over the kitchen range and poured some coffee for me into a thick cup; then she dipped into her basket, where the cakes from the bakery still seemed to be in good shape, judging by the smell, despite the mishaps of the journey. But she did not offer me a Danish pastry; she gave me a bun instead. For myself, I would rather have chosen a Danish pastry with green sugar icing and raspberry jam; but buns were good, too – they had currants in them, which you don't find in Danish pastries, and often a lot of cinnamon right in the centre.

But then it turned out that she had only bought one Danish pastry; and I had no doubt that she had bought it for a particular purpose, for although there was no lack of hospitality at either end of the churchyard, nothing was ever wasted and nothing was ever bought at random. The old woman now sliced some bread, spread it with butter and meat-paste, put the slices on one side of a decorated cake-dish, then divided the pastry into three triangular pieces and laid them on the other half of the plate. Then she poured some milk from a little tub into a jug, and said,

"Since I'm now so night-blind, I want to ask you to encourage my laziness and go over to the cow-shed for me and put this plate and this jug of milk up through the hatch into the hayloft for the poor mouse."

"What mouse?" I said.

"What mouse?" she echoed. "One cannot even begin to answer a question like that, Álfgrímur dear. And be careful of fire if you strike a light."

"I'm afraid the mouse won't be able to reach the milk in the jug," I said. "And if it ever managed to get up to the rim, I think it would topple in and drown. When I leave milk for mice, I always give it to them in a saucer."

"Just listen to the child!" she said. "Fancy thinking that the mouse hasn't learned the knack of drinking out of jugs! Off you go now and stop your nonsense, little one. And take care not to frighten the poor creature; everyone is always trying to destroy it, not just people but dogs and cats as well."

I struck a match, and found a stump in the candlestick. Then I started up the steps, going as carefully as I could so as not to spill the milk, and not to scare the mouse either. But I could not resist putting my candle up through the trap-door to see if I could catch a glimpse of this strange mouse which it was unseemly to serve with anything less than Danish pastry and bread with meat-paste, and a whole jug of milk to boot. Or was there no particular mouse that the old woman had in mind, but the Mouse in general, the mouse-race of the world?

This loft was divided into two, a hayloft and a lumber-room, with a partition between them. The part of the loft that was nearest the hatch was almost empty; summer was almost over, and the few hay-trusses that the grass-patch at Hríngjarabær yielded had long since been stored away; and from the loft there came the smell of hay fermenting. But when I raised the candle I could see that in the nearer compartment, on this side of the partition, some hay had been spread out on the floor for a bed, and that on it lay a large bundle carefully wrapped in foreign newspapers, that is to say some copies of the London *Times*, which in my young days was called the greatest newspaper in the world and sometimes reached Iceland as wrappings for goods from England.

What treasure could it be that old Kristín of Hríngjarabær was keeping here in the cow-shed loft wrapped in that world newspaper, *The Times*? I would perhaps have pursued the question no further if, just as I was about to take the candle downstairs again, I had not caught sight of a shining pair of shoes standing beside this bundle, with a stiff collar laid neatly on top of them, and a spotted tie. Then I began to shine the light over it more carefully. And now, if I was not mistaken, it seemed to me that inside the London *Times* something was beginning to stir; a rather careful movement, to be sure, as if from a realization that the newspaper was after all made of paper. And while I was studying this phenomenon, some toes appeared at the end of the bundle nearest to me! It does not really concern the story just how I felt at seeing this sight up in Kristín's hayloft in the middle of the night, nor do I intend to try to describe it here.

"Bring the light up to the edge of the hatchway, my friend, I have to talk to you," said Garðar Hólm.

While I was setting the candlestick on the edge of the hatch the singer wormed his way out of the cocoon of newspapers; he had a special way of doing it so that the papers were not dislodged. Then he folded them all up neatly and laid them aside with great care, slipped his shoes on and put on his collar and tie. He took a small comb in a case out of his pocket and combed his hair with practised gestures, and ran his fingertips down the creases of his trousers: and now this was a man that no one would have believed was staying anywhere other than at a luxury hotel, if not in the house of the Governor himself. I have seldom been so relieved as I was then that it was not considered proper for a youngster like myself to speak to an older man without being spoken to first. I sat down on the edge of the hatch and brought out my pair of pliers and busied myself with pulling nails out of my boots.

"Listen, friend," said Garðar Hólm when he was quite ready. "As I told you the other day, I thought you were standing too close to the edge of the grave while you were singing. If I may be permitted to offer you some good advice, the singer should stand at a suitable distance from the grave."

"But if it had only been a sea-scorpion?" I said.

"In that case, it's splendid," he said. "But anyway, thank you very much for the singing. Always sing just as you sang that day. Sing as if you were singing over a sea-scorpion. Any other singing is false. God only hears that one note. Anyone who sings for other people's entertainment is a fool, but not quite such a fool as the man who sings for his own entertainment. I want you to be quite clear about that right from the start, my lad, because I too was brought up here in the churchyard, just like you."

"Do you think I could learn to sing, then?" I asked.

"Tcha, no one learns to sing," he said. "On the other hand, I see that you are rather badly shod, and I want to give you my shoes."

"That – that's quite unnecessary," I said.

"No," he said, "it's not unnecessary. We are friends. You sing. I give you shoes. And help yourself, here's some meat-paste. Or would you rather have some Danish pastry?"

And so we two singers up in the hayloft ate the snack that Kristín of Hríngjarabær had bought for the mouse. And there was no getting out of it – I had to put his shoes on, and he changed into my battered pair.

"I want to ask you to do me a little favour," he said. "It is to lock the door carefully on the inside and sleep here in the hayloft with me tonight. I want to ask you to be on your guard if anyone knocks at the door, and to go down and say to anyone that asks that Garðar Hólm the opera singer is not here."

When I had complied with his request and locked the door of the byre on the inside, and was back up in the hayloft, he picked up the conversation where he had left off.

"Dear friend," he said. "You asked me whether you could learn to sing. I don't know. It could well be that you have the makings of a singer. It could well be that the world will give you the best that it has: glory, power, honour, what else is there? Palaces and parks, perhaps? Or merry widows? And then what?"

"I wanted so much to ask you to teach me just a tiny bit about singing," I said, "even if it were only to sing Der Erlkönig for me just once."

"There is only the one note, which is the whole note," said

Garðar Hólm. "And he who has heard it does not need to ask for anything. My own singing doesn't matter. But remember one thing for me: when the world has given you everything, when the merciless yoke of fame has been laid on your shoulders and its brand has been stamped on your brow as indelibly as on the man who was convicted of the worst crime in the world – remember then that you have no other refuge than this one prayer: 'God, take it all away from me – except one note'."

27

THE CHIEF JUSTICE

Someone was trying to open the door. I woke up at the creaking of the warped door and the screeching of the battered hinges; I could not remember clearly where I was, but I felt I had not been sleeping for very long. The smell of hay was heavy in my nostrils. High in the gable-wall, right under the ridge, there was an open, square-shaped window, and through it streamed the red rays of the rising sun, swirling with dust-motes. What on earth was I doing here?

The door downstairs went on creaking. I looked around me in the hayloft and saw that I was alone. How had I managed to get here? Then I remembered that I had been sent to see to the mouse. But when I looked around there was neither jug nor plate in sight; nowhere any sign that anyone else had been here except I; not even a scrap of the great London *Times*. It must all have been a dream, I thought. But if someone finds me here, what will he think? At long last the door was pushed open and a young female voice called out, "Where are you?"

"Here," I replied, getting to my feet, and began to clamber down the stairs.

And who should be standing there on the threshold in the crimson rays of a new morning but little Miss Gúðmúnsen, this plump and glowing girl? It was quite plain to me that she was disappointed at finding me there.

"Jesus!" she said. "What are you doing here?"

"Nothing," I said.

"Are you alone?" she asked.

I said yes, and asked in return, "What do you want here?"

"I must be mad," she said. "Jesus! Are you quite sure there's no one else in there?"

She ducked her head under the lintel and squeezed in through the doorway, clambered halfway up the stair and peered into the hayloft. Then she went back to the doorway again in despair.

"Tell me what you were doing here," she said again.

"N-nothing," I said. "I just fell asleep."

"Alone?" she asked. "Are you sure there was no one else there?"

I replied, "None other than those who sometimes visit people in their sleep."

"Did you dream about someone, then?" she asked.

"That's another matter," I said. "But now I'm awake."

"I haven't slept a wink all night," she said, and was now nearly in tears.

I asked, why not?

"Why not? What business is that of yours?" she said. "Because my daddy and my mummy locked me in my room, of course. Until I managed to crawl out through the window when it began to grow light."

She flopped down on the flat stone outside the door, with her hair all tangled and tear-stains on her face, completely exhausted. Her clothes were loose on her and she had made no attempt to fasten them; she was almost like some shapeless bundle inside her dress as she dropped carelessly there on the door-slab, with these big knees sticking out from under the hem of the dress; she put her elbows on her knees and buried her face in her hands and went on muttering the name of the Saviour. At last she tore herself out of her despair, took her hands away from her face, looked at me in sudden anger, and said in the kind of tone that went with the words:

"You're in league with him! Where is he? Bring him here!"

"Whom?" I said.

"Whom?" she repeated. "Whom do you think? Do you think

I'm an idiot? Do you think all this pretending is doing any good? What has been happening tonight?"

I replied, "Nothing that I know of. And I am not obliged to account to you or anyone else for what I dream."

"You have always been a beastly pig," she said, and looked down at my feet. "You've stolen his shoes! I could well believe that you've murdered him!"

It was not until I myself had actually seen the shoes I was wearing, these glossy shoes from a foreign land, that I was convinced that I had not been dreaming; my shoes were more remarkable than any dream.

"If you are asking me about one particular man," I said, "I know nothing except this: that he gave me his new shoes, and he got my old shoes."

"And where did he go?" she asked.

"I think he must have gone to the warship," I said.

"There isn't any warship," she said. "Ah-ha-ha-ha! You're lying! Uh-hu-hu-hu! You ought to be ashamed of yourselves! Ih-hi-hi-hi!"

I said nothing, and let her howl to her heart's content. To be honest, I felt it a little improper to be exchanging words with a person who came out with the sort of wild accusations that this girl had done against me; we in Brekkukot were not used to this sort of talk. She went on pouring out her anger and despair into her tear-drenched hands something like this: "And my daddy who for years and years has been paying his bills at the best and most expensive hotels so as to make him famous throughout the whole world. Hundreds and hundreds and hundreds. Thousands and thousands. A million. The gold he scatters around, it's all Daddy's gold. That's how he treats us. That's how he disgraces us when it really matters. And the *Ísafold*, which my daddy keeps going with these miserable few *krónur* which the fishing yields – that's the paper that Garðar Hólm makes a national laughing-stock. Dear Jesus! Oh, God! And he's the one who had promised to show me the whole world. I could well believe that he really is married to that hag of a fishwife with the lice-ridden children."

I was slowly beginning to realize that in circumstances like these it is difficult to communicate with people at all; words cease to mean anything at all when people begin to bawl. As soon as the scale becomes natural sound, all music ceases. I made no reply, and looked silently at this plump girl sitting in a heap on the threshold of this creaking old cow-shed, so decayed through and through and dried up and long since ceased to be a house.

She had said everything and there was nothing more that could be said. And I had seen a girl disintegrate in water. She made an effort to take solid shape again by lifting the hem of her dress to her eyes to dry her face as she sat there. She had not come to herself enough to consider me a person, much less a man, when she lifted her skirt all the way up to her face. When she had wiped her face dry she stood up and breathed out her sorrow in a great sigh. The light of the early-morning sun still lay red on the blue mountains beyond the water and the green, dew-covered after-grass in the home-fields and the summer-weary tansies on the graves. It was so early in the morning that there was not even a wisp of smoke showing yet from my grandmother's chimney to the south of the churchyard. I collected my thoughts and realized that there was nothing to wait for here – better be off home before people started getting up.

"Goodbye, I'm off," I said.

She pulled her stockings up and smoothed her dress down and sniffed vigorously with an air of finality, as if she had come to the conclusion that there was no point in this sort of behaviour. Half in helplessness and half in defeat she asked me not to leave her behind like this.

"Don't make me go into town alone," she said. "There are fierce dogs and drunkards in the streets." She brushed her hair back from her forehead and said, "Am I an awful sight?"

"Yes," I said.

"Do I look a terrible mess?" she said.

"Yes," I replied. "But it doesn't matter."

"Of course it matters," she said. "But how can you expect to look any better when you have to crawl out through your own window at home? Let's get going, then."

When we were a good way down the path from the churchyard, she started up again:

"Why do you dislike me so much?"

"You mean, why do I like you so much that I accompany you all over town at this time in the morning instead of going home to sleep?" I said.

"Do you dislike me because you're poor and I'm rich?"

I was at a loss to know how to answer her, and looked at her in some amazement. I had never before now heard that I was poor – such a thing had never even occurred to me. I took it as a rather ill-chosen bit of teasing.

"If I dislike you it is because you are poor and I am rich," I said.

"You should be ashamed of yourself!" she said, and I thought she was going to begin all over again. "You should be ashamed of yourself for wearing his shoes and not even telling me what has happened to the man himself."

"What do you really want with him?" I asked.

"I'll tell you that if you will tell me where he is," she said.

"That's quite a different matter," I said.

"Well, then it's none of your business what I want with him."

"Oh well, this is as far as I go."

"No, don't go," she said, and took hold of my arm. "I won't ask any more questions. I won't say another word. I know I have no claims on anyone. I'm just a stupid girl who sneaked out through a window. But there's one thing you can tell me: do you actually know where he is even though you won't tell me?"

"I know nothing about anyone," I said, "and least of all about him."

Outside the office of the *Ísafold* in Löngustétt and all the way out to the Theological Seminary the festivities were still continuing. A remarkable assembly had gathered to ensure that there should be no premature end to the party that had been held the evening before; and this was no mean company either; as far as I could see it was the millennium itself that had come on the scene, as it is portrayed in holy writ.

In the middle of the street a train of fifty pack-ponies stood tied, nose to rump, unable to move off in any direction; many of the beasts had fallen asleep where they stood with lower lips sagging and pack-saddles under their bellies; the bundles of fish-heads had fallen off and in the confusion lay like debris in the mire. A few loose horses from the town itself had arrived on the scene along with some foals to keep their colleagues company. Three hoarse farm-workers in skin-boots were sitting on a doorstep trying to sing *O'er the Icy Sandy Wastes* while they kept the bottle circulating. A committee of exhausted mongrels had lain down on the edge of the pavement with their tongues hanging out. Two sporty Danish shop-assistants who looked as if they were on their way up Mount Hekla, were standing nearby leaning against their bicycles and studying this aspect of national life in a Danish colony. Up on the balcony of the *Ísafold* office with its handsome lathe-turned pillars sat a handful of cats, above it all in more senses than one, because they pretended not to see one another nor their enemies, the dogs, down in the street below. Two French fishermen had lain down in the gutter and were sound asleep with their clogs for a pillow in the light of this unbelievable midnight sun right up at the North Pole. On the steps of the Theological Seminary across from Gúðmúnsen's Store there was a man who was making a sunrise-speech while the world still slept; from the circumstances one might have thought that this was the holy St. Francis of Assisi, or some other of the famous saints who preached with such skill to dumb animals:

"Dear brethren, ha,
ponies and Frenchmen,
cyclists and mongrels,
horsemen and cats!
When the Chief Justice comes –
that's the very thing!
Thirty seasons at sea.
The man who rows for Gúðmúnsen needs a battleship.

"The woman who had the children, ha,
She has given you fish,
and you can see a blade of grass and a star
through the prayer-window at Brekkukot.
But the man who rows for Gúðmúnsen needs a battleship.

"When the Chief Justice comes, ha!
Good day to you!
That's the very thing.
Thirty seasons at sea.
The man who rows for Gúðmúnsen needs a battleship.

"After thirty seasons, good day to you –
you are sent home,
home to this bone-dry, motionless dung-heap
they call land,
and that's the very thing;
(the woman went east alone to Landbrot)
and besides I had something wrong with my eyes;
this dry, still, dung-heap
whose name I have forgotten –
but when the Chief Justice comes, ha,
when the Chief Justice comes, ha-ha,
when the Chief Justice comes, ha-ha-ha,
yes, good day to you –
that's the very thing!
Dear brethren, ponies, and Frenchmen –
he who rows for Gúðmúnsen needs a battleship.

"The man who commands warships has no pouches.
But a fragrant star shines through the window
when you come home from the cess-pools.
To know him is to have the battleships
he would give you
if he had a battleship.

"The man who owns the pouches,
he's the one who gives other people battleships,
so you struggle out of the miracles at Skildínganes
and the wonder cess-pools of Grótta,
and live it up;
that's the very thing,
because he who rows for Gúðmúnsen needs a battleship.

"Now there's only the one blade of grass.
But when the Chief Justice comes, ha-ha,
dear brethren
ponies and Frenchmen
cyclists and mongrels
horsemen and cats,

"When the Chief Justice comes, ha-ha-a-a,
yes, good day to you,
that's the very thing!"

"That drunkard is trying to get at my daddy," said the girl, and tightened her grip on my arm and quickened her stride: "Let's cross the road quickly."

We hurried past. We practically brushed past the nose of the man who was making the speech. But either he did not see us, or else he thought we were ponies and Frenchmen.

28

SECRET DOCTRINE AT BREKKUKOT

One day, late in the winter, a man half-carried his wife through the turnstile-gate at Brekkukot.

"Her name is Chloë," said the man.

"Glowy?" said my grandfather wonderingly. "Where does that name come from, if I may ask?"

"It is the Greek shepherdess whom Daphnis loved so much", said the visitor. "And one of the poet Horace's favourite ladies."

Then I realized from what I had learned at school that the woman's name must be Chloë, but as everyone can see, a name like that is extremely difficult to write in Icelandic, and even harder to decline. After a while we had no other choice than to call her Kló.

"Tut tut!" said my grandfather. "Really!"

"But in this life," continued the visitor, "she is descended from one of the oldest families in the north."

"Well, just as you say," said my grandfather. "I only hope she doesn't come from a family older than Adam's. Do come inside and have something warm to drink on that. Who are you, by the way, if I may ask, my friend?"

"I am called E. Draummann," said the visitor. "Ebenezer Draummann. My family comes from the Thingeyjar district, and I'm an agronomist and secondary school graduate by education."

"And what has drawn you both down from the north?" said my grandfather, and began to help the visitor support his wife, for she seemed more than a little numb in the legs.

This woman had long fair hair, blue eyes and a Mother-Iceland expression, as was then the fashion; she had handsome features with one of those noses which are sometimes described in Danish novels as Grecian; but she was rather plumper than was becoming. The reason for this may well have been her illness, with long periods in bed and lack of exercise.

"We have come south in search of a cure, Björn," said the husband of this distinguished woman. "And I would like to ask you to let her lie in some comfortable corner in your house while we are finding ourselves accommodation here in the south."

The couple were given a bed in the mid-loft beside us, in the cubicle in which the undersigned is said to have been born, and in which the woman from Landbrot had died.

Ebenezer Draummann was somewhere between thirty and sixty years old when he helped his wife through our turnstile-gate in Reykjavík, a short, stooping, broad-shouldered man. His head dithered slightly, and his hands trembled. He was incredibly pale, and yet there was some underlying colour in his skin, red and blue at the same time. His hands were freckled, and he was bald in the way that some people become from having a disease of the scalp – he had perhaps had ringworm in childhood. In place of eyebrows he had long red patches which looked sore, as if the eyebrows had just been plucked out by the roots. One could see that he had a sparse, rather patchy growth of beard, reddish in colour, but he removed this stubble secretly, using,

I think, some other implement than a razor. He had clear blue eyes, the most piercing ever seen, so penetrating that if one ever saw such eyes in an animal, in a seal, for instance, it would be difficult to avoid crying out in amazement and jubilation and saying, "Good heavens above, that creature has human eyes!"

When this couple came to stay with us, E. Draummann was wearing a waistcoat with horizontal stripes. His blue Cheviot jacket was too tight across the shoulders and rather short in the sleeves. He had a white rubber collar and a loose shirt-front of the same material, with the collar fastened to it at the front, but he never used a tie: the loose front served as a substitute for a shirt, for he was rather a shirtless man. He wore threadbare trousers of undyed homespun which were much too short, and this was all the more unfortunate because the man never wore any socks. He wore foreign-made canvas shoes, scarcely the ideal footwear here in Iceland during winter.

I do not remember which one of us it was who asked him, on that very first day, why he did not wear socks; but he replied, "The Masters do not wear socks either."

He spoke in a low voice, and when he had given a reply to anyone, he had the habit of smiling to himself and blinking and moving his lips as if he were continuing a silent conversation with himself.

After a while he added, to explain his lack of socks, "The man who wears no socks can acquire things which bestockinged people can never obtain. By saving on socks, one can afford stamps for letters to philosophers throughout the world and get from them the correct interpretation of obscure words in Sanskrit. For example, what does the word *prana* mean? Or *karma*? And *maya*?"

Obviously there was no one at Brekkukot who could answer this.

"And you don't know either, young man – and you a pupil at the Grammar School?"

"No," I said.

"There you are, then," said Ebenezer Draummann. "Everyone wearing socks, and no one knows what *prana* is. Not even this young man from the Grammar School."

"Where did you find yourself such a beautiful wife, lad?" said

Captain Hogensen, whose nature was so chivalrous that he always spoke of women in the way in which people with sight would do.

"Everyone has heard tell about the Langahlíð folk, of course," said E. Draummann (he said "fol-k" in the German pronunciation, as they all do in the north). "In that family there have been government officials, poets, and factors of royal estates, as you know. My wife is from the side of the family that inherited the intelligence and the virtues but rather less of the wealth and position. These folk always had well-educated private tutors for their children, of course. Chloë had fourteen brothers and sisters. I cannot claim that these people's good fortune in their children has always matched the excellence of their teachers, if it is measured by the yardstick of this world, which many have proved and still more have yet to prove is a trifle short at one end. But I know one thing, that there was no teacher there before me who could understand Chloë. Because the moment I set eyes on this young girl for the first time, I knew that a higher incarnation had been born into the Langahlíð family. And I said to myself, 'Aha! One of these Egyptians'."

"One of those Eyfirðings, quite so," said Hogensen. "But the most important thing is that you liked the look of her right from the start."

"Liked the look of her? No, certainly not," said E. Draummann, "I didn't like the look of her. I don't really like the look of anything. I know perfectly well that all life is *maya* – a mere illusion. But the previous summer I had had the good fortune of being given access to the *Secret Doctrine* by a man in Akureyri who had just arrived from London. To be exact – this incarnation, this higher being, if I may so put it, this woman whom I call my wife, belongs to a remote sphere; and she is of another age."

"Quite so, yes," said Captain Hogensen, "with a cast of mind inclined to the Saga Age, perhaps, as so many of the Langahlíð family have had."

E. Draummann smiled to himself, blinked, and moved his lips as if he were reading some text to himself, but he made no reply. And Runólfur Jónsson said not a word but drew up his legs, now that the discussion was becoming uncomfortably remote from life on board fishing-smacks, and the miracles and modern wonders which were happening on Seltjarnarnes.

The door of the woman's cubicle had been closed and she could be heard settling down in bed in great distress. Ebenezer Draummann went in to tuck her up in bed. Whenever he rose from his seat, it was his custom to square his shoulders as if he were going to lift a barrel.

"Now I shall tuck you in carefully, my lamb," he could be heard saying behind the door.

But the pains did not leave the woman; she went on groaning.

"Now I shall pat you a little, my lamb," said the husband.

But all to no avail; the woman went on groaning as if she were far gone. Then her husband said, "Now I shall lay my hands here on your temples, my lamb."

It seemed as if the woman's pains eased a little at the patting and laying-on of hands, but not entirely.

"Now we shall have the Indian prayer," said the husband, and they recited it together.

Then the woman fell asleep.

E. Draummann came back to join his room-mates.

"What did you say your wife's name was again, lad?" asked Hogensen.

"Her name is Chloë," said E. Draummann.

"Ah, yes, Klói; just like a mongrel," said Hogensen. "And she's a bit low. I don't suppose her illness has anything to do with her name?"

"It is a great and difficult task to be her doctor," said Draummann. "Her spiritual maturity is more advanced than mortal flesh can bear. She stands on the brink of a new incarnation."

"Oh yes, it often happens that the power drains out of a family," said Captain Hogensen. "And the Langahlíð family has lasted very well. There have always been quite exceptional clergymen in that family, in the north: outstanding womanizers, tremendous drinkers, and great men for a fight if it came to that; and also renowned fishermen, famous horsemen, and great versifiers."

Ebenezer Draummann nodded his head rather piously at this information.

"We can thank our lucky stars," he said, "that the Almighty does not let there be any spiritual kinship between relatives. Your sister could be the queen of Atlantis even though you were a sheep-thief from Rugludalur."

"Ach, I'm beginning to hear badly now," said Captain Hogensen, and indeed the distance between people there in the darkness of the mid-loft was lengthening. And Runólfur Jónsson had started snoring.

29

A GOOD MARRIAGE

E. Draummann had long suspected, according to what he himself said, and had at last found proof the previous year, that although his wife came of this famous Langahlíð family, she had nothing in common with her father and mother nor with anyone else in Iceland or in this part of the world in this century and this millennium.

"When I was talking to her," he said, "she would often not hear for hours at a time what I was saying, but just stare out into the blue; so I tried putting her into a trance. And when she was hypnotized, I took hold of her little finger and began to question her. And then it turned out that in another life she had looked after goats and played the flute: that is to say, she had been Chloë. Later she was born again as a famous courtesan in Rome. But that was only the beginning. All around this woman was an unbroken, strange world. She had been born into the world yet again, probably because of some trifling peccadillo in her former life, or even some untimely act of kindness, just like the Master Santajama who had to be born again and again for eight thousand years, sometimes as an ox or some other domestic animal, because he had taken pity on a woman who suffered from nymphomania."

It had accordingly become the vocation and life's work of this scholarly gentleman from the Thingeyjar district to support this woman who was bed-ridden most of the time because she was too spiritually advanced to live in this world. He had married her when she was sixteen and cared for her ever since.

His mind was completely taken up with how he could best serve this mystic creature; her origin in space and time obsessed him to such an extent that he paid scarcely any heed to other matters; he worshipped the woman in the way that is given to idolaters more than any other religious believers, and to those believers who have their god in substantial form rather than in books or dogma. But he eschewed no learning, however remote or far-fetched, in his quest to understand this higher being, this incarnation as he called her, and to acquire whatever material benefits were likely to make her existence tolerable in this mundane world in which she was condemned to live for yet another span. As was mentioned previously, the *Secret Doctrine* had been of some guidance to him in the matter; but that book had reached the north of Iceland only recently. He made every effort to find capable doctors for the woman; but this couple considered all true medical art to be supernatural and magical, even the most conventional mixtures, and the husband never tired of trying out on his wife new prayers and magic formulas of various kinds, such as breathing-exercises from yoga and drinking salt water through the nostrils, as well as laying-on of hands and many other ploys that will be referred to later.

In just the same way as the woman was to her husband the kind of phenomenon that never ends and which no one can ever fully understand, so did she look up to her husband as the only man who was capable of guiding her life in her chronic illness and in the absolute dichotomy that had developed between the coarse substance of mortality and the spiritual maturity her soul had reached after many reincarnations. The husband was his wife's sole and utter refuge and stay, even though he had neither house nor home to offer her, much less a marriage-bed, and scarcely even a scrap of clothing to cover her nakedness, and had now moved with her into our mid-loft at Brekkukot away in the south.

And however much the woman was to her husband a Greek shepherdess, Horace's mistress, and a few other things that have not been recorded yet, she was probably above everything else a soul – the soul itself; I think I can state categorically that if anyone here in Iceland in my youth owned a soul, it was Ebenezer Draummann. Acquaintance with this couple was at least bound to raise doubts in every intelligent person as to whether having a soul is the monopoly of fish, as some modern philosophers believe. And even so I am well aware that to call this woman her husband's soul is saying very little, for she was also his flower, his bird, his fish, his jewel of jewels, saint, angel, and archangel. Her husband had a little Oriental mat, a prayer mat, which he always carried under his arm and which he called his all; he would spread the mat on the floor beside his wife's bed and take up Buddhist postures. Often he would sit for hours at a time on the mat at his wife's bedside and practise breathing-exercises from yoga; he would try to concentrate all his thoughts to be able to move some inanimate object that was lying on a certain shelf somewhere up north, and transmit thoughts telepathically to the Masters in the East, and practise taking leave of his body. He also drank great quantities of salt water through his nostrils. At night-time he would lie down on this prayer mat and sleep on it beside his wife's bed.

I listened with only half an ear to Draummann's long lectures about this woman's reincarnations and transmigrations as I sat there, an immature coltish boy, with my schoolbooks on my knees; and since Captain Hogensen was now so hard of hearing and Runólfur Jónsson had gone to sleep, the audience-numbers would have been rather below average if our superintendent had not occasionally arrived late at night to listen. He was the sort of man who misunderstood no doctrines and said yes to most people as if he believed them, even though he himself usually followed only what the bee in his bonnet inspired him to do.

And Ebenezer Draummann went on talking about his wife:

"Invariably when I tried to give her some lessons in arithmetic or Danish," he said, "I saw from her eyes that she was miles away. And before I knew it she had started writing down some weird symbols on the paper in front of her, or else on the table itself. If she were left to herself she could go on with this strange script for hours at a time. Her mother told me that if she got hold of a needle and thread she would immediately start sewing symbols on to her handkerchiefs or even her clothes if there were nothing better to hand. I took it upon myself to try to get hold of every likely and unlikely alphabet in the hope that I might succeed in interpreting these symbols, but all to no avail. I sent some specimens of the script to learned men both in Iceland and abroad to ask what it was. Most of them never replied, probably because they thought I was not learned enough myself; but finally I heard from one dean who pointed out to me that these were not alphabetical letters in our sense of the term, but some sort of pictorial script not unlike the Chinese lettering on a tea-urn from Hong Kong. Another scholar said he thought they were pictures of insects, and a clergyman on the east coast thought they represented reindeer-moss. Just about this time I had started delving a little into the *Secret Doctrine* and had come to the conclusion that there are more things in heaven and earth than are dreamt of in our philosophy, as the poet said; so from that moment I started saving up for stamps so that I could write to oracles in distant lands. The smattering of English that I had learned in secondary school came in useful here, and now I wrote to both spiritualists and occultists in London and laid before them specimens of my Chloë's symbols; but not a single person in England proved to be learned enough to interpret these runes. And then at last it occurred to me to address myself directly to the sages of the Orient; and finally I received a reply from no less a man than that renowned bishop, scholar, and higher incarnation, Dr Leadbeater of Australia. He thought the script so remarkable that he consulted one of those almost transcendental Masters of the *Secret Doctrine* who have permission to read the Akashic Records – and that book has more knowledge collected in it than any other book, because one finds recorded in it everything, both great and small, that has ever happened in the universe since it was first created, and one needs to have taken a fearful number of degrees before one is allowed to pry into it. I have been led to understand that it was a profound Indian higher incarnation who finally discovered the truth about the script: it is the script of the Lepsky tongue, which was spoken in a kingdom which flourished at the roots of the Himalayas some forty thousand years ago. And the sages thought they could deduce from the script that my wife Chloë had been a princess in that kingdom."

E. Draummann reckoned he had no other task in life than to cure this supernatural woman of the supernatural ailments that plagued her, and he had not only become a doctor himself from experimenting on her, as has already been described, but he also left no stone unturned to obtain the aid of other health experts in the matter, just in case one of them might be harbouring some method which might be of use. No sooner had he arrived in Reykjavík than he started to seek out all kinds of healers. He was such an artist at talking about his wife to lay people and learned alike that no one could help starting to brood about her; and he talked about her with those robust "k's" and "p's" that they use in the north and which are always so much admired by the more soft-spoken southerners.

He began by dragging up to our mid-loft all the more accessible doctors in the capital, the horse-doctors, blood-letters, and enema-givers. He also managed to lure in certificated doctors who wanted to see what sort of a woman it was who had been a shepherdess in Greece, a princess in the Himalayas, and Horace's mistress, and was descended, what's more, from the Langahlíð family; they gave her strong-smelling mixtures that made Captain Hogensen and even Runólfur Jónsson sneeze; and on one occasion the chief medical officer himself came along with his cane, lorgnettes, and high collar. There was a female herbalist who came too, carrying an alpenstock and wearing a hood and smoking a pipe. Finally, Ebenezer Draummann got hold of that obsolete race of physicians who applied turf, not forgetting those who specialized in dung, who were then unfortunately beginning to die out but who deserve to have books written about them. Some writers maintain that the special purpose of medical treatment is to comfort the doctors themselves, and one thing is certain, that doctors are always extraordinarily keen to treat one another. E. Draummann, indeed, had no other means of recompensing all this medical treatment except to offer to treat the doctors or their families in exchange, both by laying-on of hands and telepathy and also by establishing spiritual contact between his patients and the Masters who are to be found in the Himalayas, according to the *Secret Doctrine*.

The woman was always ready to undergo any and every medical experiment in the hope that the pains, particularly the pains in the head, would be eased. Seldom has a woman been more convinced of her husband's power and intelligence, both natural and supernatural, than this woman was. It was quite unthinkable that she would ever question his arrangements at any point whatsoever. Nothing was more natural to her than that turf-sods should be fastened round her thighs in order to increase her earthly strength, or that people should try to stop up her nostrils with warm cow-dung at the behest of some southern dung-doctor with a cleft palate, to see if such treatment could not ease the head-pains.

I think that few marriages in Iceland at that time were as good, and certainly none better. But unfortunately, no sooner had the doctors vanished down the stairs than this supernatural shepherdess and princess inside the cubicle began once more to groan and whimper in her sore distress.

It was never properly light in our mid-loft, because the little window above the bed I shared with Hogensen was too small for anyone except blind men, philosophers, and those with salt-burn in the eyes – indeed, it was hardly possible to read Latin by it; but it was even darker in the little cubicle, where people had never until now required light for other tasks than being born and dying – what tiny glimmer there was filtered in to Chloë from Hogensen and the rest of us through the crack above the door. Nevertheless she used to the best of her ability this murky light which had never been sufficient to be shared in the first place; whenever her pains left her for a moment she started pottering with her sewing. I once heard her tell my grandmother, just as a matter of course, that the pictures she sewed were her memories from the Himalayan Mountains; she added that these memories so beset her that she could not help cutting up every single garment she possessed and covering them with sewing;

and also that her husband had never managed to keep his socks since they got married, because she always unravelled them for sewing yarn.

At first she sewed these extraordinary insects and rare Himalayan plants side by side on to her patches of cloth, and then, when there was no room for more, she would sew new insects over the first ones and roses over roses, until the pictures stood out in high relief; she decorated them with locks cut from her fair hair and feathers she plucked from the pillow; eventually the cloth had become as stiff as a board and could be stood on its edge. She made these solid pictures so expressive that it was unlikely that anyone who set eyes on them once would ever forget them.

She never seemed to acknowledge people's existence unless they were her doctors in one way or another, or her nurses. When there were no doctors she said very little. She never talked to the rest of us in the mid-loft, but asked for the door to be kept shut. Many days would pass without my seeing her at all, except for a brief glimpse of her in bed if someone walked into or out of her cubicle: this sun-bright, milk-white Mother-Iceland face with the blue eyes under the shining hair, and the eiderdown drawn right up to her chin – even when she was sewing she drew it up to her chin with only her hands and bare arms out, and in that way she would hold the bed-clothes to her breast, sewing away.

But now it so happened that down town the very spirit that Ebenezer Draummann championed was in the air: the *Secret Doctrine* was beginning to rear its head all over the place. Even up in the Grammar School one began to hear remarkable sentences such as "All life is *yoga*", or "All life is *maya*". A philosopher like Ebenezer Draummann now became a welcome guest in many houses, not only in the homes of the doctors and other healers he visited because of his wife, but also in the homes of their friends and their friends' friends; he was considered a highly intelligent person. As time passed, he no longer had time to look after his wife except now and again, because he was too busy preaching about her all over town. Considering the woman's state of health, it was not surprising that she grew impatient waiting for her husband when she thought he stayed away too long on some

spiritual expedition; and indeed the only words she was heard
to utter from her cubicle were requests to Captain Hogensen to
oblige her by having a look out of the window to see if there were
any signs of her husband coming home.

30

THE SOUL CLAD IN AIR

In Löngustétt, where the girls promenade, a girl came towards
me. By habit when I met girls I took care to look the other way;
I did not feel quite safe with these creatures, and could not exactly
think of them as people at all, any more than I could "the authorities". She was tall and shapely, and I felt her looking at me. When
she saw that I was going to sidle past her, she put her hand on my
arm. She looked at me with that strange smile that seemed to live
in the air itself but manifested itself in her face as a flash from
some unknown light: the air clad in a soul, or the soul clad in air,
and light – Blær. Her voice was slightly breathless as she bade me
good day. I stiffened up completely, just as I had done before, and
could see nothing; the world melted away in a white fog. This was
the moment that I had dreaded in my innermost being ever since
I had fled from her, the moment when I would meet her again.

"What beautiful shoes you are wearing," said the girl, and gazed
at me from out of the air.

I said nothing.

"Why do you avoid us? What harm have we done you?" she
asked.

"Nothing," I mumbled, almost in a whisper.

"Could you not see how much we all thought of you? Daddy
says I must have annoyed you. What did I do?"

I suppose I was going to say something, and I looked at her
face. Then I saw how her face quivered behind the smile when she
looked at me; and I felt as if I had been seized by the throat.

"Why?" she said, and went on looking at me.

In the end I blurted out, "When you were near, I – I – I felt I could not bear it."

"What a thing to say!" said the girl. "Am I as boring as all that?"

"Goodbye," I said.

"Aren't you even going to give me your hand?" she asked.

I gave her my hand.

"Goodbye," she said. "And remember that even though I may be boring, Daddy is still waiting for you. He says that you have absorbed everything concerned with music. I have also heard from another source that you are good at everything and anything. What do you want to be?"

"I'm thinking of just staying at home at Brekkukot," I replied.

"May I not invite you to come home with me, please?" said the girl. "I know how delighted Daddy would be. He always thinks I must have done something to you."

"I must see to my lines," I said.

"See to . . . what?" said the girl, for she did not understand fishermen's idiom.

"My grandmother sent me to Friðriksen's bakery shop," I said.

"So you're never going to come and see us, then, so that we can have a proper talk about what I don't understand?" said the girl.

She did not know that it was because of her that I could not speak.

Was it that same evening, or perhaps the following evening, that I went to see a certain woman down town? She was Danish. She had a black moustache. Astride her nose, which was one of the sharpest and most prominent aloft in Reykjavík in those days, there rode an immense pair of lorgnettes tethered by a black silken cord. Her name was Madame Strúbenhols, but many Icelanders called her the axe "Battle-Troll". She was related to the Danish wife of a civil servant in the capital, and some extraordinary misfortune which I cannot account for had caused her to be left high and dry in Iceland for the last twenty or thirty years.

She managed to keep body and soul together by teaching the daughters of the gentry three or four grips on the guitar or mandolin, and was held in particular esteem socially in better class homes. This woman had also been engaged to play Liszt's piano rhapsodies at every single public tombola for as long as I can remember. Later I discovered that workmen and shop-assistants and even a few seamen went to Madame Strúbenhols to learn music; and this was because of something that appears to be immutable – that it was the classes which were considered uncultured or unrefined, or at the very least only half-refined, that really cared for music, while total unmusicality and a basic contempt for music went on being one of the most conspicuous characteristics of the educated and upper classes in Iceland.

It was to this woman that I made my way one evening. Madame Strúbenhols squinted at me over her lorgnettes and asked who I was and what I wanted. I told her I wanted to learn singing and instrumental music.

"Well I never!" said the woman.

She looked me over carefully, up and down, raising and lower-ing her head in turn because she had to study me from beneath her spectacles, through them, and over them; and this took quite a time because I was so lanky.

"Are you a joiner's apprentice?" she asked.

"No," I replied.

"A fisherman's boy?" she asked.

"I fish for lumpfish," I said.

"Can you make a living out of that?" she asked.

I was aware that she was referring to money, and that rather disconcerted me because I had not realized that music costs money.

"Well, I have to live too," the woman said. "I hope at least that you are an honest man?"

In the end she invited me inside, into a room full of furniture upholstered in red plush with tassels. Framed family portraits stood in serried ranks on what are called *chiffoniers* – gentlemen in frock-coats and top-hats, fine ladies in pleated dresses with enormous bustles behind and carrying parasols. There was a piano against the middle of one wall, and a harmonium in the corner.

"Let me hear what you can do," the woman said.

In this Danish room in the home of a woman with a contrap-tion on her nose, a woman so un-Icelandic in speech that I cannot possibly reproduce it, I had suddenly arrived in a place where no one knew me. I was no more shy with this foreign woman than if she had been a piece of wood. I went straight to her harmonium, sat down, pulled out the diapason and *vox celeste* stops, and sang *Der Erlkönig* to my own accompaniment, without the music. Madame Strúbenhols looked at me in astonishment.

"God help you!" she said when I had finished singing. But she was not all that angry, nevertheless. And she did not criticize me on that occasion beyond saying, "Well, you had better come twice a week and we shall see what we can make out of that monstrosity."

This was my last year at school, and I really had no comrade now that my friend Grandpa Jón had left for Norway, that country where Bible story-books are bigger and better than here in Iceland and where Christianity is held in higher esteem, as was mentioned in the chapter about Thórður the Baptist; and where there is also more concern for the spiritual welfare of the Chinese.

I would come home with my schoolbooks tied in a scarf just after midday and my grandmother would give me something to eat. I looked in silent joy at her gnarled blue hands when she passed me meat and fish, and I tried to stretch the meal-hour as long as possible by recalling in full detail exactly how the weather had been since that morning, as if this were the thing that really mattered instead of the mere fact that she should still be there and I with her; then I went up to the mid-loft and tried to do something to pass the time, having a look at my sums or thinking about the essay I had to do for homework or else bringing out my beautiful shoes and examining them. These were Garðar Hólm's shoes, and it was often difficult to believe that such precious objects, which aroused the admiration of men and women alike, could be my own; and indeed I never wore them except on special occasions. On the whole, the afternoons seemed to drag very heavily towards late winter. Captain Hogensen was now so enfeebled by old age that he had difficulty keeping awake for that particularly long part of the day, so he usually just lay down and slept. This was the time of year when we had the fewest visitors; everyone stayed at home while the land was fettered in ice; nothing really significant happened except that the blade of grass kept on tapping ceaselessly against the little window in the bitter cold, and the star rose at night if the skies were clear. And the woman from the north groaned in her cubicle.

Truth to tell, I had at first hoped that this woman would die soon, like the other one who died in there a few years ago, the one from Landbrot. We at Brekkukot really felt a less pressing duty of charity towards this one than towards the woman from Landbrot, for she had been a widow but this one had a husband. On the other hand I felt it rather unnecessary of her husband to be constantly busying himself with miracles all over the place for anyone and everyone instead of performing the more necessary miracles on his wife, even if only to change the cold compress on her head when it was obvious that warm cow-dung had little effect.

I tried to pretend that the woman's health did not concern me in the slightest and never looked at her on purpose even when her door happened to be open, and so I was relieved that she never in any way acknowledged my presence. I reckoned that any man could call himself lucky who was so completely involved with *tamas*, the third and lowest strand of being in the fundamental order of this couple's philosophy, that he himself counted as nothing compared with the highly developed reincarnation that this woman was; but on the other hand I saw no particular reason to invoke special floggings for her, as Horace did when he wrote:

> "*Regina, sublimi flagello*
> *tange Chloën semel arrogantem.*"

On one occasion, as so often in the long quiet period in the middle of the afternoon late in winter, I went up to the mid-loft as usual with my books. Captain Hogensen had put his feet up and lain down to sleep on his bed as was his custom at this time of day, and his snores doubtless drowned my footsteps and the creaking of the stair. But when I was halfway through the hatch into the loft I saw a sight that stopped me in my tracks, for I had never seen anything like it before: it was a naked woman. Despite all the Latin I had studied, I was so ignorant that I thought at first that this was some animal that had been omitted from the natural histories by oversight; or perhaps a fairy creature. I stood there rigid in the middle of the stair and gaped at her, spellbound.

She was standing on the bed at the feet of the sleeping old man and had bent over to peer through the little window where the blade of grass was beating against the pane. Her fair hair was tied together with a bit of string just behind the ears and hung like a tail far down her back. I saw from her profile how pretty her cheek was, rather thin, with that straight nose and well-formed chin, and that mouth which was somehow absolutely correctly shaped; and all that glowing hair.

But in other respects this human body was so close to being a caricature of itself because of its exaggerated shape that it was difficult to imagine that anyone who had such a body could suffer from anything but excessive health, if such a disease exists. Perhaps I did not think of it at the time, but I have often thought since then that if Iceland has ever witnessed the rebirth of that goddess who in olden times brought forth the horn Cornucopia, which was famed for abundance and grew on a famous goat, then it was this woman – in addition to the fact that she was a Lepsky-speaking, forty-thousand-year-old princess from the Himalayan Mountains, the shepherdess who tended goats with Daphnis, and Chloë whom that great poet Horace so earnestly begged the goddess of love to flog. Yet this was the poorest woman in Iceland I have ever heard of, the naked woman without a spindle, so naked, so utterly spindle-less, that there is not even a proverb about her; and if she ever came into possession of a rag of clothing to cover her nakedness, she cut it into pieces and used them to sew works of art with yarn from her husband's unravelled socks.

"May God help me and forgive me!" said the woman when she became aware of someone standing behind her at the hatch and looking at her. "I was just having a look through the window to see if my husband was on his way."

And with these words she jumped down from Captain Hogensen's bed and disappeared into her cubicle and got into bed and pulled the bed-clothes over herself. And it was not very long before she once again succumbed to her sufferings, and her dreadful groans suggested very little hope or none at all.

The precentor's vegetable garden lay neglected in the March

weather, but the house continued to be as red-painted as ever, and I recognized again the steps where I thought I was going to drop dead in my colossal boots; and also the door with the threshold where I had sometimes stood and waited for someone to answer the door, dreading that some fluting squeak would come out of my throat when I had to say good day.

It was raining. Inside the house, the lamps were lit. But I did not dare to sit on the precentor's wall for fear that someone would come out of the house and see me. I sat down on the stone dyke of a garden-patch beside a tiny hovel on the other side of the road, opposite the precentor's house. I gazed and gazed up at the windows in the hope that a shadow would show against the curtains. It was lucky that my grandmother did not know where I was or what I had in mind: that I was going to steal a shadow. If she got to hear of it, she would most certainly send me to see the precentor's wife with a big pot-bread the following morning.

I sat there all evening, and it rained on me. An old man transparent with age and using a stick and a crutch came out of the hovel and started having a look at the weather from his vegetable garden. He asked me my name.

"I'm called Álfgrímur," I said. And like all men who are hard of hearing, he thought I said Ásgrímur.

"It's very moist," said the old man.

This was his little joke, because one never spoke of it being "moist" except during the hay-making, when one meant that the grass was damp and easy to mow.

When he had gone inside again I noticed that I was soaked to the skin. I stood up and walked across the old man's vegetable patch. The whole garden had been covered with iron sheets, flotsam of some sort; I had no idea why, and had never seen that sort of thing before. I sat down on the dyke at another spot and went on gazing up at the windows on the other side of the road. But no shadow came. After a long time the door of the cottage opened again and the old man came out for another look at the weather portents.

"Are you from outside town?" he asked.

"Yes," I replied.

"What's doing?" he said.

"Nothing," I replied. "But why are these iron sheets here in the garden?"

"I use them in summer to warm the beds," he said. "They draw the heat of the sun into the earth. You get bigger potatoes that way."

Time passed, and I sat on the wall in the rain. But however long I waited, no shadow came. At last I noticed that I was not only soaked through but that my teeth were chattering. Then the old man came out to forecast the weather for the third time.

He walked right round his hovel peering in all directions, and discovered that I was still there sitting on the dyke.

"Ach, what was your name again?" he said.

"Ásgrímur," I replied.

"And what are you waiting for?" he asked.

"I am waiting for a shadow," I replied.

31

PERHAPS THE GOD

"Álfgrímur," said the woman.

I was up in the mid-loft once again towards evening, and I seem to recall that I had started working at my sums – I was at the stage of trying to solve second-degree equations with more than one unknown; and Captain Hogensen was lying on his bed as usual. I could hardly believe my ears when I heard the woman call my name. Until then I had thought that I was much too low in the reincarnation scale for a higher being to take any notice of me, let alone know my name.

"Álfgrímur," she said again, and now there was no mistaking it: she must be meaning me, for there was no one else to be found with that name in the whole of Iceland. I laid down my mathematics book, got up, and eased open the door of the cubicle. The woman had drawn the bed-clothes right up to that Grecian nose, and her hair flowed over the pillow.

"Would you please," said the woman, "go down to the water-barrel and fill this bowl with some really cold water for me?"

Without a word, of course, I went off with the bowl down to the door of the cottage and came back with the cold water. The woman went on groaning with pain.

"Indulge my laziness and make me a cold compress," she said.

"Are you getting worse?" I asked.

"That's hardly the word for it," said the woman. "I wish I knew what I had done wrong in some life long ago. My head is like a furnace. Feel my forehead."

I laid my palm on the woman's forehead as she wanted me to do. There could well have been a furnace there as she said, but in that case it was quite obviously internal, because on the outside I thought her forehead rather cool, if anything.

"Don't you think it's terrible?" said the woman.

"Yes, I suppose so," I replied.

"Or the way my heart's beating!" said the woman. "Put your hand here! Feel it!"

She took my hand and steered it down to her breast under the bed-clothes.

"Do you feel it?" said the woman.

"No," I said, because in actual fact the only thing I felt was how very much softer a woman's breast was to the touch than the chest of a man; and besides I did not know the difference between right and wrong heartbeats in people.

"Put your hand a little higher and wait until you feel it," she said, and I did as she asked; but I felt nothing except that her nipple stood up into my palm.

"I'm burning," said the woman. "Put the compress on me quickly."

That evening everyone was at home in the mid-loft and the door of the cubicle was half open so that Chloë could console herself with the sound of people's voices. And then she suddenly spoke up from inside her cubicle:

"There is undoubtedly something more than a little spiritual about Álfgrímur's hands," she said. "He changed the compress on my head today, and lo and behold: no sooner had he touched my forehead than I began to feel a current, and after a moment I got the right trembling and then I fell asleep and woke up feeling better than I can remember for ages. I am quite sure that he has greater talent for laying-on of hands than most of the spiritual healers who have tried their skill on me so far."

The woman's husband got up and came over to me and began to examine my hands. He fingered them knowledgeably and then was lost in thought for a moment before he said solemnly:

"These are spiritual hands. It was obvious, I suppose, that Chloë would instinctively perceive anything spiritual in her presence. In these hands, even though they are on the large side and indeed a little clumsy-looking, there is rather less of *tamas* and more of *sattva* than many people would suspect. Who knows but that the boy might be *bodhisattva*? There is something about these hands that reminds one of seal's hands. Pharoah comes most readily to mind."

"Ah, pickled seal's hands!" said the woman. "Can you imagine anything more delicious – if only one dared to eat them because of one's soul!"

"You mean because of one's redemption, Chloë," said E. Draummann.

"We used to call them flippers in Breiðafjörður," said Captain Hogensen.

"Well, seals are of Pharoah's race, as we know," said Draummann, "and that's why they have eyes and hands like human beings: that much at least we ought to know; and they were drowned in the Red Sea, I always thought. It was that nation which stood highest in the life-scale in its time, if only such a heavy *karma* had not lain on it."

"What *karma* was that?" someone asked, because *karma*, *prana*, *sattva* and such-like had become everyday talk in the mid-loft at that time.

"We shouldn't need to ask about that," said E. Draummann. "That's the least we should know. They forced people into slavery and then made them build the pyramids and carry all the stones on their backs."

Some overnight visitors from down south at Njarðvík were quite

prepared to believe in the healing power of laying-on of hands
and other spiritual and supernatural treatments, no less than in
the dung-cures which were still practised down on the south coast;
but they found it harder to believe that the lout cowering there
over his Latin books could be Pharoah reborn.

"Is the northerner not just being a little eccentric?" they said.

It was late in the evening, and contrary to custom the superintendent was at home; the weather had been rather poor and
people had not been venturing out of doors, so there was no one
for him to superintend. As always when he was present, people
turned particularly to him when there was need of philosophical
answers. Finally he replied:

"On the contrary," he said. "Since the Draummanns came to
the mid-loft here, I feel that for the first time in my life I have
been free from eccentrics."

He was asked if it weren't just another of those old wives' tales
to say that seals were Pharoah and his people reborn.

"I won't say anything about that," said the superintendent, "but
I do know that belief in *karma* and the laws of cause and effect
and the doctrine of rebirth and transmigration of souls is at least
a more widespread belief throughout the world than, for instance,
Christianity. I think that the great masses of Asia profess more
or less the same beliefs as this worthy and respectable couple. We
in Europe are just an unimportant little headland – those of us
who aren't merely an out-skerry like us Icelanders. What we in
Iceland believe is out-skerry wisdom. I feel that I have come home
at last when I meet people who hold the same beliefs as the largest
population group in the world."

"Is one then to believe the majority unquestioningly, instead
of listening to the wisest?" they asked.

"I'm not saying that a raven isn't a bird," replied the superintendent. "And it's often comforting to hear him croaking in
winter when the other birds are far away; and it may well be that
he is right to start laying eggs nine days before summer. But the
tern is in a certain sense a hundred times more a bird than
the raven, even so."

Then one of the visitors from the south said, "Well, I always thought that the largest population group in the world was the one that knew nothing at all, either about Pharoah's rebirth or anything else. I was taught that it was only knaves or fools who had ready answers for every question."

"That's a very different matter," said the superintendent. "And yet I think it's true to say that there is an answer to most questions if they are framed correctly. On the other hand I think that few answers can be found to questions asked by fools, and even fewer to those put by knaves."

"Well," said the man from Njarðvík, "then I'm going to put to you two questions which an ordinary fellow without a prison record, and no more of a fool than people in general, might ask: does man belong more to heaven than to earth? And what do you say about the Barbers' Bill?"

"Tcha!" said the superintendent. "The eagle would not like to dig itself into the ground. The eagle lives in the hall of the winds, as the poem says. Is it then so easy to fly, perhaps? Well, that all depends; the little mouse doesn't think so, nor even Pussy herself. It's not so easy to give an answer that covers everybody equally. On the other hand I would like to mention to you one person who answers all questions for himself but never bothers about those answers which are valid for eagle and mouse alike, and that is Björn of Brekkukot here, with whom we are staying tonight. But as for the Barbers' Bill, I would say this: have a shave wherever you like, whenever you like, and in whatever way you like, just so long as you don't get in other people's way."

"Allow me to thank our superintendent," said E. Draummann. "There are few men here in the south who will stand up for people from the north. Indeed, I never asserted that this boy who laid hands on my wife today is Pharoah reborn; obviously, no one could make such an assertion unless he had read it in the Akashic Records. What matters is that the boy has healing hands, and that my wife is feeling better. Perhaps he is the god Vishnu."

32

POLITICAL MEETING IN THE TEMPERANCE
HALL: THE BARBERS' BILL

"Put your hand on me, Álfgrímur."

It was the same story every day after this: as soon as I came home from school, I went into the cubicle in the quiet of the afternoon, laid my hand on this woman, and sent a current through her. The woman invariably reacted with the proper trembling. As I have said already, the improvement in health that the woman obtained from this current was both spiritual and supernatural, according to her own judgement and that of her husband and of the doctors and other healers who were closest to this couple. But those scientists who carefully count the bones in dogs but cast doubt on the soul on the ground that its ownership cannot be assigned to people either by notarial certificate or by urine test, would perhaps have had different opinions about that. Whatever the facts of the matter, I just want to mention here, while I remember, that one fine day in the spring this excellent couple went away from Brekkukot, the woman completely recovered and unsupported, her husband an acknowledged pioneer in the spiritual field in this future capital of the nation, a clairvoyant, intellectual, soothsayer, psychologist, disciple of the Masters and I don't remember what else which was then coming into vogue, and had started writing spiritual reflections in the newspapers – besides the fact that he was wearing a brand new suit, and a pair of socks into the bargain.

The first time I laid my hand on this woman I felt deep down inside me almost like a man who is being attacked in his own house. When it was repeated next day I was perhaps even more astonished at the woman – and even further from understanding myself. Afterwards I was assailed by the question: which of us was the fool, I or the woman? And I no longer felt it did not matter.

This was just before the town council elections, and there was a public meeting in the Temperance Hall. The Barbers' Bill was on the agenda as usual. I was not in the habit of involving myself in politics, but somehow or other I found I had drifted in and started listening to what people were saying.

The Barbers' Bill had been a very delicate subject in Reykjavík for a long time. The question was whether barbers' shops should be allowed at all, and if so, to what restrictions they should be subjected. Was the community to tolerate barbers opening their shops at six or seven in the morning and giving people shaves right up until midnight? Or should one find some suitable opening hour round about nine o'clock, and then legislate for some reasonable closing hour in the evening?

The debate had been going on for a long time when I reached the meeting, but there was still a long list of speakers to come. A builder was making a speech, a dignified-looking gentleman with a huge moustache and some difficulty in articulation, like so many intelligent people. He said that in his opinion shaving in the mornings was a bad habit, and he did not think it right to encourage the man in the street to take it up. He reckoned that shaving was the kind of titivation that men should permit themselves when they were going to gatherings or functions or when young men were going to meet other young people to enjoy themselves in a dignified and proper manner, but most especially when upright young men who were officially engaged went to meet their betrotheds, say, once a week. He said that such titivation was not proper when a man was at his everyday work. His view was that since shaving in public was unfortunately permitted at all, it should be limited to evening shaving, for instance between seven and eight o'clock, and then exclusively for men who were going to public or approved functions held by leave of the authorities; in which case it would not be unreasonable to require these men to show proof that they had no opportunity of shaving at home.

Next a bearded man, a former farmer from the east, came striding up to the lectern; he had bought himself a certificate of citizenship and become a grocer up in Laugavegur, and now played an influential part in local affairs. This speaker maintained that it was a sign of the indolence and slothfulness of modern times for people to drop into a barber's shop in the middle of the day and hang around there waiting their turn, thus wasting their time in the most deplorable way, often indulging in pointless gossip and irresponsible slander about their fellow-citizens along with carping criticisms of the municipality, just so that they could throw their money away on those rascally so-called barbers. He said that Gunnar of Hlíðarendi had never allowed himself to be shaved, any more than the other saga-heroes, apart from those who had been born with the infirmity of never being able to grow a beard, like Njáll Thorgeirsson of Bergthórshvoll. He said that those who wished to be in the fashion in these matters ought to be content to shave once a month, and to do it, what's more, quietly and unobtrusively, each in his own home, without calling in perfect strangers from town – for shaving was a private matter that each and every person ought to keep to himself; at the very most, perhaps, one might get one's wife to help if one's hands were a bit unsteady, rather than waste time and money on establishments that had no business to be there in the first place.

The next speaker on the rostrum was a black-haired man with sunken gums who chewed tobacco incessantly and spat all round the platform. He was a highly articulate man but inclined to be rather excitable. He said he no longer wanted to live in this town if he was not to be free to go at any time of the day or night to craftsmen and offer to pay them for any task that he required of them. He said that one might just as well forbid doctors to keep their surgeries open at night, as barbers.

He said it was a downright lie that Gunnar of Hlíðarendi had ever grown a beard, and he challenged the previous speaker to prove his claim with an affidavit. No sane or healthy man had ever grown a beard. There was no conceivable work at which a beard did not get in the way. The only people who grew beards were men with tender skins, and the only cure for that ailment was to seize them by the beard and drag them back and forwards through the whole town. There were few people who were so indispensable to a community as those who shaved men's beards.

In olden times the function of doctor and barber was one and the same profession. These people not only shaved men's beards off but also lanced boils and excised tumours because they had such good knives. All respectable men shaved every day, he said; it was a good custom to go to the barber's and talk to one's fellow-citizens about the common good and the needs of the nation while one was waiting one's turn; so it was money well spent that went to barbers, whether by day or by night.

The next person to speak was a lean man with a face the colour of yellowing parchment, wearing a frock-coat, lorgnettes, and an enormously high collar. He submitted that although medical treatment and shaving had gone together in former times, and it could be argued to a certain extent that shaving was actually a cure for a beard, it could hardly by its very nature be called moral, Christian, or in accordance with socialism to let someone else wait upon one in this way: that was tantamount to making another man your slave, or at least your servant. Such degrading service ill became any of the parties concerned, both the one who accepted it and the one who offered it; service of this kind had no place except within the family.

It was quite true: people ought to go about clean-shaven; but it was equally true to say that people ought to shave themselves. There was only one possible excuse for going to someone else to have one's hair and beard seen to, and that was if one suffered from ringworm or beard-rash, in which case one ought to see a doctor. This speaker said he wanted to emphasize that the views he was putting forward that evening about immoral and antisocial behaviour were in complete accordance with the Communist Manifesto which Marx and Engels had brought out in 1848 and with other doctrines from London, and finally with the revisionary theories of Bernstein.

After him there appeared another speaker, in his own way no less erudite, who put forward quite opposite views on the matter. This was a red-haired, half-bald man with a dishevelled moustache and a soiled collar and rather few teeth; he had a comfortable paunch and took snuff, and the points of his waistcoat stood out like pig's ears. As everyone knew, he said, he had been *studiosus perpetuus* in Copenhagen for thirty-five years, and he had never before heard such opinions expressed. He said he had no intention of arguing with people on the basis of communism and other London doctrines, nor the revisionary theories of Bernstein, nor even on the basis of Christianity, whether or not shaving was a curing of beards; but he would permit himself to contend that if this were so, then it was a singularly unsupernatural cure, consisting simply of applying soap to people's faces in order to facilitate the removal of the beard, which was a considerably more agreeable treatment than trying to cure headaches by smearing people's faces with warm cow-dung, as had been customary in Iceland for a very long time, even though the esteemed previous speaker, bank-manager, socialist, and theologian had so far not criticized this practice.

"I consider it absolutely imperative to have public barber's shops in Iceland where there is a pleasant smell and where people say good morning in a friendly fashion and wear white coats and take care to handle their sharp knives deftly so as not to cut people's throats too often every day, which is undeniably a considerable temptation in this community. But as for the other question, namely whether it is a misdeed to be shaved by someone else, then naturally a lot depends on what a person means by morality, and indeed what value one places on it. I shall now tell you a little parable about how differently people value morality in different countries. As you all doubtless know, old Goethe, the German, once wrote a little book which he called *Faust*; it's about a man who became a candidate for Hell by sleeping with a woman. Obviously various other things happen in the book, but that's the kernel of it. Towards the end of the book Goethe stops short of actually despatching the man to Hell even though he so richly deserved it, and instead lets him be saved by God's mercy and because of his interest in draining marshlands, and sends an angelic host to fetch him and lift him up to Paradise. But now I shall tell you a story which goes in quite the opposite direction. When I was in Copenhagen recently there was an excellent fellow there called Pedersen. He was red-haired and balding and had blackened teeth and seldom used soap, not so very unlike me, as a matter of fact, in character and appearance, except that he happened to be engaged to forty-five girls at once. For some strange reason the Danes dragged this excellent man into court and began to interrogate him and his sweethearts. The poor little sweethearts stood there in the court all in a row, crying their eyes out, and even though they scratched one another a little at times and tugged at one another's hair now and again, yes, and even weren't above spitting a little on one another, they all had this in common that they all begged for mercy for their betrothed; for each and every one of them was convinced that she was the Gretchen (or should we say Maggie) whom he truly loved.

"Each one of them had truly given him her heart; each and every one of them was prepared to let him have her last shilling at any time so that he could go out and buy himself a beer. All of them, separately, had discovered something in Pedersen that could never be valued too highly, and his excellence continued to grip the imagination of each and every one of them quite unblemished, regardless of the fact that it had been proved that he had been carrying on with forty-four others simultaneously. They not only forgave him before God and man but also announced one after another that they were prepared to give up everything for him; many of them begged to be allowed to go to prison in his place, if anyone had to go to prison at all. Some said, 'If anyone is guilty in this case, it's not him but me!' And the judges sat for hours pondering which was the greater crime: that one man should be carrying on with forty-five women, or that forty-five women should be carrying on with one man. The outcome of it all was that Pedersen was fined fifty *krónur*. And since Pedersen was broke, as philanderers always are, the sweethearts had to chip in to pay the fine, and according to my reckoning they must have had to fork out one *króna* and eleven *aurar* each. You see, that's how the Danes looked at the problem: what the German wanted to punish a man for with nothing less than Hell itself, in Denmark it cost no more than one *króna* eleven *aurar* apiece. Isn't it rather the same sort of thing where the Barbers' Bill is concerned . . . ?"

Good deed or misdeed? My mind was reeling with all this

dialectic about the Barbers' Bill when I emerged from this keen debate into the open again.

For some time I had felt in my heart a certain uneasiness, as all guilty people do; I felt I had done something against my better conscience, something which was not worthy of my dignity. But what was the value of Better Conscience if it forbade people to bring others better health and a little romance? And what did the Dignity of a stupid slip of a boy matter? As if God and man cared one little whit on which side of the rump he rode or whether he had a saddle! Could a good deed be a misdeed? The Master Santajama had chosen to wait eight thousand years in order to break the cycle of incarnation and had preferred to risk being reborn over and over again as a domestic animal rather than deny himself the chance of being of use to a woman who was probably very fond of him anyway – assuming nothing worse than that. What do eight thousand years matter to the soul? Is there any hurry, is there not plenty of time to complete the circle from Nirvana to Nirvana? Or is there perhaps anything on earth that is more perfect than a fine head of livestock? Maybe I was the god Vishnu, too, as Ebenezer Draummann had suggested when his wife told him what had happend.

But one thing at least was clear to me: I would never see Blær again. This was in fact my only sorrow. I had betrayed the unincarnated woman, the woman of heaven – "eternity in woman's form", as it says at the end of the book that the red-haired man had made so much fun of at the Barbers' Bill meeting. With my laying-on of hands I had dragged this ideal down from its heaven and laid on it the shackles of incarnation, crammed it into the prison of the flesh. Now there was no longer any hope of seeing a shadow against the curtain; the mirage had disappeared.

33

FAME

On the day I graduated from school as a university student my grandmother made hot chocolate for everyone up in the mid-loft. It was that thick, fatty, sweet, strong chocolate which is never brewed any more, with cinnamon-bark in it, and with cold pancakes with sugar to boot. It was a great moment to be allowed to drink chocolate in the company of these people who symbolized peace in the world, and I was fortunate to have lived among them. But once again, just like the time some years back when my grandfather had told me his plan to send me to school, I felt apathetic and just a little bit apprehensive. Once I had been apprehensive about losing the security which reached as far as the turnstile-gate at Brekkukot; now I was apprehensive about the new paths which would open up when I stopped treading the well-worn route up to school in the morning, in a half-circle round the Lake, and back home again in the afternoon. Where was I to go on all the mornings which I had yet to wake up to after this?

"And what are you now thinking of becoming, friend?" said the superintendent. Contrary to all custom he had allowed himself to play truant for half an hour from his supervisory labours in order to share this excellent chocolate.

I must have been slow to reply.

"I have never dreamt of anything less than the office of sheriff for our Álfgrímur," said Captain Hogensen.

"Does the blessed child not know what it wants to be?" said Runólfur Jónsson. "I wouldn't have thought that would ever be a problem."

But he did not say what I ought to become, at least not on that occasion; he was perhaps unable to recall for a moment what the job was called. But I knew perfectly well that as soon as he acquired another battleship he would remember: I knew that deep down he would not be satisfied on my behalf with anything less than studying to be a Chief Justice.

"Oh, I suppose it will be the lumpfish," I said, half in jest and half seriously, because no matter how many Latin inflections I learned, I could never stop putting this fish above all other fish in the south.

"Tut tut!" said my grandfather, with a suggestion of a grimace. "Really!"

In other words, he did not like the reply.

"Perhaps Björn had been thinking rather of cod for you," said the superintendent.

"Lumpfish," said my grandfather, "are only a momentary joy in the spring, even though it cheers so many people when the season starts; but some years they fail completely. And now Gúðmúnsen's Store and the rest of them have got big ships which in one haul can catch ten or twenty times as much as my little boat can carry, and with that I and people like me are finished here in the Bay. On the other hand, Runólfur Jónsson here can tell us what it's like to catch cod for Gúðmúnsen. And therefore I suggest, my boy, that you study for the church – that has always been a useful occupation here in Iceland; what pastors don't get paid in fish they get paid in butter."

I opened my eyes wide in amazement, and I was now almost ready to believe that my grandfather was actually making a joke. Or did people perhaps become pastors in Iceland on the sober advice of some grandfather who, because of some caprice of the history of religion, read Vídalín's Book of Sermons on Sundays instead of sacrificing to the bird Colibri, the bull Apis, or the idol Ra?

But I simply had not taken it into account that when Björn spoke, it was not always Björn who was speaking; there was someone else even closer to Björn of Brekkukot than Björn himself – my grandmother.

She said, "Björn here has always wanted little Grímur to have something from us that people could not take away from him any time they felt like it."

"Oh, they come and take it all away, my good woman," said Runólfur Jónsson. "'When one goes, another comes, and all on chestnut horses'."

My grandmother said, "Anyone who does no one any harm cannot be harmed by anything that others do. 'Learning gladdens the heart and brings renown.' Riches are what others cannot take away from you."

"On my shelf are two pouches," said the superintendent. "Time passes in them as in everything else. Actually they are both empty, except that in one of them there lies a gold coin, and it is yours, my friend. Do you want it today or later?"

"Later," I said.

That evening when I went to see Kristín of Hríngjarabær, it so happened that she was not alone; there was someone with her. I felt it the moment I went in; as I opened the door I saw a young woman sitting there, well-dressed and perfumed, wearing a broad-brimmed hat and red gloves with tassels: little Miss Gúðmúnsen. She was reading aloud from a newspaper to the old woman. On the table between them there were flowers and fruit.

"Congratulations, Álfgrímur," said the girl when she saw me at the door, and she offered me her hand without standing up.

"Eh?" I said.

"You are placed first in the paper here," she said. "'Álfgrímur Hansson, Brekkukot'. I thought you would be wearing a student's cap."

"But I find it even more remarkable that you two should know one another," I said.

"Bless the child, she doesn't know me at all, but she comes all the same with oranges," said the old woman. "Oh, how good they smell, much too good for poor old wretches like me."

"How can Garðar Hólm's mother talk like that?" said the visitor. Then she silently handed me the latest issue of the *Ísafold*, which she had just been reading aloud when I came in. The big picture of Garðar Hólm had been brought out once again and put on the front page; and the article that accompanied it was written in that extraordinary epic style which in my youth was used for momentous news in the newspapers, for instance anything

concerning the king or for major disasters at sea or if some
important person died:

"Tidings have reached us from beyond the sea that Garðar
Hólm, the world singer, will be setting foot again on Icelandic soil
shortly. The great world celebrity is on his way here from the
realm of France; during the winter he has been gladdening men's
hearts with beautiful singing south of the Alps in all the greatest
cities in that part of the world. The singer has been given an overwhelming reception by the populace in all these places, as well
as by the most important princes and other men of rank, and even
by the Pope himself, in the greatest pleasure-domes and fairy-
palaces of the goddess Thalia in those countries.

"It is rumoured in the south that when the Pope summoned
Garðar to sing for him in St. Peter's Cathedral, His Holiness
declared that this was a voice that reached the higher heavens and
glowed with a reflection of the good light. The Pope had the
singer brought to his presence and invoked a special blessing on
him, and added a papal intercession for all Icelanders."

This text went on for another two or three columns, but I
thought it unnecessary to read any further and handed the paper
back to the girl.

"Jesus!" said the girl. "So you're too high and mighty to read
what it says in the paper!"

"Isn't everything that appears in print just as true whether I
read it or not?" I said. "Isn't it?"

"I say!" she replied. "I do wish you wouldn't be so conceited,
Álfgrímur; excuse me, but I'm older than you are. I think it would
do you no harm to wear a student's cap like other students, yes
and even to read what it says in the paper, especially when it's
about your own relative. By the way, is it true that you're going to
be a singer too?"

"Who says that?" I asked.

"Our friend Madame Strúbenhols, who teaches me to play the
guitar."

"I'm off," I said, "and I'm sorry for disturbing you, I didn't know
that Kristín had visitors."

"I must be going too," said the girl, and stood up and kissed the old woman. "May Jesus be with you, Kristín dear, I'll come and see you again soon if I may. Álfgrímur, you can accompany me into town, I want to talk to you."

The outcome was that I went with her; and when we were outside on the paving I could not help reminding her that this was not the first time I had walked with her down this hill.

"Jesus, yes, there's the shed," she said, and pointed towards the old out-house in whose doorway we had met one morning the previous year. "Wasn't I completely mad?"

"Yes," I said.

"Yes, but you were stupid too," she said. "You were wearing his shoes."

She said nothing for a while, and we walked down the path together. Eventually she started up again: "What an incredibly strange woman that is."

"What woman?"

"His mother. This is the third time I've taken her flowers, and I'm no further on. I'm sure there isn't a single living person who knows what that woman thinks. She hasn't even heard her own son sing."

"Why are you bothering about her?" I asked.

"Have you ever heard him sing?" she asked.

"No," I replied.

"Try to be sincere for once and tell me the truth," she said, "you who know all about music. Speak!"

"I have heard the song of Iceland," I said, "the bluebottle for whole summers on end; and a little chirping from the birds in between. And sometimes, in the autumn, the screeching of the swan, which is called the swan's-song in Danish novels. And then of course the bawling of the drunks when the ships are in. And *Just as the One True Flower* here in the churchyard."

"Do you think it's a lie, then, that he has sung for the Pope?" said the girl.

"I don't know," I said. "Who was present when Jesus redeemed the world?"

"The woman ought at least to be able to confirm or deny whether her son is married," said the girl. "But I haven't even been able to get that out of her."

"What concern is that of yours?" I asked.

"What concern is it of mine?" said the girl. "You've always been a beastly pig."

"Will you tell me quite honestly what you want with Kristín of Hríngjarabær?" I asked.

"I don't make any secret of the fact that I have never thought about anyone else except this man ever since I was a little girl; always only him. I know he is greater than all other men. Even though he were married I would be ready to be his mistress for ever and ever. But now I've had it investigated and, thank God, if he ever was married, he has now renounced his former life completely."

"Have you poured out all this hysteria to Kristín?" I said.

"Call it what you like. I'm not talking to you because you're a decent person, but because you're related to him; and now a student. And because I simply have to say something to somebody. You know yourself how frightened I was last year. But here's the letter."

She pulled a letter from her handbag and gave it to me. It was from Denmark, and I half-thought I recognized the name on the postmark until I remembered that I had seen it on a photographer's stamp the previous summer. The photograph had been found on a man who was sleeping in the churchyard; a picture of a work-worn, rather gross woman, and two children.

I ran my eye over this Danish letter. It said something to the effect that, in reply to an inquiry, the name Garðar Hólm was unknown in these parts, and that there was no Icelander living in this town as far as was known; no one in any way connected with Iceland at all apart from a certain Hansen from Schleswig who was married to a woman who owned a little butcher's shop in the square; he was a reserved man who did not mix much with the other residents and was away from home for long periods, besides; he had once or twice signed on as a deckhand on board a ship which carried salt-fish from Icelandic ports to Spain. At the end of the letter there was some kind of official stamp and an illegible signature.

"Why are you showing me this?" I asked.

"So that you can see it was only my imagination, or some misunderstanding. Don't you know that he's coming here soon, don't you know that Daddy has invited him home to Iceland to sing at the golden jubilee of Gúðmúnsen's Store? It was perhaps childish of me to write and inquire. But I couldn't help myself, I wanted to be absolutely sure. Because I'm the one who is waiting for him. And he has written to me again. Now I know that when he comes, he is coming because of me; he is coming because he is beginning a new life."

34

GARÐAR HÓLM'S THIRD HOMECOMING

We Icelanders have always felt grateful to the Pope ever since he wrote a letter of consolation to Bishop Jón Arason shortly before the emissaries of a certain King Kristian III, a German malefactor in Denmark, led this chief clergyman of ours out to his execution. We have for a long time suspected that Popes are higher than emperors. But in one respect we had always, until now, considered what he said rather far from the truth and sometimes even a little laughable, and that was when he opened his mouth about religious faith. Yet we had now arrived at the point where we believed implicitly in his infallibility over a bit of news which came into the category of faith to the extent that we had been nowhere near when it happened, just as we had been far away when the world was being redeemed. We had fallen into the paradox of believing in one of the most improbable of the many doctrines which, rightly or wrongly, have been ascribed to the Pope.

I think I can assert that during this summer after the concert in St. Peter's Cathedral, the sun of Garðar Hólm's fame stood higher in Iceland than ever before. So it was little wonder that the student at Brekkukot had difficulty in believing that he himself had actually exchanged shoes with this man up in Kristín of Hríngjarabær's hayloft last year.

"I gave them to a Danish seaman who was sailing on a fishing vessel to Trékyllisvík," said Garðar Hólm when I asked him what had become of my boots.

At the instigation, I think, of Gúðmúnsen's Store, I had been commissioned to wait upon the world singer during those late-summer days when he was staying here in order to entertain the townspeople on the occasion of the Store's golden jubilee. This time the singer was here as the guest of the Store, and naturally there was no question of offering him accommodation in anything less than a three-roomed suite in the Hotel d'Islande.

Garðar Hólm sent me out at once to Friðriksen's bakery shop to buy twelve five-*aurar* cakes and to Mikael Lund the chemist to buy sodium bicarbonate. His suit was different to the one he had worn on previous occasions, no better than the other one indeed but brand-new from the tailor's; and the singer himself was not so physically worn as he had seemed previously, except that the heavenly light which I remembered so well from his youthful portrait was almost completely dimmed; in its place had come the smile of world fame; it never left his face when he was talking to people, but quickly, alas, turned into a tired grimace when he was by himself. Often his expression was dominated by something of the reserve that made so many people find him unapproachable, not unlike the expression characteristic of the inmates of lunatic asylums this century, but which seems to have been the permanent distinguishing feature of the faces of the more outstanding geniuses and world-famous men of the nine-teenth century, particularly the poet Baudelaire, if we are to judge by the lithograph on the title-page of *Les Fleurs du Mal.*

He kept on walking over to the mirror and practising facial expressions while he was preening himself, each one more improbable than the last, putting brilliantine on his hair and rubbing glycerine into his hands. He took out his coat and exam-ined it minutely inside and out, and carefully plucked out all the loose threads. He made me help him stack all his heavy travelling cases in various ways, but when he had rearranged them so that each case in turn had been top and bottom of the pile, he suddenly remembered that there were servants available in the building and started ringing bells. He ordered a knife to be brought so that he could tackle the cream cakes, but when at last the knife arrived it occurred to him that a fork would be a more suitable implement, and when the fork arrived he sent out for a spoon. Finally he ate the cakes with his fingers and rang for someone to find him a napkin, but when the napkin was brought he wiped his hands on his handkerchief.

He often talked in mysterious phrases which somehow only contradicted one another, and sometimes he stopped in the middle of a sentence, because it could just as well end in one way as another; or rather, perhaps, in no way at all. Often, too, it was as if he were thinking about something entirely different to what he was talking about, and he did not always hear what was being said to him, at least not coherently; but sometimes he would react with a start, like a sleeper waking up, to some perfectly ordinary remark that someone might come out with in conversation with him; he would rise from his chair with a sparkle in his eyes as if this insignificant remark had revealed some hidden truth to him. But the very next moment he had withdrawn into himself again. If he were asked something important he invariably made some irrelevant reply. Was he making fun of people? It was impossible to think of anything more hopeless than trying to question him about his private affairs, such as for instance what he had thought about the Pope.

I was now noticing peculiarities in his behaviour which had escaped me before, perhaps because I had never been with him for any length of time. When least expected he would suddenly pull pencil and paper out of his pocket, often just loose scraps, and start scribbling on them complicated figures and working out sums by some system I could not fathom; nor did I think it seemly to ask him, or to try too hard to read what he was writing. When he had engrossed himself in this arithmetic for a while, frowning heavily and often sighing deeply, he would come to again, look around almost absent-mindedly, and then smile at anyone who was present as if he were asking forgiveness for having been lost in thought, and yet with a slightly defiant look as if he were really saying, "I know the result, but I'm not telling anyone." Were they perhaps only money-sums that he kept working out apparently so endlessly?

One thing was certain, he had in his pockets an inexhaustible supply of bank-notes, carelessly rolled together, and he never bothered to bend down and pick up any money he might accidentally drop on the floor, even though it represented the price of a sheep. When he sent me out to buy cream cakes he thrust a fistful of bank-notes at me.

"That's far too much," I said. "A *króna* will do." Or as a joke I asked, "Is there perhaps a certain place one can just walk into and collect as much money as one likes?"

"One night you discover to your great surprise that you have not spent all your money that day," he said. "Next morning you wake up early and go out and buy yourself a hat – and when you have got the hat you realize that you now have even more money in your pocket. You invite a friend, two or three of them perhaps, to come with you to a restaurant, and you eat your fill of all the best food and wines available there. When you simply can't force down another bite and you leave the restaurant, you discover that you've made yet another haul while you were sitting inside. You become flurried and go and buy a house with a garden to try to rid yourself of this trash, but no sooner have you paid for the house cash down than you notice that your money has multiplied through the purchase. Now you are seized with a kind of frenzy that Björn of Brekkukot would never understand, far less your grandmother. You set off travelling round and round the world, pouring out money with both hands to other demented vagrants wherever you go, and you don't even dare to open your letters because you know that they will all say the same thing: your deposits at I don't know how many banks all over the world are still growing with ever increasing speed."

"What has happened?" I asked.

"Nothing," he said. "It's the old fairy-tale: you wanted to conquer the world, and apprenticed yourself to a sorcerer. He has taught you a couple of formulas. One morning he asks you to fetch some water and fill the barrel at the door while he is out begging. It's a contemptible job, fetching water, and you choose instead to try a magic formula. You recite Formula One and the bucket goes off on its own accord to the well. But when you see that it is going to carry on fetching the water after the barrel is full, you try Formula Two in order to stop it; but the only effect is that the bucket works even faster and fills up the whole house. In your terror you try Formula Three, and now all hell is really let loose. Soon the land sinks. And the bucket carries on and on."

"But what happened to the sorcerer himself?" I asked.

"He is sitting huddled on some steps somewhere down town, holding his hand out, and the wind knifes through the holes in his rags. The sorcerer, you see, is the person who pays no attention to profits."

35

RIBBONS AND BOWS

On the afternoon of the day he arrived, he said to me, "Go home and tidy yourself up, I'm going to take you to a party at the Hotel de la Guðmundur tonight."

It was a long, old-fashioned shop-building; older men often called it after a merchant with a Jewish surname who came to Iceland from Schleswig or Holstein in the last century. The shop was in three sections. The first section: food, which people were then beginning to call "colonial wares" after all the aromatic produce from distant corners of the world, such as pepper, cinnamon, and cloves. Next to it was the department for dry goods and small wares, with the name GUÐMUNSEN'S STORE painted in black on a rotting board above the door; and finally there was "The Schnapps", called by a Low German word that the Danes had imported to Iceland, that is to say, the liquor department. Food and schnapps had once been in the same department, until the increased fishing gave people so much more ready money that the drunks began to silt up the doorway to the shop, singing and brawling and denying entry to women who were trying to shop for food; so liquor was then moved to the other end to give the food some peace.

The merchant's residence was on the first floor, four or five drawing-rooms in a row at the front of the building. But the floor was not well enough insulated to prevent the shouting and singing of those down below from being heard upstairs.

As usual in these old merchants' houses the ceilings of the rooms were rather low. On the white-painted window-sills stood earthenware pots with weeds from the tropics like geranium and fuchsia; these pots were placed in polished copper containers, and round these containers were tied green ribbons with great big bows.

In this house there were ribbons tied in a bow round practically every single thing. The window curtains were tied up with an enormous bow at the top and held together by small silk bows at the bottom. A broad silk ribbon was tied diagonally across the sofa-back with a bow the size of a bull's rump, and one had to take care not to lean back, otherwise this gigantic knot caught you in the back. The porcelain dogs had bows; there was a bow on the bread-tray and the coal scuttle. There was a blue silk bow on the canary's cage. The cat came in with her tail in the air, stepping as carefully as if there were burning patches hidden in the floor which would scorch her pads; and Pussy too had a blue ribbon round her neck carefully tied in a bow – in this house the cat wore the same uniform as the canary. Such ribbons and bows were certainly the fashion in well-to-do homes everywhere in the Danish empire in those days, wherever they might have come from originally.

Now I had seen all the ribbons and bows in the house; but what else was there?

I think that what aroused my interest most after this was the older generation of this family, particularly the elderly women, some of whom were very ancient indeed. Here one could see a living example of that mixture of great farmers and little shop-keepers which characterized genteel families in this future capital of the nation in my youth. Foreigners have recently stated in the papers that this capital is a town in which the big wholesale merchants have the taste of little shopkeepers; and perhaps it would have been no further from the truth to say that when I was growing up, the great farmers liked the kind of things that little shopkeepers usually find beautiful, and the little shopkeepers had a taste for what the great farmers liked.

In itself it was quite astonishing that these typically Icelandic women, wearing the national costume, used an incredible number of Danish words and idioms, and I heard some of them actually conversing in this shopkeepers' Low German dialect which is more unlike Icelandic than any other tongue we know. And when they spoke Icelandic, they used the most guttural pronunciation they possibly could, as is done in northern Germany and Denmark – used it with feeling and even, I am tempted to say, with actual enjoyment; perhaps the real difference between Icelandic culture then and now lies not least in the fact that if young people have the misfortune nowadays to develop this guttural pronunciation, they go to a doctor to get the "r" moved forward to the tip of the tongue. On the other hand, there was nothing in the behaviour of these elderly ladies to remind one of Danish kindness, or good nature, or humour.

These ladies and their husbands – book-keepers, civil servants, or senior clerks of various kinds, men who have all been completely obliterated from my memory – these people all belonged to the female side of the younger Gúðmúnsen's family; the male line was represented only by his father, old Jón Guðmundsson himself, the founder of the Store. He was actually a bit "off his food" by then, as we used to say at Brekkukot, knotted, bent, and withered, and had to use a stick all the time. His face could best be compared to those rock formations in mountains; perhaps it would be closest to the truth to liken such old men to fearsome idols – and indeed they come to be worshipped often enough; and it's no disadvantage either if they happen to own more ships than other people. But I have no reason to doubt that old Jón Guðmundsson had been as highly intelligent as he was said to be; at least he was undoubtedly intelligent in the way that liquor merchants always are in comparison with their customers.

He came originally from Miðnes, one of the poorest fishing

villages in the south. In his days, a penniless person in an Icelandic fishing village had no other alternative, if he wanted to become wealthy, then to economize on food to the point of absolute starvation and use the money he saved to buy drink and sell it at a thousand per cent profit to his comrades when they were stormbound ashore. Over the door of the middle department in this old Danish shop-building there still hung, as I have said already, a small rotten board, the same one that old Jón Guðmundsson had had made to put over the door of a stone-and-turf shed in a fishing village on Reykjanes when he began the chapter in his commercial career that followed the episode of supplying his comrades with liquor from his food-box. It was a sign of his ambition that right at the very start of his career he should paint the Danicized name GUÐMUNSEN'S STORE above his door; but the name "Gúðmúnsen" had never attached itself properly to the old man himself.

"Now who is this young creature?" said the old man to his grand-daughter, and poked me with his stick after he had grunted some sort of greeting towards his former shop-assistant, Garðar Hólm.

"Grandfather, this is Álfgrímur, the student," said little Miss Gúðmúnsen. There were red blotches on her neck and beads of sweat on the tip of her nose, and she was almost gasping for breath.

"Ásgrímur?" said the old man. "Who are his people?"

"He's the foster-son of Björn of Brekkukot."

"Björn of Brekkukot!" said Jón Guðmundsson the merchant. "I should certainly know him all right. We rowed together for the late Magnús of Miðnes. We had one thing in common, neither of us drank; but the difference between us was that Björn never had any ambition, and indeed he has always lived in the most abject poverty. I'm told that his threshold is never crossed by anyone higher than workhouse paupers, vagrants, and emigrants to America. But he was always a thrifty fellow, old Björn. And there's no one who cures dried lumpfish as well as he does in the whole of Faxaflói here. I would have no hesitation in taking any boy of his to work behind the counter downstairs."

I must not forget to mention three other distinguished guests whom it would be difficult to overlook. First there was Madame Strúbenhols, whom some Icelanders referred to as the axe "Battle-Troll", my music teacher, who has already received honourable mention in these pages if I remember correctly. Next to her I must mention Professor Dr Faustulus, who had been summoned from Copenhagen with doves in a top-hat to display his art to the public at the Store's birthday party along with Garðar Hólm. This Dr Faustulus reminded me of that odd German fellow Faust who had been discussed at the Barbers' Bill meeting, except that this one turned out to be from the island of Falster originally and had earned himself fame at fairs, particularly in Jutland. Dr Faustulus played an important part in livening up this rather stiff family gathering with his genuinely Danish cheerfulness and inexhaustible inventiveness.

And I must not forget to mention also that imposing frock-coated magnate who was so often to be seen in the streets with a silver-headed ebony cane and gold-rimmed lorgnettes and an imperious air and hawk-like gaze that was often directed all the way up to the rooftops, and iron-starched cuffs and waistcoat-creases filled with snuff: the editor of the *Ísafold*, Member of Parliament, and – I will not say "national poet", because every second person of any importance in Iceland in those days claimed to be that, but rather just "poet", as will soon be proved in these pages. But within the Gúðmúnsen family circle he laid aside his sovereignty and bowed right down to the ground when he greeted the other guests; he even bowed to me in some confusion and bared his teeth, which were green with tartar, and congratulated me on having graduated from the Grammar School, called me "man of promise", "Iceland's white hope", "student Hansen", "our nation's hope of future glory", and various other things of a kind that was reckoned sheer hysteria in our own house.

But the greeting I received from the host himself was scarcely less meticulous.

"*Bonjour*, my dear fellow-countryman and *Herr Stu-dent*," said merchant Gúðmúnsen, accenting the "*-dent*" heavily, as was the custom in those days among people who knew their etiquette.

"An unexpected honour! *Italia terra est. Sardinia insula est.* May I have the pleasure of introducing the stu-*dent* to this world-famous professor and doctor who has come here with doves in a hat? And also to our most distinguished Danish Muse, the axe "Battle-Troll", whom I shall nevertheless permit myself to call Madame Lorgnette; she has promised to play Liszt's Rhapsodies for us after dinner."

I think that Gúðmúnsen himself was the only person in that whole family with some remnants of a Danish disposition in his blood, combined with a certain lightness of demeanour, as well as a humour which often partly or, indeed, entirely, hides the inner person – or can at least give a misleading impression; but it could well be that he had to a certain extent adopted this demeanour in Denmark, where he had been a shop-apprentice in his youth.

He took me by the arm and led me over to a wall, where he showed me a huge oleograph of a lion.

"My dear student Hansen," he said. "I'll bet you've never seen anything like that at Brekkukot! That's a lion."

"Indeed?" I said. "No, I'm afraid I've never seen a lion."

"That's exactly what lions in zoos look like, except of course that this one is twice as large as an ordinary lion," said the merchant. "It's not so funny if a beast like that comes at you and wants to bite you."

"Do lions bite?" I asked. "I thought they just gobbled you up."

"*Oui, oui,* yes, *oui,* of course a lion gobbles you up," said the merchant, and roared with laughter. "So it's better to have a care, eh? *You have a map and a ruler,* ha-ha-ha!"

Nature in some fit of absent-mindedness had neglected to give this fully fifty-year-old man the proper marks of age. He had a little toothbrush moustache on his upper lip, and his hair was cut equally carefully; but now as before, when I had first looked at his cheeks, I could not help thinking of the plums in my grandmother's rhymes. But even though he was such a cheerful ruddy-cheeked fellow, or perhaps just because of this, he could suddenly become very serious and start saying something sharp in the middle of his boyish antics; and because he was not quite sure whether his words of wisdom were appropriate, or the phrasing opportune, he would peer round rather furtively to see whether his remark had gone home; and if he saw no signs to that effect he would burst into loud laughter so that people would think he had not really meant what he had said but had merely been trying to shock people for fun with some dubious contention, even trying to test their credulity, but was ready to take it all back again. I imagine that underneath it all, merchant Gúðmúnsen suffered from shyness and fear of ridicule, which was how in my youth we described all manner of things which are now given Freudian names. There was one face in particular which he always studied like a barometer to see what success he was having, and that was the face of the person who had tied ribbons and bows on both the cat and on the birds that the cat most wanted to eat. And this was really no surprise, for Mrs Gúðmúnsen came of both an older and a better family than he did; and though her lineage would not have been reckoned in Brekkukot better than that of Adam in age or quality, I can at least say to her family's credit that Iceland had won as regards this woman's bearing and appearance, and no doubt her very soul as well, because she never wore Danish dresses and never let herself be lured to visit Denmark.

Icelandic national costume, as we all know, has three grades, and even its lowest grade is loaded with more gold and silver than any other costume with the exception of the get-ups of emperors and army generals; thus the national costume of Icelandic women was the most unlikely national costume in the world to become the uniform of destitute mountain-crofters, as was the case with the national costumes of other lands. Mrs Gúðmúnsen was wearing the grade suitable to an occasion of this importance, namely the second grade, and I will not attempt to say how much wealth she was wearing on her bodice in gold and precious stones; but it would be generally agreed that few emperors or army generals would have borne their gold with greater authority than this genuinely Icelandic Mrs Gúðmúnsen (despite all her Danish gutturals) as she sailed majestically through her rooms and saw to it that no article was without its ribbon and bow.

In accordance with the peculiar custom that used to be followed in Iceland if one wanted to show exceptional hospitality, visitors were first of all offered coffee and cakes before the meal itself; it could be that this custom was a relic of the times when there was no other fuel available than peat, and slow-burning stuff it was too, so that visitors often had to wait for hours for the roast meat and pudding, and therefore there was no alternative but to serve light refreshment to blunt the keenest edge of hunger during the waiting. There was no question of slow cooking in this case, however, but rather a loyalty to an old tradition of hospitality in Reykjanes; and not until the guests had regaled themselves on pancakes, doughnuts, fruit-cake, tart, pastries, and about twenty other kinds of biscuits along with coffee and cream was there any attempt made to prepare the table for the banquet itself.

I said earlier that I had thought the party rather heavy going. Was it not remarkable that a pillar of the community like Gúðmúnsen should be content to eat with his family in honour of his protegé, a famous Icelandic world-figure, on the day of his homecoming – a man who according to the Store's mouthpiece had recently been giving a concert for the Pope – instead of holding a banquet for him and inviting to it other pillars of the community? Did not such a guest have a right to an even grander reception than this one from his patron and protector? What did this family party signify? Was this feast an invitation to Garðar Hólm to become a member of the family without further cere-mony? Despite the ribbons and bows on the cat and the canary, the gold-laden cousins and aunts, the Rhapsodies by Liszt, and the most lavish hospitality imaginable in Iceland from bramble-berries all the way down to porridge, I still could not fathom the meaning of this party. The family's attitude to this famous man was, to put it mildly, rather ambiguous. Granted that the appreci-ation of a famous singer was somewhat lacking among people who did not know what singing was – but what exactly was this man in their eyes? Or had the former shop-assistant Georg Hansson from Hríngjarabær just been fished out and tied with a ribbon and bow for this one evening because they wanted to mislead someone about something? And if so, whom, and about what? What had happened since little Miss Gúðmúnsen had been locked in her room the previous summer? It was only a few weeks since she had confided to me that it was she who was waiting for Garðar Hólm, but all evening I saw no sign that any understanding had been established between the singer and the merchant's daughter; it was quite obviously a rule in this house that the daughter should not know this guest better than any of the others; they pretended scarcely to see one another; but on the other hand it was not clear to me who was putting on an act for whom.

Was this an act put on for my benefit and for Madame Strúbenhols? Or for Professor Dr Faustulus? It was surely not for the benefit of the Store's confidant, who wore such an imperious mask every day in Löngustétt but put on a lackey's face when he was invited in behind the counter? But there was one thing that was not play-acting – the red blotches that came and went like fleeting clouds on the neck of the daughter of the house.

The first of the courses that were sent through to the large table in the centre room consisted of sugar-browned potatoes accompanied by all kinds of jams and sauces so thick as to be almost solid; then came, one after the other, such varied commodities as toasted white bread and smoked lamb, pickled whale and sardines; and then, as sudden as a Jack-in-the-box, there came steaming hot blood-sausage. Hard on its heels came singed sheeps'-heads and bilberries mixed with lovely red brambleberries; and then other provisions that it would take too long to enumerate. It was almost as if one had broken into a food-shop. Here each and every person could eat his fill according to his own particular fads and fancies about nourishment, and each in his own way too; some started with the toasted white bread and ended with the pickled whale, others began with brambleberries and ended with the sheeps'-heads or sour whey – for drinks were served as well, cows' milk and French red wine in addition to the liquid already mentioned. Bringing up the rear came a soup tureen filled with incredibly thick porridge, which was set before the old patriarch Jón Guðmundsson; in accordance with some doctrine from Scotland, this particular dish was at that time considered particularly wholesome for the stomach.

When the torrent of food from the kitchen began to abate,

merchant Gúðmúnsen invited the guests to take their places at the table, and people seated themselves wherever they liked, with the exception of the hostess who, by old Icelandic custom, stood in the middle of the room and supervised the serving. Merchant Gúðmúnsen called upon Madame Strúbenhols, who was sitting beside Professor Dr Faustulus, to produce her mandolin. The editor of the *Ísafold* reached into his pocket and distributed copies of a table-song which he had composed and printed, entitled *Table-song for Family and Friends, to be Sung at the Table to the Tune of* Don Giovanni *by Mozart.* Surprising as it may seem, there was no mention in the title of the occasion for this "Family and Friends Party", so people had to decide for themselves whether they were there to celebrate the jubilee of Gúðmúnsen's Store or to welcome a friend and compatriot who had carried Iceland's fame throughout the whole wide world, even to the Pope as well as to Mohammed ben Ali. But whatever the nature of the party may have been, and for whatever reason the people were assembled, or whether this was just a normal evening meal in the house, people now began to sing the poem printed for the occasion. Unfortunately, the singing was less robust than it might have been, for several of the guests were without their spectacles. The poet himself, however, seemed to enjoy his own poem tolerably well, and not only had to lead the singing but even to sing whole verses solo; but merchant Gúðmúnsen let loose great bursts of song every now and again, and his voice rose above everyone else if he was lucky enough to hit on the right line in the printed text. Garðar Hólm listened to the singing with inscrutable grimaces and gestures; the patriarch Jón Guðmundsson, on the other hand, paid no heed to such tomfoolery and straight away started on his porridge, and mumbled to himself throughout the singing. No sooner had Madame Strúbenhols laid aside her mandolin at the end of the song than Professor Dr Faustulus pulled seven eggs and a small dried fish from the top of this talented lady's dress.

This was the opening of the poem, according to the printed copy which can be found among the pamphlets in the National Library:

"What the gods like most, they say,
Is yeast done up in their own way;
But smoked lamb, berries, curds and whey
Are quite enough to make my day.
Smoked lamb, berries, curds and whey
Are what I choose whene'er I may;
But what the gods like most, they say,
Is only yeast done up their way."

One of the elderly ladies in national costume turned to the world singer Garðar Hólm, whom she had managed to confuse with Professor Dr Faustulus, and asked with great dignity:

"Are they not very short of meat in Denmark, Doctor? I have heard that the poor people over there live on practically nothing but cabbage and beans."

The singing had only just stopped echoing in people's ears. Suddenly it was as if from out of the singer's dark enigmatic grin there stepped an old spinster, dressed up to the nines, who began to whine in a ghastly falsetto a nonsensical verse to the same melody from *Don Giovanni*. I was not very sure what meaning the company saw in this extraordinary performance; some of them perhaps thought that this was the final verse of the table-song, and indeed there is no doubt that the poet's face lengthened as he listened. Everyone stared at the singer except the patriarch Jón Guðmundsson, who went on eating his porridge. For all I know, the people there were thinking that this very sound, this old woman's whine, was the famous world-singing that had so charmed the Pope. Certainly, no one smiled. Madame Strúbenhols merely raised and lowered her head in order to be able to study this man from beneath her spectacles, through them, and over them. Professor Dr Faustulus stopped pulling food out of the top of Madame's dress for a while, and stared dumbfounded; it was as if no dove from anyone's top-hat had ever taken this conjurer quite so much by surprise before.

This must have been the first time that the world singer was heard singing in Iceland:

"Cabbage is all they have to eat,
Dear lady, since there is no meat;
The guttersnipes sit in the street,
And utter their pathetic bleat.
The guttersnipes sit in the street
And chorus their pathetic bleat,
Cabbage, when there is no meat,
Is all, dear lady, tradara . . . "

There was dead silence for a moment after Garðar Hólm had finished this extraordinary number. Young Gúðmúnsen glanced quickly round the table to study the reactions of the guests, and saw at once that no one was even smiling. As if to cover up for this unexpected entertainment he burst into a roar of laughter, shouted "Hurrah! Bravo!" and clapped vigorously. Then he looked round again and suddenly stopped laughing. No one else had clapped. The guests ate and drank in silence for a while. And then soon afterwards the merchant rose from his seat, placed two fingers to his lips, and cleared his throat genteelly; he adopted the attitudes and gestures of a trained orator, although he could not help looking a little like a small boy who was pretending to make a speech. He pushed his chair back carefully, raised his head with affected composure, and blinked a few times while he was searching for the right opening; and then the speech came:

"I am going to permit myself to say a few words to welcome our world-famous friend, who is so famous that if we could for a moment imagine just how overwhelming his fame really is, no one here would dare to talk to him, but only talk about him – yes, and scarcely even that."

The orator now threw a glance at his wife to see whether she was not feeling rather proud at having a husband who knew how to get up and make a speech.

In the style of some skilled orators or other he had in mind he now conjured up a little text on which to build his thesis; it was from the German Primer:

"As it says in a famous book," said merchant Gúðmúnsen:

"*Ein Englander der kein Wort Französisch sprechen konnte reiste nach Paris.*"

At this the orator looked hard at his wife. There now followed a long and pregnant silence, and a few beads of sweat appeared on the tip of the orator's nose.

"Did I say a famous man? Did I say a great man? Ahem. Yes, and I stand by that. Woe unto those who cast doubt on that. Isn't that true, Herr editor? And yet Garðar Hólm is not too big to have been more or less a member of this family at this table for more than ten years, even though his fame is now at its height, not least since he began to earn his living in front of Mohammed ben Ali and the Pope. To put it briefly: *Italia terra est.* Ha-ha-ha! Cheers, my dear compatriots. May I drink your health?

"Now then, to get back to what I was going to say. Ahem.

"For all those years, ever since he was a shop-assistant downstairs in the liquor shop here, Garðar Hólm, otherwise known as little Georg from Hríngjarabær, that is to say Georg Hansson, has been my brother and son; and not just my brother and son and my wife's and my father's, but also my wife's and my daughter's brother and son. As it were – *Sardinia insula est.*

"We live in a new age. In the old days, when my father was in his prime, people contented themselves with a drop of liquor, which only cost them twenty-five *aurar* a quart anyway; and the most that sober fishermen could achieve was to put aside a few sovereigns in their sea-chests for their heirs. But now the only way to run a fishing business is to own a bank; or at least to have connections with money institutions. And indeed, we have not only put machines in our ships and we are not only buying trawlers as fast as we can, but we have also founded a bank in which the populace can hoard money. And we have hired a famous accountant, theologian, and socialist to manage this bank.

"Selling salt-fish to countries in the south isn't enough any more. One day you go to Copenhagen as a fine gentleman, and what happens? The papers call you a salt-fish baron. Because although salt-fish is one of the most expensive cargoes that can be carried between countries by sea, because it's so heavy when it's pressed, salt-fish is nevertheless a laughable commodity in itself.

And what I am trying to say, my dear children, friends, relatives, and worthy compatriots, is this: salt-fish has to have a ribbon and bow. And it isn't enough that Icelandic fish should have Danish ribbons and bows; it has to have the ribbon of international fame. In a word, we have to prove to the rest of the world that 'the fish can sing just like a bird'. And that is why we who sell the fish have made great efforts to improve the cultural life of the nation to show and to prove, both internally and externally, that we are the people who not only haul the grey cod out of the depths of the sea but also tie a ribbon and bow round its neck for the delectation of the world, as it says in the book: *er ging in ein Wirtshaus hinein um zu Mittag zu essen.*

"I know that it surprises you, my love, that I am an educated man, because my father made me start working in the Store instead of going to Grammar School when I was a boy. I have had to learn languages at night when you had gone to sleep, my love, so that I could hold my own in refined company out in the world. But there was one thing I learned in the liquor shop downstairs, and that was never to get drunk. My motto, as my father knows, has always been 'Machinery, not Alcohol'."

"Yes, Guðmundur," old Jón Guðmundsson said, raising his head from his porridge. "You are right. I have always been a teetotaller. I have always said that people should not have liquor, but should save their money and stay at home when they are stormbound; that's the best entertainment for the people. And then people are glad to get away from home and out to sea again. People who drink are nothing but damned cookhouse-lubbers and idle louts. I have suffered more losses from drunkenness and idleness than any other ship-owner in Iceland."

"Quite so, my dear father," said young Gúðmúnsen. "Absolutely. We are involved in progress. Machinery is with us now. And country clergymen like my forefather Pastor Snorri of Húsafell are no good now, even though they knew how to exorcize ghosts. Now we have to have culture. The best-looking girls want to have famous men – all except my wife, she fell in love with me. Good health, my dear, may I have the honour of proposing a toast to you? – *er setzte sich an einen Tisch und nahm die Speisekarte.*

"We here in the Store have sent you out, my dear opera singer Garðar Hólm, to preach Icelandic culture abroad . . ."

"Eh?" said the old man. "That's a lie. To the best of my knowledge we sacked him, to put it bluntly, because he was negligent, unpunctual, and impertinent, and caused nothing but trouble in the Store."

Merchant Gúðmúnsen went on as if nothing had happened.

"Ahem," he said. "I admit that we didn't have the good fortune to understand the opera singer to begin with. Who has the courage to acknowledge a singer here in Iceland? Begging your pardon, but who knows the front from the back end of singing here in Iceland? On the other hand, I was the first person to acknowledge his recognition immediately it was achieved in Denmark.

"I shall never forget how dumbfounded I was the year after Georg was sacked; I was on a visit to Copenhagen as the guest of my faithful old friend, Jensen the butcher, and also the hard-tack bakery manager from Aalborg. You see, as you no doubt remember well, Herr opera singer, we had sent you to a slaughter-house in Copenhagen when it became quite obvious that you could not be of any use in our liquor shop; we had your welfare at heart, despite everything, my dear compatriot.

"Anyway, Jensen now said to me, 'The story of Herold has repeated itself: the Icelander you sent me has a bigger voice than anyone else in the slaughterhouse. I had him into my office along with my brother-in-law Sörensen, the manager, who plays the tuba at Aalborg. There's always a terrific din in slaughterhouses, as everyone knows,' Jensen the butcher said to me, 'especially when you are slaughtering eleven hundred pigs a day. The number of times I have said to my brother-in-law Sörensen, Sörensen, there is only one slaughterhouse in Denmark which can drown the orchestra at Aalborg, and that's my slaughterhouse. But when we had heard the Icelander bawling all those songs about the trolls, outlaws, and ghosts that you have in Iceland, we were absolutely flabbergasted; we sent the man straight to a professor. Next day he came back with a certificate'.

"'Bring him in here,' I said, 'as my name is Gúðmundur de la Gúðmúnsen!'

"And what do you think my fine friends in Denmark had pulled out of the hat? None other than our little Georg Hansson here from Hríngjarabær, whom my father had sacked from his liquor shop the year before! And the certificate was as genuine as any royal official certificate in Denmark can be, with a proper stamp and everything from the Conservo-lavatory: 'This man is a world's wonder, he only needs some German and Italian schooling to become world-famous'.

"Or was it from the Lotterio-observatory? I won't go into any details, except to say that I put my hand into my pocket without a word, pulled out my wallet, and said to Denmark's manager, 'Here you are, how much do I pay?'

"To this little story I just want to add that I had an inkling that my friends in Denmark had already arranged among themselves to send this Icelander to Germany and Italy. I thought this rather a poor show, and so did my dear respected father, despite the fact that he has never been considered exactly extravagant and has always lived in more straitened circumstances than any other man in Iceland of his time and has tasted nothing except porridge for a whole generation and worn only clothes which our shop-assistants have discarded; we both thought it would be the crowning disgrace for the nation if a young good-for-nothing, whom Gúðmúnsen's Store could not even find a use for in the liquor shop, should be exalted by Danish butchers to become world-famous, perhaps even to become a genius, as the Danes had done for Albert Thorvaldsen and Niels Finsen. We are Independence men, my father and I, we want separation from Denmark, and so does our newspaper, the *Ísafold*. I asked, and father asked, and the whole Store asked: is it not now time that we Icelanders, who are busy moving out of the rowing-boat age into the machinery age, began to acquire something ourselves to prove that Iceland is no longer inhabited by the same seals that lived here before the year 874 when that first merchant, Ingólfur Arnarson, set up shop here in this very place where we are now? Since the leaders of reputable Danish enterprises took their oath on it, and there was a certificate available from first-rate Danish professors, that here was an Icelander who could sing louder than a slaughterhouse in which eleven hundred pigs were being slaughtered a day, not to mention the tuba at Aalborg, was it not obvious that we here at home, who until then had only hauled in silent fish, should pull ourselves together and spit in the pisspot and stop merely being damned salt-fish barons as the Danes say, and start making the fish open its mouth to some purpose?

"And with that I gave orders that this man was to be given a new frock-coat and a tile-hat and made into a full-size genius, all at the Store's expense, and sent out into the wide world in order to make Iceland famous. The time has come to stop talking about Egill Skallagrímsson who vomited in people's faces. The time has come to realize an ambitious Icelandic paradox, like the one I referred to earlier:

> 'The fish can sing just like a bird,
> And grazes on the moorland scree,
> While cattle in a lowing herd
> Roam the rolling sea.'

"I say, and have always said, and will always say: the fish that does not sing throughout the whole world is a dead fish. It is high time that we here in Iceland started to have singing fish with a ribbon and bow. Welcome home, my dear compatriot, to your old and new table here in Löngustétt! We believe in you! You are this nation's singing fish, even though it is I, de la Guðmundur, who says so! Your health!"

Merchant Gúðmúnsen had scarcely finished his speech nor begun to reap his due applause, nor even had time to peer at his wife's face to see how she had liked it, before Garðar Hólm the opera singer was on his feet and had started his reply.

"I have the honour," said the opera singer, "of being present at one of the most magnificent banquets and sumptuous out-pourings of hospitality that has ever been given for gold-braided people in Europe in our time – in this new age which has started in the almanac, even though we have no proof at all, far from it, that time moves forward. Anyway, the day has come, whether time moves forwards or backwards, that I must say the few words I owe to this house, this fine house that not only ties ribbons and bows round the cat and the canary but has bought fame for fish and has refuted the old saying: 'livestock dies'.

"Once upon a time a king and queen were in their kingdom and a peasant and his wife in their cottage: I shall try to tell you the story as far as it goes. In this house, in that very place downstairs where our beloved patriarch Jón Guðmundsson has been emperor over far more non-singing fish than any other Icelander has ever been before, a little peasant boy began his singing; or rather, here he became notorious for bawling and bellowing. It was during the years that our host, de la Guðmundur, so called because it was the fashion to speak French here in Löngustétt in those days, was improving himself out in Copenhagen along with those pork-worshippers, hard-tack bakers and double basses he has described for us this evening. In those days the Store was patronized by Icelanders who no longer got any enjoyment out of begetting children in sobriety, and some with some justice, for dry land in Iceland has always been just as dangerous for the children as the sea has been for their fathers. When they had returned half of their children, or even more, to mother earth, many Icelanders started the habit of investing the rest of their income in a battleship, to quote old Runólfur Jónsson, one of the greatest cookhouse-lubbers and Chief Justices there has ever been in Iceland. When these people had acquired their battleship they screeched *O'er the Icy Sandy Wastes* until they started weeping. Then they sobbed *Oh, Thou Sweet and Cooling Well of the World* until they lost the power of speech and lay flat on their backs on paths and thresholds – that's what is called being 'dead' in Iceland. And respectable ladies who wanted to go into the Store to buy pepper for their eternal fish had to step over these men."

"I have always been a prohibitionist," interrupted Jón Guðmundsson; he had leaned forward over his porridge and was using his hand as an ear-trumpet in order to hear the speech. "And I can't help it if stupidity is so ingrown in people. When I was young I liked cod-liver oil; but I mixed it with tar so that I would not drink too much of it. I am eighty-five years old now, and I have never drunk anything to speak of other than whey, although I use skim milk on porridge. And there were some people who never sang at all, thank God."

Garðar Hólm the opera singer went on: "When the people had finished burying these forty or fifty out of every hundred children which it was then the custom to bury in Iceland, with wholesome and genuine sorrow, they used to challenge the Store to a battle of singing, and wheeled out no less formidable war-chariots than the Andrew *rímur*, in which people are knifed like tallow or sliced like meat-paste. Then there was nothing for it but to give a good account of oneself, ladies and gentlemen! My voice had only just broken round about then. I am not going to describe for you in any great detail the greatest of all the victories I won, when I realized that in a singing combat with one of the biggest louts and braggarts in this community I had managed to make him so hoarse that he could not raise a single squeak, and the concert could only be finally settled with fisticuffs. Yes, the singing combats I waged in defence of the Store's good name are without number. Indeed I am not boasting but merely stating a fact when I tell you that before I was fully eighteen years old there was scarcely a single bawling baboon whom I did not sing down to hell the moment he came through the door of the Store. My dear old sea- and liquor-man, Jón Guðmundsson, you who have never seen the southern nesses sink beneath the horizon, and have never drunk anything other than whey; and you, dear de la Guðmundur, Knight of the Danish Order of Dannebrog and linguist and so much more than I can count – accept at last the thanks of your counter-jumper from the liquor-shop whom you wanted to make a butcher's-boy in Denmark."

36

EVENING AT THE ARCHANGEL GABRIEL'S TOMB

"Perhaps you are going to accept their offer and become one of their shop-assistants?" said Garðar Hólm when we were outside in the street again.

He had not stayed for very long after he had made his speech

of thanks; excusing himself by saying that he had promised to
look in on the King's Minister, he rose and made his farewells.
But once we were outside he made no attempt whatsoever to
set course for the Governor's house, but headed straight for the
churchyard.

"Who knows?" I said. "My grandfather actually wants me to
study for the church. But I was unlucky enough to be dux of the
school, and it's said that duxes never become anything."

"I have no doubt they will send you to music college and pay all
the expenses if they discover you can sing louder than the drunks
downstairs in the shop – but most particularly if the Danes tell
them that you can bawl louder than pigs. But I want to tell you
in advance that no one gets a double-chin from becoming their
spiritual table-guest. Christmas-time will see you turn into some
side street in a foreign city and fumble for any loose change that
might be lurking somewhere in your pockets, and try to work out
whether you have enough for a cup of coffee in some bistro where
there may be a fire in the grate. You see, the cheque you were
expecting from Iceland has not arrived in time for Christmas,
any more than it did the previous year. You have no friends. You
walk home. You huddle under the threadbare strip of blanket
that goes with the rented room and you put your tattered overcoat
on top to try to get the Christmas shivers out of your bones. I
know that it takes a real man to attain that one pure note; many
have given all that they had, even their physical and mental
health, and died without ever having attained it. And yet they were
to be envied, compared with those others who became famous
singers without ever knowing that the one pure note existed; and
they were happy in comparison with those few who came near it
for a moment, or even actually attained it."

We were sitting on the low bench-shaped tombstone on the
grave of the late Archangel Gabriel.

"Does the cheque never arrive, then?" I asked.

"Your heart misses a beat every time the postman rings the
bell, sometimes thrice a day, sometimes six times. You have been
hoping against hope that the miracle would happen now, during
this last quarter of an hour before holy Christmas Eve comes

in at six o'clock. Christmas after Christmas you wait in foreign cities for the postman's last call on Christmas Eve; but the famous cheque from Iceland never comes. No creature in the whole universe is so deeply embedded and hard to dislodge as the cheque from Iceland. It is not because Gúðmúnsen's Store is a bad shop. But it's not exactly a music shop. When he has provisioned something like twenty ships with hard-tack biscuits, and tied a ribbon and bow round the coal scuttle, and found a new cord for the editor's lorgnettes, and supplied a packet of pins for the forty-ninth aunt, it may well be that Guðmundur suddenly thinks, 'Oh, hell, I almost forgot all about culture itself, where on earth did I put Zoëga's English Primer that I was going to study tonight when my wife had fallen asleep? And wait a minute, didn't the Store have some singer or other wandering around abroad somewhere?' But it might well be March by then, perhaps even April. Who knows, you might see a few pound notes before spring."

"I think I would rather try to get myself a job in the fishing industry abroad, rather than wait until I was quite dead," I said.

"And give up singing?" he asked.

"I suppose so," I said. "At least, my grandfather reckons that fish comes first in every man's life."

"If you are not prepared to starve this Christmas, like the last one, and like next Christmas and the Christmases thereafter, and wake up with numb fingers and shuddering with cold on Christmas night, and feel the weight of all the sorrows of creation upon you, that is because you lack the string."

"I'm afraid I'm too stupid to understand that," I said. "What string?"

He replied, "The one that does not give you power over heaven and earth."

"What does it give, then?" I asked.

"One tear-drop for the creation of the world," said the singer.

We sat silent for a while under the marble statue of the Archangel in the late-summer dusk, and there was scarcely a breath of wind to stir the tansies.

"Then there are other days," said Garðar Hólm. "*Im wunderschönen Monat Mai, als alle Knospen sprangen*. Schumann. Heine.

And the Rhine. One morning a group of young people go on a pleasure-trip up the river, and you are out the whole day. You come to an old orchard and dance a reel, you go into a cool medieval inn and drink out of age-old tankards. The girls in the party are wearing national costume, in peasant tradition. And in the evening when you are sailing home and the moon is riding high in the heavens, before you know it one of the girls is snuggling against you in the night breeze as you sit there in the stern of the ferry boat looking out on the wake streaming away behind you. It's the same girl that came right into your arms during the dance. And now she's tired, and nestles her face against your cheek. She pretends to sleep. And when it's time to part she whispers, 'Are you going to see me tomorrow?'

"But tomorrow, of course, she's no longer a folk-dancer in national costume. She's a well-bred and educated girl, dressed in big-city style, even rather grand in manner. The restaurant where she had arranged to meet you especially recommends its caviare. She asks you when you will have finished learning singing. Later she calls it 'this singing'. Finally she says 'this blessed singing'. In other words, 'When are you going to stop this damned bawling?' How do you answer then?

"If you answer, 'Never', she thinks you're exceptionally droll and laughs and laughs; and her laughter, moreover, is absolutely real. She asks you what in the world you are going to do when you have finished learning singing; and if you reply, 'Nothing', she laughs again. It's rare to meet such an unusually amusing man. You are older than all other people. You must be a millionaire since you can afford to permit yourself to be so droll. 'I'm from Gúðmúnsen's Store in Iceland', you say; is it surprising that she wants to meet such a droll fellow as often as possible? Finally she takes you home to meet her parents: Sunday lunch with white wine, and a polite stroll in the park afterwards. Then she says, 'Won't you give up singing, if only for my sake, and come and work in my daddy's office, he's got a business that bakes a hundred tons of hard-tack biscuits a day' (or slaughters eleven hundred pigs – or was it eighteen hundred pigs?) 'and plays the double bass on Sundays. Perhaps we'll get married; and in a year you'll be a head clerk there. And the following year perhaps a sub-manager. Finally we would own the bakery' (if it's a bakery – the slaughterhouse if it's a slaughterhouse) 'you and I. And you will play the double bass with pork-worshippers and hard-tack biscuit bakers on Sundays'."

When Garðar Hólm had told me this part of my life story he asked me one of the most difficult questions that has ever been asked on the Archangel Gabriel's tombstone. He said to me: "What do you do now?"

Many a man has had difficulty in answering this question.

"My grandmother would say, 'You are what you are yourself, and nothing else'," I said.

"That's where she's wrong, the old woman," said Garðar Hólm. "What a man is himself is the one thing he is not. A man is what other people think he is. Do you imagine that the Emperor of Japan is an emperor, really? No, he's just like every other poor wretch. And therefore you say to the girl, 'No thanks, I'm going to be a world singer.'

"I know this is a difficult hour in your life," Garðar Hólm went on. "You study the girl from tip to toe, you note what a healthy complexion she has, how neatly she does her hair; or let us say, the way she walks with her head held high, as they say in Iceland, heavens above! Do you imagine that a better match could be found anywhere else in the world? The story has now reached the point where the peasant's son has met the king's daughter: you will get both the princess and the kingdom on the day you give up singing. So what do you do?

"Words fail you," said Garðar Hólm. "She looks at you expectantly, awaiting your reply. But you remain silent, because the woman hasn't been born yet who can understand you. If you had never suspected it before, you realize at that moment that there is nothing on earth more perfect than a woman – in her own way, and within her own limits. And you silently take your leave of her and walk away – for ever.

"In the evening, when you get back to your room, you pack the few things you own: one pair of socks and a shirt; and the old shoes you wear when it's wet; and two neckties because you're a fine gentleman; and seven handkerchiefs because Franz Schubert only owned seven handkerchiefs when he died, and besides that, you are rather prone to colds, like all singers. And don't forget your book of voice-training exercises; and the book of Passion Psalms from your mother in Iceland, don't forget that, dear friend, for that's to be laid on your breast when you are dead. You catch the night train out of the city. And you never go back there again."

My life story had now reached the point where it made little difference how I replied; so I said nothing.

"Listen, don't look so depressed, old fellow. This is what all of Heine's poems are like, it's only peasants who don't laugh at them; or rather, perhaps, Calvinists. Abroad, it's the normal practice that if someone is looking really sad in the street, a horde of fat men comes running over waving cheque-books and hire him for a circus; they teach people like that to ride a bicycle which disintegrates when they try to mount it, or else make them play a stringless fiddle with a broomstick.

"Listen, would you not rather go with a choir to America, my friend? A hundred dollars a month and all found. And now your luck is knocking at your door, horse-luck, fluke – the only luck a good Icelander ever recognizes: good fortune.

"And very soon there arrives in America one of these solemn, self-important German-Scandinavian choral societies which are representing European culture on a goodwill mission and trying to increase mutual understanding between the two continents. Such a decorous society is of course all dressed up in the ceremonial clothes that the Danes call white-tie-and-tails, but which the Americans use chiefly for corpses. In America, on the other hand, choral singing is never heard except as a comic turn, so it arouses twice the mirth when the buffoons come on stage dressed like corpses. The sprinkling of lumberjacks who bought tickets because they were related to the singers quickly fall asleep or flee, and there is no one left except a few caustic newspapermen and some girls who are looking for a husband; or some circus-managers looking for an act. And now it so happens that you are asked to sing the solo part in a choral work, let's say it is something by Handel. You step forward when your turn comes; and the spotlight falls on a face that is more serious-looking than a frozen spruce-cone in this company of shroud-covered berserks.

"You raise your eyes; and it's as if all the people wake up. And when you open your mouth and the first notes are forming in your throat, pumped out from the depths of your heart – hmm, no, we won't talk about that, no one understands the heart. But anyway, it's a long time since such a serious face has been seen in a country where the glossy magazine smile is a public duty. Besides, the Mosaic Law of singing is Always Smiling – *sempre sorridente*. You start singing with a voice-tone that vacillates between a pastoral poem and a war-cry. A pastoral poem sung by a heroic tenor, that is comedy itself raised to the nth degree. And the laughter comes rolling at you in waves."

It was little wonder that I now began to grow hot under the collar, and I asked abruptly, "Is that how I sing, then?"

"Yes, that's how you sing," he said. "And that damned Icelander had thus managed to ruin this triumphal German-Scandinavian tour right at the start, and now it is the conductor himself who says to you, 'It's odds on that if you ever show your face in this choir again, we shall all be drowned in laughter here in America.'

"You shut yourself in your hotel room that evening and start trying to think, even though it's rather pointless the way things are now. Perhaps you also say to yourself, 'This is Garðar Hólm's fault, the man who sat on the late Archangel Gabriel's tombstone and listened to me singing *Just as the One True Flower* over a man without a face – it was he who put the idea into my head that I possessed that string of grace, that note which reached the heart and could call forth that useless salt water we call tears.'

"And then, that very same evening that your singing career has been shattered, suddenly the door of your room is thrown open and a well-known concert organizer is standing in front of you and starts to embrace you and kiss you. 'Dearest beloved act,' he says, and waves his cheque-book, 'you are almost as good as the man who plays a stringless fiddle with a broomstick. You have those tired, despairing, bloodhound's-eyes which almost equal Grock himself. I'll dress you in a seaman's blouse and send you across the length and breadth of the United States with a company of comedians. I ask nothing of you except that you sing that funny solo by Handel, and sing it for yourself just as you did this evening without paying any heed to the people who come to listen – just so long as you promise to lift up those incredible Icelandic eyes of yours a few times during the recital!'"

When my life story had reached this point, Garðar Hólm paused again in his narrative and asked, "What do you do now?"

"I don't want to be a famous half-wit," I said.

He said, "Fame is just as good however it is achieved, my friend. Fame is like the Koh-i-noor jewel that miscreants from the Punjab stole and gave to the English king to put in his crown. That German-Scandinavian European cultural association you were committed to has told you to go to hell; and at the same moment an American comedy troupe arrives and offers you all the money and all the fame that a clown can possibly earn in this world. What do you do? The choice is to become a funny dramatic singer who is shown the door wherever he goes, or a sad clown for whom all doors are open. Now you have to be very clear about what a man seeks in his art. Did you want anonymity? Or were you seeking fame?"

I said, "Unearned fame seems to me no fame at all; at the very most it would be someone else's fame."

Garðar Hólm said, "Does the English king deserve to wear the Koh-i-noor diamond?"

"I think the only person who can wear it is the man who can match its value within himself," I said.

"That's a misunderstanding, my friend," said Garðar Hólm. "The man who is worth anything never gets a jewel. What are you going to do?"

I said, "I suppose I would just go back home."

"You can't go back home," said Garðar Hólm. "You have no money. And your grandmother is dead. You could, of course, go out and wash motor cars at night or wash up dishes in a hotel, in the hope of saving enough money for your fare in three or four years – and then come back home like a castaway to the liquor-shop in Gúðmúnsen's Store, from which you had originally

set out. But your problem is still unsolved. Why don't you want
to gain wealth and fame instead of standing behind the liquor
counter in Gúðmúnsen's Store?"

"If I don't attain the one pure note, I have no wish to be
famous," I said.

"Ah, if only that note were the guarantee of fame!" said Garðar
Hólm. "But unfortunately it is much more likely to be the way
to total anonymity. If you read an encyclopaedia, you will find
that common thieves, to say nothing of murderers, particularly
multiple murderers, command much more space than the greatest geniuses and men of intellect. You set forth to seek wealth
and fame as a young singer; and you are offered the world on a
plate as a clown – perhaps as a criminal. Choose! Make your
choice here and now!"

I replied something like this: "Oh, most of the things I am
told about fame and such-like go right over my head, although
I'm rather fond of singing. I'm so bound to Brekkukot, somehow.
I have always hoped to be allowed to become a lumpfisherman;
and I know that when I am ninety and have lost all sight, hearing,
sense of smell, taste, and feeling, I shall sit in a corner somewhere
and think about when I was seeing to the lumpfish-nets with my
grandfather in Skerjafjörður late in the winter before another
living soul was up and about, and there was no glimmer of light
anywhere except in one little cottage on Álftanes."

"You're a strange boy," said Garðar Hólm, and looked at me
in the late-summer dusk. "You don't believe in anything, not one
single thing; not even in the Barber of Seville."

"Who's he?" I asked.

"The Barber of Seville?" said Garðar Hólm. "You've never heard
of the greatest barber in the world ? What do they teach you in
the Grammar School if they don't teach you about the barber
before whom all other barbers pale into insignificance?"

"I'm afraid we haven't got very far yet in the art of barbery,"
I said. "Forgive me for being so ignorant. Where does this barber
do his shaving, if I may ask? And whom does he shave?"

"That's another matter," said Garðar Hólm. "You see, it's more
than doubtful whether the Barber of Seville ever knew how to

shave. At least, everything certainly went wrong when he tried to shave Don Bartolo in the Third Act, because Don Bartolo suddenly jumped to his feet with the soap all over his face and started fighting with Count Almaviva. All that we know about this barber is that he tried, with the help of a guitar, to make total strangers fall in love with one another. But if it were now to be proved that Figaro could not shave, would you then reject the Barber of Seville out of hand, and Rossini himself and the whole orchestra as well?"

"I have listened to great debates on the Barbers' Bill, which is one of the biggest political issues here in Iceland," I said. "But I have never heard before that one should believe in a barber who actually could not shave."

"But you believe in ghost stories, I hope?" said Garðar Hólm.

"Oh, ghost stories be blowed!" I said.

"Really," he said. "Is that so? I can see that you're rather an arrogant youngster; a little above the rest of mankind, if I may put it that way. Because mankind has an inclination to believe in ghost stories. That is its strength. If you don't respect this fundamental truth about mankind, I'm afraid you may suffer for it, my friend."

"I think that ghosts don't exist," I said.

He said, "Mankind's spiritual values have all been created from a belief in all the things that philosophers reject. I asked you just now: What do you choose at this crossroads in your life? But you didn't give me an answer. Now I ask you: How are you going to live if you reject not only the Barber of Seville but also the cultural value of ghost stories?"

"I'm going to try to live as if ghosts didn't exist," I said. "And concern myself as little as possible with this world-famous barber who never shaved anyone."

Garðar Hólm asked, "If it were to be proved scientifically or historically or even judicially that the Resurrection is not particularly well authenticated by evidence – are you then going to reject the B-minor Mass? Do you want to close St. Peter's Cathedral because it has come to light that it is the symbol of a mistaken philosophy and would be more useful as a stable? What a catastrophe that Giotto and Fra Angelico should have become enmeshed in a false ideology as painters, instead of adhering to realism! The story of the Virgin Mary is obviously just another falsehood invented by knaves, and any man is a fraud who allows himself to sigh, '*Pièta, Signor*'."

37

NIGHT IN THE HOTEL D'ISLANDE

My life story was over for the time being, and Garðar Hólm rose from the Archangel Gabriel's tombstone.

"Go down to the hotel and sleep there for me tonight," he said. "If someone asks for me, I'm dining with the Government."

He was up and away. I heard the tansies brushing against him as he walked away and disappeared into the darkness between the tombstones. I walked down to town again as he had asked me to do.

There was a light on in his many-roomed suite. Little Miss Gúðmúnsen was sitting there and waiting. And it was I who came in. She stared at me dully and said without any preliminaries, "Where is Garðar Hólm?"

"He's having dinner with the Government," I said.

"Have you, too, started telling lies now?" said the girl.

"Too?" I said. "Like whom?"

"Everyone," she said. "Can't you hear how everyone tells lies; if not deliberately, then involuntarily; if not out loud, then silently? But I don't care if he lies. It's just that he has no cause to despise me even though he despises all my family. I haven't done him any harm."

"What on earth makes you think he despises you and all your family?" I asked.

"You've seen how he behaves," she replied. "And you've heard how he speaks. He greets me like a complete stranger. He never even looked at me – even though he had written that he had started a new life and that when he came, he would be coming because of me. He doesn't have to lie to me because of that; I don't care in the least if he doesn't live in palaces in various countries whose names I don't even know. And he doesn't have to be ashamed of himself on my account, either, even though he knows that I know it. If you're fond of someone, you don't care even if he doesn't live in a palace and even if all the banks where he has deposits and all the world-cities where he is famous don't exist."

I said nothing. She dried her eyes, but the tears continued to come in showers just the same.

"Will you take me to him?" she said at last. "I won't survive the night unless I talk to him."

"He is sleeping at the Governor's house," I said. "Haven't I just been telling you?"

"Oh, I know perfectly well he's lying up in that horrid old byre-loft," she said. "But you can take me there nevertheless. You know everything, anyway."

"Know what?" I said. "I don't know a single thing. But you must at least realize that since he didn't make any appointment with you, he doesn't expect to meet you tonight."

"You're just the same beastly pig you've always been and I should have known!" said the girl; she had stopped sobbing for a moment, and her face had even hardened a little. Then she said, "As if I didn't know that he was making a fool of me! He's making a fool of all of us. I don't really know whether he himself has made up all these stories; but at least he's been clever at finding plenty of disciples and other runners to spread them around. And he's not bashful about making us do the paying."

"Oh, I don't believe your father would spend money on things other than those he thinks he can get something out of," I said.

"That's just like you!" she said. "Actually, I don't care a rap about singing any more. I don't even know what singing is. I don't care whether he sings well or badly. I was just a little girl who loved adventure stories, and I swallowed all the descriptions of those huge concert-halls where the people held their breath when he opened his mouth; and these great hotels where everyone bowed to him; and those bank deposits which kept piling up. No sooner had he arrived in the country than I felt I was beginning to float on air, and our little country which is known only as a colony of an even less-renowned country – God knows, one was almost becoming part of the world itself. When I walked by his side here in Löngustétt, I was raised above the life we live here; and he would pull out gold coins from his pockets for anyone who wanted them. But now I've long since stopped caring about all that; I don't care if all his gold coins were counterfeit."

"What has happened?" I asked.

"Happened?" she said. "Nothing has happened. I just love him. I wrote to him that even though he were a labourer in a country no one knows and is called Jutland and isn't even a country, yes, even though he had a wife and children there, I was ready at any time to give him everything he wanted. He is the only man I have ever fallen for, and no other man except him can ever have me. And you can tell him that from me since you won't take me to him; I had to tell it to somebody!"

"It is considered unwise to whisper one's secrets to the wind," I said.

She looked at me after long reflection and asked sombrely, "Are you the wind?"

"Part of it," I said.

The cathedral clock struck one; or perhaps it struck two. There was nothing more to say for a while. At least there was nothing I could say, I who had sat on a stone dyke in pouring rain one night the previous winter waiting for a shadow on a curtain, and had lost this shadow for ever.

"It's getting late," I said.

"Late?" she said. "What do you mean, late?"

I said, "It's well into the night."

"I don't call that late," she said.

She stared stiffly into the blue, as people do who are recovering from sorrow. "It's only a new day," she added.

Her red gloves with the tassels lay on the table.

She sat huddled on the sofa, with her hands dangling over her knees; she looked bigger when she was sitting down than when standing upright in a long gown. She had one characteristic that distinguished her from most women of her age and class, in that she never tried to be smart in her movements and did not know any affected poses. Only her red gloves contradicted the impression that she was the reincarnation of that Gretchen who brought Faust so close to damnation that things would have gone badly for him if some angels had not arrived and rewarded his interest in ditch-digging and swamp-draining.

For some reason or other the world has never really taken the tears of plump women very seriously, and a fat martyr has always been considered contrary to the laws of reason – and quite unthinkable in a portrait, moreover. In any cultural concept, the only valid salt water is that which a thin and haggard person pours out in Christendom. Yet the kind of story that the girl was telling me is much more natural if it is served up with a salt water dressing. But now I had the impression that the story was at an end, and with it the tears.

"Don't you think it's time to be going?" I asked.

She woke up from her trance and answered curtly and angrily, "Go yourself! I decide where I'm going to be. This is my home. It is I who provided this apartment; and it is I who pay for it."

"So sorry," I said. "All the more reason for me to be getting off."

I began to look for my cap.

"What's all the hurry?" she said. "That's something new, if you have become the part of the wind that blows quickly past."

I went on looking for my cap until I found it.

"Aren't you going to sit with me a little to comfort me while I wait?" she asked.

"If you're going to wait, I'm afraid you will have to wait until morning," I said.

"Should we wake up the staff and have them bring us some refreshments?" she said.

"Refreshments?" I said. "After that dinner tonight?"

"I haven't had anything to eat or drink all day," she said. "Do you think that the dinner tonight was held so that people could eat and drink?"

"I ate my fill," I said.

"Yes, but you have no soul," she said.

"If you're hungry," I said, "I seem to remember that there are some five-*aurar* cakes on a shelf in the cupboard."

"Bring them over," she said, and dried the last traces of her tears from her nose with her handkerchief. "They're my cakes, anyway."

Without a word I brought her the remains of the cream cakes from earlier in the day.

"It's as if you were throwing food to a dog, you don't even say so much as 'Help yourself'," she said.

"Didn't I put out that knife, fork and spoon for you there?" I said.

"You're surely not going to leave me behind like a rat among his cream cakes? Presumably you're gentleman enough to keep me company and eat with me. Go on, have a seat."

"No thanks," I said. "I've come to the wrong place. And I'm not more of a gentleman than that. Goodbye."

She reacted to this farewell like a leaky vessel that has been abruptly filled with water and weeps through every seam.

"Dear Jesus, you're the beastliest pig of a person I have ever heard of in my whole life!" she said through the torrent of tears. "I never dreamt that such a foul person could exist. And you stink of soot and fulmar's feathers."

It had never actually occurred to me that I was so wicked; and the result of it was that I sat down beside the girl and began to try to comfort her. And as always happens when a child has to be consoled or a misdeed forgiven, reason goes into abeyance and other laws take over; perhaps even life itself, as it is.

And the few, brief nocturnal hours passed in the Hotel d'Islande.

At first light, just about the time when the harbour-workers were getting up, Garðar Hólm found little Miss Gúðmúnsen and myself in his apartment. He greeted us with a handshake and smiled his inscrutable mathematician's smile at us. The night's revelry had left no mark on him, there was no blemish or wrinkle to be seen on him except perhaps a tiny wisp of hay on his back; and he was a little pale. He pulled out of his pocket a few copies of the world newspaper, the London *Times*, and laid them on the table. When he had greeted us he walked over to the mirror, studied his face, and stroked his chin.

"How very nice of you to wait for me here," he said while he was inspecting himself in the mirror. He bared his teeth and inspected them carefully as well. "I hope you slept well, children. The party I was at lasted all night. Hmm. I need a shave. Then we'll have some coffee."

"I'm rather afraid we've finished all your cream cakes," I said.

The girl had not spoken a word; she was just finishing making her hair tidy, and finally she said as if from afar, "Where's my other shoe, Álfgrímur?"

I searched the room for a while until I found the shoe under the sofa on which she had been sitting the previous evening. Garðar Hólm had taken off his jacket and was putting soap on his face in front of the mirror.

"I dropped into Paradise on the way from the party," said Garðar Hólm.

"Indeed – the place where the angels took Dr Faust?" I said, because I somehow could never get the Barbers' Bill out of my head.

"It's a very pleasant place," said Garðar Hólm. "The only place here in Reykjavík that smells more like a chemist's shop than a chemist's shop itself. My good friend sits there in the mornings at his open hatchway and looks out over the sea. And all the gulls in the North Sea fly past him."

"I suppose only famous people talk like that," said little Miss Gúðmúnsen. "Isn't that right?"

"Don't bother to make my bed, dear," he said. "There are plenty of servants in the place."

"I must talk to you, Garðar," she said. "In private. As soon as possible."

"I'll go," I said.

"No, that's one thing I know you won't do, my friend," said Garðar, and went on soaping his face. "To leave little Miss Gúðmúnsen and myself just when we're going to have morning coffee! I didn't think we three had any secrets from one another. By the way, aren't there enough cream cakes?"

Little Miss Gúðmúnsen had sat down in a chair.

"Álfgrímur and I," she said, "are engaged. We got engaged last night."

"Hurrah, bravo!" said Garðar Hólm. "Isn't that fun? My warmest congratulations. Now I'm going to shave. Then we'll have an engagement party. We'll get some champagne."

I stood over by the window and looked down into the street, where a farm-hand was herding some cows; and now, when the night was past, I honestly could not help holding back a little.

"Isn't it a little early to say that, little one?" I said. "Should we really be bringing up this sort of thing in front of Garðar Hólm?"

"What do you mean?" she asked.

"I mean, er, that in reality, perhaps, nothing so very much happened; except that we are just like all other human beings," I said.

"Nothing very much happened!" she said. "Human beings, indeed! Speak plainly! Show us the kind of person you are!"

"I mean, nothing happened except what usually happens under similar circumstances: a man is a man and a woman is a woman – anything beyond that is external, incidental."

"So nothing happened, is that it?" she said. "Nothing except the usual! Ha! In other words, I'm just a common slut – isn't that what you mean?"

"Álfgrímur," said Garðar Hólm. He had now put enough soap on his face, and came over to me at the window and gave me some bank-notes from his pocket. "I think we need some cream cakes. Would you mind popping over to Friðriksen's bakery for us?"

He got out his razor and began to whet it on the edge of his hand, and I abandoned my unsolved problems to go and buy more cream cakes.

I had to wait a good while in the bakery, because it was not yet quite seven o'clock: "Friðriksen is still squirting the cream cakes," said the shop-girl.

I was rather impatient at having to wait, because although I had not read very many Danish novels, I was suddenly a little anxious at leaving the singer's sweetheart alone with him and a razor on a morning like this.

"I think," I said at last, "that I don't have time to wait for any more cream cakes at present. I'll just take the ones Friðriksen has squirted already, and come back for the rest later."

38

SINGING IN THE CATHEDRAL

When I came back with the cream cakes, Garðar Hólm had finished shaving. Little Miss Gúðmúnsen had gone. The singer was sitting at the writing desk engrossed in doing sums on little bits of paper. He did not become aware of my presence for some time, or else he could not tear himself away from his sums. Finally he thrust the closely written scraps of paper into his pocket and turned round in his chair to face me. The smile came and went.

He said, "I've been thinking something over in the few minutes since you went to the bakery shop. I'm thinking of giving a special concert tomorrow."

"Yes, it's been in all the papers: the Gúðmúnsen's Store jubilee in the Temperance Hall," I said.

"That's not the one I mean," he said. "I'm going to give another concert in the forenoon: a church concert. It will be for invited guests only: my invited guests; those who would never dream of hurrying to a Store function at Gúðmúnsen's. I want to ask you to give me a little help with this concert."

"Then we'd better hurry up and get the invitations out," I said.

"Today we'll invite the guests," he said. "And I'll see Pastor Jóhann about the church."

"Madame Strúbenhols will be available, of course?" I said.

"I was thinking of asking you to play the accompaniment for me," said Garðar Hólm.

I cannot say that this absurd suggestion took me completely by surprise, but as can be readily understood I demurred and raised all kinds of objections; and these were actually not merely pretexts, because no one knew better than I myself that anything like that was quite out of the question.

"I have scarcely ever been near an instrument, except your battered old harmonium at Hríngjarabær," I said. "Until a short time ago some of the keys in it did not even play. In the cathedral, on the other hand, there is a pipe-organ which needs a special man to tread it, and that in itself is a difficult enough task."

"There's a handy little instrument in the vestry that we can use," said the singer. "Every second note in it was silent when I was a boy. Let's hope that the other half has fallen silent by now as well."

This kind of melancholy jesting about music from the lips of the maestro left me speechless. But what really showed up my naiveté was that I did not start laughing, instead of trying to find rational excuses. The world singer looked at me and smiled again that extraordinary smile – which was perhaps the reverse of its negation.

"Drop in at my mother's on your way home and tell her that she is invited to a concert in the cathedral tomorrow morning," he said. "I'll come and fetch her."

When I was on my way home in the middle of the forenoon, there was an old long-beard walking in front of me, smoking a pipe; he had a pile of tabloid-sized advertising posters under one arm and a paste-pot in the other, and he was pasting these big posters up on buildings. It was an advertisement about the Store's function in the Temperance Hall the following night; each poster had three portraits printed on it, a large one of Gúðmúnsen himself with cigar and decoration, and underneath it two smaller pictures, one of Garðar Hólm in his youth, when one gazes at heavenly chariots, and the other of Dr Faustulus with his top hat and a dove. Round the pictures were columns of print in that ever-valid classical narrative style, full of obligatory praise for these excellent men, but particularly about the Store.

When I walked past the Temperance Hall I saw that the building had been painted grey-pink, or as they would say nowadays: grey-violet. In later years, when I tried to recall this colour to mind, I have often doubted whether such a colour ever existed; my memory must be deceiving me in this matter, I thought; until I saw this remarkable colour with my own eyes inside hotel rooms and other dwelling-houses in Paris, many years later – and even had the odd experience of staying in a grey-violet room myself in that capital of culture, what's more. The Pope calls it a penitential colour, and it is used on Maundy Thursday. Garlands of linen flowers and greenery were being put up here and there in the Temperance Hall, both inside and out, so that a simpleton who had never come across this sort of thing except in Biblical pictures could not help being reminded of Palm Sunday.

Part of my daily round, as I said earlier, was to look in on Kristín of Hríngjarabær every morning and evening, particularly since she had become unsteady on her legs through old age, and poor of sight and hearing. This time I had a more momentous errand with her than to bring her fish and milk.

"You can't be right in the head, child," she said. "My son left here only a short time ago, and he said nothing about a concert in the church."

"But it's true, nonetheless," I said. "This is going to be a concert for his own specially invited guests, the ones who wouldn't fit in with the Store's guests."

"Is that so?" said the woman, and began to think. "He wants, of course, to show the authorities appreciation because they supported him with almost a hundred *krónur* a year while he was studying to be a singer."

"And perhaps he also wants to sing for his mother," I said.

She replied, "Yes, he should know, my little Georg, that it's always been my hope and dream to be allowed to hear him sing. But I have now had so many dreams; and though few have come to pass, to have had this boy makes up for it. I've really nothing against him singing not just for old Jón Guðmundsson the liquor merchant and his people, but also for the ones who deserve it, like the ministers and bishops, and of course the Danes. Yes, and not forgetting the Catholic bishop at Landakot here. But tell my little Georg that there's no need to invite an old woman like me who's not fit to be seen in public."

I roamed around Hríngjarabær for a long time, up in the churchyard and out in the fields, in a strange fit of depression; and I began to envy some ponies because they did not have to play the accompaniment at a concert the following morning, but could just carry on grazing. Surely this must be some sort of joke on his part, I thought: or is he somehow planning to get his own back on me because I had inadvertently and involuntarily ended up with his sweetheart whom he had come to Iceland to fetch? Was he now cast up on a skerry in his life, perhaps? Was the tide creeping up on him? And was it perhaps I who had driven him out on to this skerry? If so, was there any way out of the dangers into which I had stumbled? Now at last I could understand people who resort to suicide to steal a march on death.

I looked in on old Kristín towards evening as she sat there on a three-legged stool with her blind eyes open, glowing with gratitude for her son. When she realized that I was there, she said, "Thank God you came, child. I simply had to talk to you. What's the news?"

"Oh, nothing very much," I said.

"Isn't the town all excited?" said the old woman.

"I should certainly think so," I replied.

"I'm so slow at thinking nowadays," she said. "I didn't remember until you had gone this morning that I wanted to ask you to do me a little favour. It's said to be a courtesy to give singers flowers. Now though I am humble as everyone knows, I am still going to ask you to pick some flowers for him and put them somewhere close to him tomorrow morning when he sings. And say nothing to him about where they came from. He will then perhaps think they came from some fine great lady."

I cannot say that the future accompanist himself had a very much clearer idea about concerts than old Kristín of Hríngjarabær; it had not even occurred to me that flowers would be required. Flowers were very far from my mind at that moment.

"We are almost in autumn," I said, "and the outfields are being mown, and all the flowers have bloomed and withered a long time ago; except perhaps horse-daisies and such-like that are considered weeds."

"Oh, come now," said the old woman. "There are all sorts of flowers all around that are still blooming while the outfields are being mown. Meadow-sweet is like an aromatic seed-pod around this time; or the mountain dandelion, honeyed and dark red, which nods its head so nicely late in summer, or the stone bramble, with the berries that are the brightest red to be seen in

Iceland towards autumn. And there's not much wrong with the heather at the end of the hay-harvest."

"One has to go miles out into the country to find flowers of that kind," I said. "There isn't enough time."

"I'm sure your grandmother at Brekkukot would lend you Gráni to go on this errand for me," she said. "There's a lovely slope near a little lake at a certain spot in Mosfell district; and two swans on the lake. The flowers grow on that slope. I walked there once when I was a young girl."

"Isn't it less trouble, Kristín dear, just to pick a few flowers in the churchyard here, for instance at the late Archangel Gabriel's grave or that of some other foreigners who have been dead for fifty years and have no descendants alive here?"

"What a terrible thing to say, child!" said the woman. "Not a petal from the churchyard, I say! Not a single horse-daisy. It would be reckoned against us. The churchyard belongs to the Saviour alone."

"Aren't there a few little flowers on the grave of the late bell-ringer?" I asked.

"But they're the bell-ringer's flowers," said the woman. "The dear bell-ringer, he never wanted to see or hear my little Georg. We'll leave those flowers alone."

I could not avoid promising to pick the right flowers for her, and she said, "Bless you for promising to do it. And now I'm going to ask you to find my best skirt for me, it's hanging in the corner there behind the curtain. I never managed to get myself a full costume, never mind all the bodice-work, because I was never more than the bell-ringer's housekeeper and therefore never had to sit in church in the place where his wife would have sat if he had ever had a wife. But I have a nice day-bodice from the old times, blue with black roses."

It was now nearly night-time, and somehow I could not be bothered making an expedition to Mosfell district for flowers; instead I made do with picking a few pansies and marguerites in the churchyard. I suddenly felt that these flowers were owed to me by the residents there because I had sung there so often when I was younger.

I had been back to the hotel over and over again all day to see Garðar Hólm; there was so much that I felt I had to say to him. But Garðar Hólm was away all day, and I never managed to track him down. That evening a card reached me, in which he asked me to sleep in his apartment that night again, since he was still at a party and would be staying up all night.

"And be ready in the church at the crack of dawn tomorrow," it said. "Enter by the vestry door."

Next morning very early I was down at the church with my false flowers like a man in a dream who has to carry out whatever the dream imposes on him, however afraid he feels. Never have I felt such apprehension about any concert. I stood behind the church peering furtively in all directions, rather like a man who is not quite sure whether he is in his right mind and would like to have it settled one way or another; and I stared in amazement at the flowers I was carrying. I was hoping that it would all turn out to be some sort of trick, and that the vestry would be locked; one thing was certain – everything was quiet in the square, there was no one within sight who looked as if he were going to a concert. Two carpenters were on their way to their work at a house farther down the road. A peasant wearing skin-boots had just set off with a few pack-ponies laden with dried cods'-heads which he was obviously going to transport all the way home to the east, doubtless a journey of several days, and I was not very far from envying him. But when I turned the door-handle, the vestry proved to be open. The nightmare went on. Had the guests arrived already, perhaps, seated in the church, and all now waiting for me?

The vestry was poorly lit and I felt my way forward until I found the door into the chancel; it was ajar. I peered in. The church was empty. I went on into the chancel. The rays of the rising sun did not penetrate here, because there are no windows in the east gable of such buildings. Inside there was only a colourless light, clear and dismal, with reflections off the gloss-painted ceiling and walls and pews; it reminded one of the glitter of a fresh-water lake under clouded skies; and this lustreless light fell on the gilded image of the Risen Lord above the altar.

I stood with the flowers in the silent chancel of the Cathedral, in front of the altar-rails, and looked around. And lo and behold – there stood a dusty old harmonium; I had been clinging still to the hope that it had only existed in a dream. But however shocked I was over this wretched harmonium, which did not concern me in the slightest, how much more extraordinary was it that I should be standing there myself! If someone should see me there now! I hurriedly laid the flowers down on the floor as if they had nothing to do with me. But then it occurred to me that the floor was no place for flowers. Should I not rather put them on the altar-rails? Or up on the altar itself? But what would Pastor Jóhann say if he came upon these flowers on his altar? – for he would undoubtedly recognize them and know they had been stolen. I picked the flowers up from the floor again. It feels as if I am still standing there with these flowers in my hand as I write these lines so many decades later. I do not remember ever having got rid of these flowers. Where was I to put these flowers? What was to become of these flowers?

Then the main door of the church opened and two guests entered: an elegantly clad, distinguished gentleman in the prime of life, and beside him a poor old woman. He led her up the aisle. She hobbled forward on her frail, numb legs, leaning heavily on her son to draw strength from him for this walk. She was wearing her pleated skirt and the day-bodice, and she had tied her best fichu round her shoulders. She had become small again, in the way that old people shrink, not unlike a little girl who has had polio; and on her face was that dull, blind expression that is directed towards another light elsewhere.

Garðar Hólm carried himself with all the air of a celebrity, an emperor of art making an appearance in the soaring halls of Thalia before the thousandfold gaze of a distinguished and discerning audience and warmed by the special admiration of a public which is deeply moved that he should be leading this poor woman, his mother, by his side: at the highest peak of his fame, he was remembering his humble origins. And he inclined his head with a modest smile towards the empty pews on either side, as if he were catching sight of some important face and did not want to fail to show his respect on this solemn occasion. There

were even a few guests here and there who required no less defer-
ence than that he should stop in the middle of the aisle to click
his heels and bow. And the old woman went on leaning against
her son as he paused in the aisle and bowed to men of rank.

He led his mother right up the aisle and into the chancel, to a
chair that had been placed up against the altar-rails. He placed
her on it and settled her into her seat with tender solicitude, with
respect and affection in every glance and gesture as if he were
assuring her that even though there were many people there of
higher rank than she, she was not to feel ashamed of herself, for
this was her place in the eyes of God and man. And now she
sat there in front of the altar, transformed and exalted in her best
pleated skirt and her best black fichu, and folded in her lap
her gnarled, rather swollen hands with their black veins and white
knuckles.

Garðar Hólm turned to me.

"Sit down at the harmonium," he whispered.

I sat down.

"Start playing," he said.

"But – but . . ." I said.

"It doesn't matter," he said.

"But I-I-I."

"It doesn't matter in the slightest what you play. I'll sing to
anything. Just start playing!"

No sooner had I touched the pedals than the harmonium began
to shrill of its own accord, so that the empty church resounded
and echoed as if the whole place were coming down in ruins; all
the vents were so leaky that the notes bellowed of their own accord,
with loud sucking noises whenever the pedals were trodden.

And now Garðar Hólm pulled out all the stops of his voice.
The concert began.

I want to repeat once again what I have often implied already
in these pages, that I am not the right person to describe properly
Garðar Hólm's accomplishments. We were born and bred each
on his own side of the same churchyard and have always been
called close kinsmen, and many people have confused us and
some have even taken the one for the other. But even if that had

not been the case, I would still be bound, in any talk about this idol of my childhood, to preserve that courtesy which each man owes himself, according to the English maestro who wrote in his thirty-ninth Sonnet:

"O, how thy worth with manners may I sing,
When thou art all the better part of me;
What can mine own praise to mine own self bring,
And what is't but mine own, when I praise thee."

People have kept on asking me: did he sing well? I reply, the world is a song, but we do not know whether it is a good song because we have nothing to compare it with. Some people think that the art of singing has its origins in the whirring of the solar system as the planets hurtle through space; others say it comes from the soughing of the wind in that ash-tree called Yggdrasil, in the words of the old poem: "the ancient tree sighs." Perhaps Garðar Hólm was closer to that unfathomable ocean of unborn song than most other singers have been. I shall not compare Garðar Hólm's singing with that of other people who may have sung in Thalia's palaces all over the world, in the Teatro Colon, Küssnacht, St. Peter's Cathedral (or was it perhaps St. Petersburg?), or before Mohammed ben Ali. But no one has ever heard the like of the singing I listened to in that least-known of all cathedrals; and I do not believe that anyone would ever have been the same after hearing it. And indeed the ears for which it was intended were deaf.

It may well be that this was the only time in my whole life that I ever really heard singing, because this singing was so true that it made all other singing sound artificial and affected by comparison and turned other singers into frauds; and not just other singers, but myself and all the rest of us as well – the woman from Landbrot no less than Chloë, Ebenezer Draummann and Captain Hogensen just as much as Runólfur Jónsson and the superintendent. And this sound affected me so deeply that I saw no alternative but to tread that old wreck of a harmonium with all my strength, heart and soul, in order to drown the singing or at least to challenge it, in the hope that I could survive.

What did he sing, people ask? I ask in reply, does it matter? No, there was no printed programme. What songs? Perhaps it was these new-style songs which will achieve recognition if time continues to go backwards towards its origins and communication becomes more simplified than at present, so that people will be content to bellow the vowel "a" to express their thoughts on everything, instead of inflecting verbs and nouns; it may also be that what was sung there was the song that the ass and the ox sang for the angels on Christmas Eve. Yet I still have the feeling that in the midst of this singing of a time still unborn there was a jumble of incoherent fragments of important old texts: *exultate, jubilate; si tu ne m'aimes pas, je t'aime; se i miei sospiri.*

He sang at first with vehement gestures which I would have thought more appropriate to a performance of drama. But perhaps this demented mixture of laughter and sobbing was nearer reality than other singing and more natural to living creatures than the stern discipline of the roles on our stage at Brekkukot. After a short while the singer had a fit of coughing, and stood there in front of the altar gasping for breath, his face convulsed with spasms, and could not produce another sound. He fell to his knees at his mother's feet and buried his face in her lap.

And this concert was now over.

39

THE STORE'S JUBILEE

Evening. There was autumn in the air, and we could hear the wind buffeting the tombstones and the rain beating down on the tansies. I walked round and round the house, stopping at the turnstile-gate in the rain every now and again to listen for footsteps, as if I were expecting someone; because his parting words to me that morning had been, "Stay at home so that you can be found if you are needed." But there was no one about – at the most, perhaps, the occasional person hurrying home down to

Grímstaðaholt; until at last the girl came running up. She stopped outside the turnstile-gate in the rain and called my name. I had had more than a suspicion that things were going to turn out something like this.

"He's not singing!" she said.

"Really?" I said.

"He's left the hotel. And I've already searched in – the other place. I expect he's already on his way abroad as usual."

"Had you ever expected otherwise?" I said.

"I've come to ask you to come to the rescue," she said. "The hall is full, the editor has made his speech, the brass band has played thrice. Madame Strúbenhols has finished with Liszt's Rhapsody, and the conjurer has done his turn twice and was just starting on it for the third time. Now you must come and sing."

"I don't know how to sing," I said.

"Everyone knows you can, come on," she said.

"No," I said.

"Do you want to make my father a laughing-stock in the town?" she said.

"What's your father got to do with me?" I said.

"I can't believe that you are a wicked person, Álfgrímur, until I see it with my own eyes," said the girl, and started crying.

"I can't see how it would help your father if I make myself a laughing-stock in public," I said.

"Madame Strúbenhols has often told us that you can sing," said the girl.

"I don't believe that even a trained singer would ever dream of singing unprepared and without notice," I said.

"I know that you and Madame Strúbenhols have been practising together from a German music-book," she said. "And you can wear the conjurer's evening-dress."

"It's out of the question," I said.

"Not even for your kinsman Garðar Hólm?" she said.

"Don't you think he would have sung himself," I asked, "if he had thought it necessary?"

"Wouldn't you like to put father in your debt – a debt he would never forget from this night onwards?" she asked.

"Oh, I imagine your father knows what he is doing," I said. "I find it hard to believe that he will be very disappointed over Garðar."

"So that's all the feeling you have for me!" said the girl. "Never mind that you won't do anything for my father – but I see now that you are also prepared to have a kick at me. So that's the kind of man you are: you seduce me when you find me weeping in the middle of the night, entice me from the man I love so that he goes away and never comes back again, and make me the worst slut in town, ahaha, uhuhu, ihihi . . . !"

The brass band had played the Björneborgernes March thrice down to the very last note. We reached the back door of the Temperance Hall just as Professor Dr Faustulus finished plucking doves out of the hat for the third time. The conjurer was immediately stripped of his clothes and I was hastily crammed into his finery. There is no need to describe how his frock-coat fitted me, we were so completely different in build; or his collar, limp with sweat from all these strenuous feats of legerdemain. But without further ado I was thrust on to the stage in this get-up, and the professor was left in the wings wearing nothing but his underpants and holding his doves and top-hat. This was the biggest conjuring trick that had been performed all evening: Long-Loony from Brekkukot was on the stage as a substitute for the world singer. Madame Strúbenhols was at the piano.

I hope no one expects me to describe the singing which now took place. But I believe I can claim that it was not done from any vanity, and that my first thought when I landed on the stage was that I was not acting in my own interest. Even though my voice was hardly born – nor I myself as a man – and even though no one knows what shape a worm would take if it ever managed to fly out of its chrysalis, my loyalty to Garðar Hólm was nothing new with me; it had always been something secret and fundamental to my vanished childhood. I sang my undivided gratitude to this world tenor who by God's mercy had lifted himself above our bass at Brekkukot; I sang because I knew that singing is testimony to the gratitude we owe to God – but not because I knew how to sing. I was so deeply committed to this task right from the first note that the peals of derisive laughter that broke out had no more effect on me than a distant breeze in the eastern mountains so rock-firm was my certainty that since I was standing there (and I had always known, deep down, that I would be the one to stand there), I was standing there through the power of things which were so high above me that I no longer mattered.

Ruhn in Frieden alle Seelen . . .

Whatever the cause of it: these little, big people, rigid and ossified for so long from being the incarnation of everything that is right and true in a little, big town beyond the seas, these unmusical Icelandic educated and upper classes in the years before we came to be reckoned as people at all, this most tuneless crowd of people that has ever been assembled in the whole world – they all began to listen. After the first song, certainly, most of them looked at the Governor and then at the Bishop; but there were one or two who involuntarily gave themselves up to some power of primitive acceptance of what was happening. People began to raise their hands a little so as to be able to clap them together in applause. I do not think for a moment that the applause was for me. But yet, people acknowledged the singing, and that is always a beginning. After the second or third song both the Bishop and the Governor applauded too – and that had the same effect as an official announcement from the authorities: "We cannot acknowledge that We are listening to bad singing; since We happen to have been invited to a concert and We are present and seated, that concert is by definition a good one." Then all the people applauded. They went on applauding long after the few songs that I knew were finished. I stood in a trance up on the stage and looked at the people applauding until someone gave me a sign to clear off; and I did not come to again until I was in the wings, and Professor Dr Faustulus had started to take his trousers off me.

The evening was still not over. As I stood leaning against a wall in a daze, one of the people from Gúðmúnsen's Store suddenly came over to me with the message that I was asked to call in at the Store's office on my way home.

Gúðmúnsen's Store was blazing with lights. Two assistants were

standing downstairs and they looked at me like court ushers as
they let me into the mid-shop; they lifted the flap of the counter
for me and escorted me through the empty book-keeping department to a door with the mysterious word *Comptoir* painted on it.
Merchant Gúðmúnsen was standing in his office wearing a frock-
coat, top-hat, and decoration, with his iron-stiff cuffs reaching
to his knuckles. He had thrown his overcoat across the back of
a chair, and was lighting a cigar. This was a very different guise
from the one he had worn at the banquet the previous evening:
he pulled down the corners of his mouth as he smoked, and
frowned; there was a dried-up look about the ruddy cheeks, such
as you sometimes see in the plump faces of old spinsters.

"Good day to you, and please have a seat, stu-*dent* Hansen," he
said in Danish; he could not be bothered displaying his erudition
in more important languages on this occasion. He himself did
not sit down.

"This was the very last thing I expected," he said when I was
seated. "If I may ask, whom were you trying to rescue?"

"No one," I said. "The little one came to me."

"Do you think I am an idiot, or something, may I ask? Did you
think that I didn't know that Georg Hansson wouldn't turn up?"

I mumbled something to the effect that Garðar Hólm must have
had a very pressing engagement since he had not come.

"Pressing engagement?" merchant Gúðmúnsen repeated.
"Whom are you trying to make a fool of, if I may ask, stu-*dent*
Hansen? What's the meaning of this pretending?"

"And you, Mr Gúðmúnsen, who know Garðar Hólm so well,"
I said, "did you believe for a moment that he would ever perform
on a stage this evening against his will?"

"Of course not," said merchant Gúðmúnsen. "On the other
hand, I told him that I would keep a look out for him all round
Faxaflói; and if he tried to get on board a ship, I would have
him arrested for fraud."

"You yourself must know best why you brought him back to
Iceland," I said.

"Why we brought him back home?" said merchant Gúðmúnsen,
and came over and stood right up against my chair. "I'll tell

you that quite plainly, herr stu-*dent*, since you have seen fit to get mixed up in this business. We brought him back home because it was impossible to carry on with this any longer. We were tired of it. He had deserted the old Danish woman who had been keeping him for the last ten years; and the pocket-money he was sent every month by mail from that eccentric old man Jón of Skagi, who looks after the urinal in the harbour, obviously wasn't enough to provide him with a livelihood. And then to add insult to injury, my daughter got it into her head that she was engaged to him. In other words, he had to be exposed. And that's why we sent for him, my dear young man."

"Allow me to deny that I ever tried to get myself mixed up in this business," I said. "I certainly gave him a little help during the days he was here, but that was at the request of the Store. Nothing was further from my mind than having anything to do with this concert. I wasn't invited. I didn't even buy myself a ticket for it. I stayed at home. But someone came for me. I was begged, implored – in your name. For God's sake. I was dragged down town; I was pushed on to the stage. I realize now that I have been made a fool of, and have shamed my people and angered you. There is no atoning for folly and stupidity; and I know it is pointless to ask forgiveness when one has no excuses. The best thing now is to hold one's tongue and be off."

And with that I started to get to my feet.

But it was Gúðmúnsen's nature that when he did not succeed in making a sale and his customer started to look stubborn, the good-natured Dane in him came to the surface, witty and gay, of which there is not nearly enough in Iceland. Even at this highly serious moment he lived up to his usual habit. He stroked me on the cheek with the back of his hand, as if he were caressing a child, and burst out laughing.

"*Poeta cum agricola pugnavit*," he said, and was suddenly a whole lesson further ahead in the Latin primer than when I had heard him quoting from it last. "May I offer you a cigar?"

I told him I was no good at smoking, which was true.

"Indeed, dear stu-*dent*?" he said. "And not even a drink, either? But there's no hurry. We need to have a little talk. Now you know where I stand, as it were, my friend, and where we all stand. You're the son of old Björn of Brekkukot, or is it his grandson? He's a good chap, old Björn, even though all these open boats are just about finished and the small-time fishermen done for. And even though the little one says that you smell of soot and fulmar's feathers, as you'd expect, coming from the most miserable hovel in all Iceland, I am nevertheless going to write down a few words for you here on this paper, just something for the road."

He sat down and scribbled something on a sheet of paper, folded it, stuck it into an envelope, and handed it to me.

"There you are," he said. "Now I must go and see to my guests, the King's Minister and the others. Goodbye."

My grandmother was sitting up late beside the fireplace with her knitting, while her wonderful pot-bread was baking. I could not bring myself to tell her all the things that had happened that evening, and contented myself with talking about the weather.

"Oh, yes, summer storms," she said, "they pass quickly."

Then I took out Gúðmúnsen's letter and told her what was in it: namely, that Gúðmúnsen's Store undertook to pay for my training as a singer abroad for five years.

"Well, well, that's quite something," said my grandmother, but did not stop knitting. "He is an excellent man, of course. Indulge my laziness, Grímur dear, and take that creel there and fetch me a few peats from the stack."

When I came back in with the peats she covered the embers with them carefully. Then she started knitting again. After a good while she said:

"I don't know how Björn will take this. As far as Gúðmúnsen's money is concerned, it has never been valid currency with us hitherto. Besides, I would have thought that the same thing applied to singing as has been said about poetry here in Iceland: 'I write for my own contentment and not my own aggrandizement'. See what happened to poor Kristín's little Georg, who could have become the bell-ringer after his step-father: he took to travelling. And the bell passed into the hands of other people."

40

ONE *EYRIR*

Autumn had just breathed in our direction the previous evening, but next morning it was away again. It glistened on the raindrops on the grass-tufts between the paving-slabs and on the optimistic late-summer dandelions and the fish-scales in the mire; and the tansies glowed red in the sunshine.

It was on this morning that our superintendent came up from the harbour pushing a hand-cart. Jónas the policeman accompanied him. They were heading towards the churchyard. On the hand-cart lay an oblong object, the size of a man, covered with canvas. They laid this object on a trestle that rested across the benches in the mortuary; but they did not take the canvas off. The superintendent had not been home during the night, but now he arrived with his companion for some morning coffee. My grandfather was sitting in the doorway of the fish-shed mending his nets, and bade the two men good day. The smoke from my grandmother's chimney went straight up into the sky on this calm, clear, late-summer morning of eternity.

I did not ask what had happened, nor how it had happened; I had no wish to know. But I heard that there were some people who criticized our superintendent for his part in the affair. Many years later I was allowed to glance through some old police records, and there I came across a report of a brief interrogation of the superintendent that had taken place that very day. In it he stated that a visitor had come to see him in his little cubicle at the harbour near midnight the previous evening. The sheriff asked what the visitor had wanted.

"Oh, nothing very much", said the superintendent. "He only wanted to be allowed to die in there."

"And what did you say to that?" asked the sheriff:

"I said, 'Please yourself, my friend'," replied the witness.

Sheriff: "And then?"

Witness: "He took a small holder from his pocket and asked me to go outside."

I shall not quote any further from these police records. After the corpse had been placed in a coffin it was left in his mother's house at Hríngjarabær. And since I had been in attendance on him during the days he had been in Iceland, it so happened that I was present when his luggage was opened in the hotel and the pockets of his clothes emptied. In his suit-cases, which were of good quality and fairly new, were found bricks wrapped in straw; and nothing else. In his pockets there were a few Danish bank-notes left, five-*krónur* and ten-*krónur* notes, barely a hundred *krónur* in all; and a number of scraps of paper covered with huge sums, for the most part ordinary mathematical puzzles which result in strange and unexpected answers.

I never saw the body of Garðar Hólm the singer, but I sang over his clay. And it was I who went to fetch his mother Kristín and escorted her at the funeral.

The funeral service was held in the mortuary in the churchyard and not in the cathedral. We, his closest relatives, sat on the front bench – Björn of Brekkukot and my grandmother and Kristín and I. Pastor Jóhann made the funeral oration. He was extremely old by now – I believe he was one of the oldest serving clergymen in Iceland by then; and indeed it was considered a sign of his senility that he forgot to mention in his funeral oration whom he was burying. He talked about those people who have no faces; those whom the Saviour loved above all others. Did he perhaps think for a moment that he was burying one of those now? Quite often I did not know very clearly what Pastor Jóhann was thinking. Nor did I know what Kristín of Hríngjarabær was thinking. I did not know what my grandfather and grandmother were thinking. As for myself, I have seldom been so certain that the man who was being buried was not in the coffin.

Oh, blessed moment when the mists are clearing . . .

Then the coffin was carried into the churchyard. The copper bell was rung. I was given a sign to step forward to the edge of the grave and sing.

It was one of those white autumn-sunshine days with a very gentle breeze. I hope that the breeze carried my singing to some little boy sitting in a vegetable patch amidst the tansies and dockens somewhere nearby, looking on death as just another innocent entertainment.

While the grave was being filled in, Pastor Jóhann tottered over to us and greeted us; first Björn of Brekkukot, then the two women, and then myself. He greeted us all by name, even me – yes, he remembered exactly what we were called; and I was most of all surprised that he should know me still, considering how old he had become, and how changed I was. I thought perhaps it was because I had such a funny name. But no. He said he wanted to see me about something.

"I still owe you some money, my dear Álfgrímur, and I am beginning to feel very ashamed of it," he said.

"You must be making a mistake, Pastor Jóhann," I said.

"No," said Pastor Jóhann, and put his hand in his pocket under his cassock. "I always remember my debts. I remember very clearly that I asked you to sing at the funeral of a man here many years ago. I promised you thirty *aurar* for the singing. But my purse was so old by then, I think it must have started to leak; whatever the reason, I could only find twenty-nine *aurar*. But now my daughter in Copenhagen has sent me a new purse."

He pulled this beautiful new purse out from under his cassock and began to try to open it with his blue, numb fingers. And to break the silence while he was struggling with the clasp, he said, "I have never known how to sing properly. But the day has never dawned that I have not known that there is one note, and it is pure."

Pastor Jóhann finally managed to open his new purse, and in it he found the one *eyrir* he had owed me for so many years, and handed it to me.

"It is good and lovely to sing," he said as he gave me the coin. "Especially if one is aiming at nothing higher than to sing over the clay of those people who have no faces."

It was quite certainly towards the evening of that same day that I happened to catch sight of my grandfather coming from the direction of town with his hat tied under his chin as if he had been out in a storm. I did not even speculate on what my grandfather had been doing down town, for there was enough to think about. But later in the evening, when I was on my way out for a stroll to pass the time, my grandmother spoke to me at the door and brought me back into the kitchen.

"Perhaps you'd like a sugar-stick, just like the old days when you were smaller, Grímur dear?" she said.

Then she handed me a generous slab of black candy-sugar.

"Listen, grandmother," I said. "Don't you think it's some other Grímur you're thinking about? As far as I can remember, you always told me when I was small that sugar was bad for the teeth."

"No, it's all the same Grímur," she said. "But it's quite true that sugar is unhealthy for the teeth, except just on special occasions. But fortunately there have not been very many special occasions in this house."

"Did you say 'fortunately', grandmother?" I asked.

"Slow good luck is best," she said.

"This is absolutely marvellous sugar, grandmother," I said.

"Listen, Grímur dear," she now said. "Do I remember right, or did I dream it, that you had some sort of paper from that wholesale merchant Gúðmúnsen?"

"That's right," I said. "The Store wants to pay for my training abroad for five years."

"That's wonderful, I must say," she said. "Indeed I've always heard that they're fine people. But I'm afraid, Grímur dear, that your grandfather is not very pleased that you should have this paper."

"I'll have to do something," I said, "since grandfather doesn't want me to be a lumpfisherman."

She replied, "Once upon a time I was allowed to decide that the name Grímur should be added to your own name. It could be that I had it in mind, both then and sometimes later, that someone named Grímur might mention my name if ever he were in need rather than the names of those people in Gúðmúnsen's Store."

"I shall gladly throw that paper into the fire and study for the church," I said. "Perhaps one day I would get far enough to hear that one pure note that Pastor Jóhann hears."

I had already taken the paper out and was going to put it into my grandmother's fire.

"No, you shouldn't put it into the fire," she said. "That would not be courteous. You should rather take it back to the Store and tell them that you no longer need it. Your grandfather would rather that any studying you do should be done on his money."

"I didn't know that grandfather had any money," I said.

"Brekkukot has been in Björn's possession and his family's possession longer than anyone can remember, but he sold it today," she said. "It's getting too much for us now. But we're thinking of hanging on here for the winter. In the spring we're going to move into a basement in Laugavegur. We haven't got so long left now, thank goodness. Your grandfather wants you to sail on the first ship to study whatever your mind is set on."

41

THE END

For some time no one had heard our clock, any more than if it had not existed. But for these last few days the living-room was quiet, and then I heard that it was still ticking away. It never let itself get flurried. Slowly, slowly went the seconds in my grandfather's timepiece, and said as of old: et-ERN-it-Y, et-ERN-it-Y. And if you listened hard enough you could make out a sort of singing note in its workings; and the clear silver bell struck. How good it was to hear once again the note of this clock in which there lived a strange creature! And to have been allowed to stay here in Brekkukot, in this little turf cottage which was the justification of all other houses on earth, in the house that gave other houses purpose.

"Tell King Kristian of Denmark from me," said Captain Hogensen, "that I know well what it is to be summoned from other lands to become a man of authority among the Danes.

They fetched me, a poor cottager with a crowd of starving children in Breiðafjörður, and placed me in charge of their warships. And that's the way they fetched him too, a poor cottager with a crowd of starving children in Germany, and placed him in charge of the whole country in Denmark; and he of course did not know a word of their language, any more than I did. That's how they put impoverished foreigners into the highest positions in the land in order to have their own way. Tell him that I do not blame His Majesty even though the Danes have committed one of the greatest blunders in the history of the world; and that was when they allowed Gúðmúnsen, together with the English and the Faroese and other such races, to use drag-nets and trawls in the most important bays in this country such as Faxaflói and Breiðafjörður and scrape the bottom clean and destroy every single living creature, big or small. And with that, obviously, people like Björn of Brekkukot here are done for. Tell His Majesty that on every New Year's Day since I came to Reykjavík I have left no stone unturned in my efforts to impress upon His Majesty's highest servants in this country, Governors, Bishops, and King's Ministers alike, my protests against this behaviour. And that's that."

I took Kristín of Hríngjarabær her milk for the last time. She was sitting in her corner-seat, quite blind now and very nearly totally deaf, with that clear, handsome look in her features, and the sun shining on her face.

"How are you today, Kristín dear?" I said.

"Oh, I have lived many lovely days here in our churchyard in sunshine and a westerly breeze like today," she said.

When I was leaving she said, "I have had a little hank of wool since years ago, and as I heard you were going I have been trying hard to knit something from it. I have knitted these two little pairs of socks that I want to ask you to take with you in your bag for me. I want to ask you, when you've crossed the sea, to look up for me a poor woman called Mrs Hansen in Jutland. Tell the woman I made these socks myself and give them to her from me for the boy and the little girl, with my greetings."

"Give me your bag, my boy," said my grandfather. "My shoulders should be broad enough still."

We walked through the turnstile-gate at Brekkukot which divided two worlds. My grandmother followed. We were on our way to the ship. It was growing dusk. Rain was falling on the autumn-pale grass. The boat which ferried passengers out to the ship had not quite arrived when we reached the quayside. I had promised to say goodbye to the superintendent. It did not take long to find him; he was sitting in his little cubicle next to the harbour sheds from which there always came a strong smell of carbolic and soap. He was sitting on a cobbler's-stool at a rickety old table, binding a brush. When a second person came into his cubicle, there was no more floor space left. Throughout his whole establishment, the so-called harbour urinals, there was not a single piece of wood that was not scrubbed white. I think perhaps it must have been the cleanest hygiene establishment anywhere in the northern hemisphere at that time.

We never called him anything other than the Superintendent, and when I was small I had thought he was some sort of superintendent for the whole town, or even for the whole country. But now when I am growing older and begin to think of various famous institutions I have seen, and their directors, I feel that here was the man who should have been the superintendent for the whole world.

"Well," he said, and stood up and looked at me with that warm, alive, cheerful look. "So it's your turn now, my friend, to set off on your travels and buy me a little of the canary-seed they use abroad."

"I didn't know you kept birds here," I said.

"Oh, I don't," he said. "But I always try to have a little titbit for the mouse that sometimes comes to visit me when the weather's bad."

Then he gave me a few *krónur* in small change for that purpose. As a joke I said, "What if I just use it to buy liquor for myself when I reach Copenhagen?"

"It doesn't matter," he said. "That's for you to decide. And now I wish you a good journey."

"Thank you very much indeed," I said.

"Oh, yes, and while I remember, and about time too," he said.

"Perhaps you remember that I once took a gold coin off you, a long time ago."

"As if I hadn't forgotten all about that ages ago!" I said.

"Here is your gold coin," said the superintendent. "And may things go well for you. May things go for you according to the deserts of all those who have a purpose in life; be it great or small, it doesn't matter, just so long as they are determined not to harm others. And if you ever need a little money, then write to me, because I will soon be having difficulties in getting rid of my monthly pay."

My grandfather opened the door and peeped in to tell me that the boat that was to take me to the ship was on its way.

I kissed my grandmother as she stood there on the quay in her long skirt, with her black shawl over her head and shoulders. I had never embraced this woman before, because embracing was not a habit in our house. I was amazed at how slender and light she was, and wondered if her bones were hollow, like those of a bird. She was like a withered leaf in my embrace for that one brief fraction of a moment that I held her in my arms.

"God be with you, Grímur dear," she said, and added after a second, "And if you should meet a poor old woman like me anywhere in the world, then give her my greetings."

My grandfather Björn of Brekkukot kissed me rather drily and said these words: "I cannot give you any good advice at this stage, my lad. But perhaps I could send you a bundle of dried fish with the midwinter ship. After that, we can see. And now, goodbye."

When the boat had gone a few oar-strokes away from land they were still standing on the beach, gazing after the boy whom an unknown woman had left naked in their arms. They were holding hands, and other people gave way before them, and I could see no one except them. Or were they perhaps so extraordinary that other people melted away and vanished into thin air around them?

When I had clambered up with my bag on to the deck of the mail-boat *North Star*, I saw them walking back together on their way home: on the way to our turnstile-gate; home to Brekkukot, our house which was to be razed to the ground tomorrow. They were walking hand in hand, like children.